OTHER BOOKS BY JOHN HEALY

The Grass Arena (Faber & Faber, 1988; revised edition
    Penguin Modern Classics, 2008)
Streets Above Us (Macmillan, 1990)
Coffeehouse Chess Tactics (New In Chess, 2010)

THE · METAL MOUNTAIN

JOHN HEALY

ETRUSCAN BOOKS

First published by Etruscan Books 2019
ISBN 978 1 901538 89 2

Edited by Nicholas Johnson; the author acknowledges
John Hall and John Welch for casting an eye over the text.
Designed and produced by Uniformbooks
Printed by TJ International, Padstow, Cornwall

Distributed in the UK by Central Books: www.centralbooks.com
and in the USA by Small Press Distribution: www.spdbooks.org

Etruscan Books
2nd Floor, Oak Passage Studio, 68 George Street,
Hastings, East Sussex TN34 3EE
etruscanpublishing@gmail.com
www.e-truscan.co.uk

For Glyn Roberts who saved lives

"Protect us dear lord from the wrath of the Norsemen, they plunder our land they pillage our churches they take our women and children."

8th century Anglo Saxon prayer

ON RAGLAN STREET

Before noon, but with the sun already high, four people assembled outside a dilapidated house in north-west London. As nine-year-old Michael pulled shut the front door, his mother Mary Jane sat his four-year-old brother Dermot into a battered pushchair. Suddenly Danny, at thirteen years old the eldest child, unfurled a flag. A small, paper Union Jack.

It was the 2nd of June 1953, a very special day, the day of the Coronation of the young Queen Elizabeth II and it had been her pleasure to allow street parties all over the United Kingdom, so that people might celebrate her new dignity and tell about it forever. Now, Danny, with much advice and fussing from the other children, began tying the jack to the front of the pushchair with a short piece of twine. When he had done this, his mother looked round at them all and, satisfied that her tiny brood were neatly scrubbed and in good order, gave a happy laugh and they stepped off, the little flag fluttering prettily before them.

Temporarily elevated from an existence which their poverty-stricken lives normally demanded, the kids' hearts were soaring as they sped alongside their mum towards the party, everyone straining to be the first to hear the sound of the celebrations. But, not until they came closer to Camden Town was there any sign of life and they all heard it at once, dimly at first, then more clearly, the sound of a band playing martial music. When they turned into Camden High Street the atmosphere of revelry hit them with force, and it was rousingly festive. From opposite windows, coloured flags stretched high across the road, royal purple draped the lamp posts. Large pictures of the Queen were everywhere, alongside adverts for Bovril, since it was discovered that the virtues of British beef could be stored in a small bottle. Many young men in army uniforms stood about joshing and drinking bottles of beer, their berets tucked into the epaulettes on their shoulders. The musicians sat in a half circle in the middle of the road while two jolly policemen laughed and joked with the bandmaster. The Pearly King was dancing with his Queen. Then the vicar, to the amusement of the children, joined in by tapping the Pearly King on the shoulder and when he looked round, slipping in and waltzing off with his lady.

The whole area was gaily decorated with pennons and flags of red, white and blue, the colours of the English Union Jack garlanding the town in celebration. Shields hung from balconies on which the royal coat of arms was emblazoned with a dash of scarlet and the leopard of Normandy. And on this day only the very churlish or then again the very sane and sober might have noticed the irony. The young Queen, along with the rest of the English royal family, were of German descent and thus in no way related to the Norman line. But this fact did not concern the multitudes who stood now silently at attention in the midst of their poverty, while the band began to play the national anthem. As the battle hymn of the English monarchy rose higher and higher, the world became too small for the Docherty children, who felt themselves expanding infinitely. No one could contain their joy and happiness. The whole place was vital, everybody was significant, as the sun's golden rays shone down, making every detail poignant. All over the land there was a trumpeting of joy, its fulsome notes rose up to the sky. The splendours which were being summoned kindled lights of great expectancy. In the jubilant street a bright gleam had caught the monarch's paper crown. Her head glittered with jewels. Soldiers issued commands, trumpets prepared the way. Their piercing notes echoed with anticipation. It was obvious that caparisoned elephants would pass, horses prance, princes and princesses would arrive. Meanwhile…

Coronation mugs plates and cutlery were being laid out on long rickety trestle tables covered with sheets of white paper. Dozens of kids, vibrating with anticipation, were beginning to sit down, with parents in attendance. But as Mary Jane started to settle her children at the table, several Raglan Street mothers exchanged meaningful glances, some whispering angrily. Mary Jane felt the stir of their interest as one of the women, with a quiver of indignation, went to speak to an official. An elderly man who, in spite of his extravagant middle class manner, did not withhold his generous attention, which encouraged the blunt raw faced woman, who did hesitate at first to convey the dark details. But, once launched, she would not be dissuaded from doing her duty. He frowned once or twice, itching to cut it short for although separated by class, Patriotism was joining them, so that when he had listened with open impatience a while more to her repetitious complaint, he nodded curtly and went over to where Mary Jane stood, pointedly tending her children.

"Mrs Docherty?" There was a quick silence. The presence of such a dignified figure caused everyone nearby to look.

"Yes?" The word came in a tense whisper. She saw how his medals shone.

"I'm afraid there's been some mistake in registering your payments," said the official. He was talking about the twelve-shilling party fee that everyone had paid over the last six months, at sixpence per week. The silence seemed to have isolated the woman, who stood now with her mouth open revealing lipstick applied too hastily by an unpractised hand on her parted lips, some of which had come off on her teeth. Her three kids gave quick, apprehensive glances at her. She looked foolish in her injured simplicity. Turning as it was into something more than just a lost helping of blancmange, their party faces had grown stiff and hollow, they had forgotten their previous joy. "The full amount was paid, sir, I have the receipts at home in a jar." The blood rushed to her face and neck. She was consumed with bitter pride. "I can send one of the boys to run back for them. Danny will you…?" She could not express herself except in fumbled gestures and in her distraction she began patting her clothes to console or mollify.

"Mrs Docherty" he began. This was a situation he might have handled better if it had only been about money since the woman had missed just one payment he would have happily paid it himself but unfortunately this involved problems of cultural compatability."I'm afraid I'm going to have to ask you to leave."

As the light was gathered in, her hopes shrank; where she had glimpsed for an instant the possibility of concealment, it now became clear that she would not remain unmasked. "Why?" she dared to enquire.

Here her accuser grew reticent but got his words out at last; "Because you're Irish."

In the pause that followed, Mary Jane Docherty's mind fumbled after some acceptable excuse as she stood firmly gripping the handles of the pushchair in a cotton dress patterned once with tiny flowers but still presentable in spite of wear. "My children were all born in England sir." She said this very slowly and deliberately. Doubt was gone now, and anger was in its place. She had not yet learned the extent of her delusion.

"Indeed," replied the official, this prospect troubled him. He had stepped into a situation that was becoming increasingly uncomfortable. He wished he could have washed his hands of the whole affair; but one of his responsibilities was to keep order. He could not afford to inflame the crowd because they had begun to enjoy war—it was one of the peculiarities which made them feel superior. There were angry nods from some of the crowd who stared at her out of their permanent positions on their invaded street.

The resentful blood had risen to their faces in their anxiety to confirm what they had just heard, tempers were up, and some of them vicious.

"I'm sorry", he quietly said. He was a cultured man and he would remember this day long after the coronation street party had been forgotten. In his eagerness to avoid a threat to public order he had sacrificed an innocent woman and her children to placate a hostile crowd.

Mary Jane did not reply. She knew her accent was against her now, and tried not to show too much emotion for the sake of the children, who had been frozen into listening, regardless of whether they had wanted to. It was all part of a complexity about denying their contempt to herself so that a kind of despondent ferocity had developed in her over the years. But, she started rousing them from their places, as two coarse-boned boys at the next table began to laugh. The youths' laughter was all the more wicked because of the incident from which it had ensued. Michael was near to tears. In fact, the hostility of the people had begun to frighten them all as it burst around them distorting their vision into ugly patternless shapes. But they were conquerors. Conviction shone from their loyal cheeks, sometimes over-spilling, running down their chins and gushing from their lips in wild heroic bursts.

Mary Jane was a pretty, Irish, country woman, with warm eyes and soft skin. She was absolutely kindly, humorous and refused to weep. She loved her children and they her. She really wanted to know all about their day at school, their work and play. There was no one in the world they could talk to as they could talk to her. But in the cool yet solid sunlight of that indifferent afternoon she might have sensed a criticism in her children which they had not meant to offer. For the moment she was neither mother nor wife not even a person but it was she who must take the initiative so she turned the pushchair in the direction of home, (a place that still might need to be confirmed) and moved off with stiff precision. She was uglier now. She could hear the wind rising to accuse her as the little group departed with their shame.

When Michael, snivelling a bit, his lower lip atremble, asked why the people had not let them stay at the party, Mary Jane, to disguise her hand in her children's disappointment replied irritably, "Because they're pure daft." The barbed humour that the whole of England, from the queen, right on down, were somehow a bit daffy and not to be taken too seriously, was not lost on Michael. It lent the disaster some dignity, and though he continued with a few token sniffles, it was noticeable that his lip had ceased to tremble. In his pushchair, young Dermot started to giggle; he knew about it too!

But no matter what face you put on it, it was still a retreat. From the first step they plodded now without music to the humiliating whine of oil-starved wheels, which was in sad contrast to the first blast of the trumpets that had played them in; nor could that jarring whine bring the same spring to their departing step as the beat and pulse of the drum, while the little flags fluttering colours were bent backwards by the wind which made their departure more uncomfortable as they pushed against it on their way back to Raglan Street, a narrow little street with houses on both sides, some of them unoccupied on account of them having taken direct hits, courtesy of the Luftwaffe. Some were tumbled ruins; others were gashed and ripped, with part of a wall or part of a roof left, the insides cruelly exposed with staircases leading to nowhere. Indeed some of those dwellings looked as if they had never been occupied. In the middle of these bombed out buildings, No.14 was still standing, a grey, shabby two-storey dwelling. Behind it lay the Northwest London railway line, and the sounds of the trains coming and going were part of the residents' lives. Mrs Docherty stopped outside No.14. Michael opened the door with his key and they all tramped inside down along the bare passage, then in across the worn lino until abruptly halted, trapped by their own bewilderment and embarrassment by a table wedged up against a wall in the tiny front room.

Seán Docherty who until that moment had been employed in sitting by the grate in his Sunday suit rolling himself a cigarette, stared at his wife and three kids. Obviously puzzled by their absence from a place where a party was in progress he asked them why they were back so early from the celebrations? The children, on account of their youth and swaying a little from lack of breath, could not be expected to take part, so naturally it was left to their mother to explain. But there are limits to what a mother might be expected to bear. Consequently she began constructing her answer along lines that would hopefully appease everyone except herself. But caution made her falter. In the effort to express herself, she was looking about the distracting room, running her hand over the patched tablecloth on which the complicated patterns were standing out in bold relief. On one wall a coloured print of the virgin mother hung. Her eyes gazed down softly while the adoration candles Mary Jane had lit in front of the picture that morning conveyed an impression of movement, so that her slip or shift, seemed to flutter gently, though here the artist's attempts at pious serenity were less believable; in those shimmering folds austerity strained to convince against the voluptuousness of the Madonna's figure. Mary Jane continued to look at the picture, pondering on the more agreeable agonies until at last she could no longer defer the moment of explaining their expulsion, so she said, "They were put out because the full fee had not been paid."

The eyes of this lean faced man—her husband—were darkening dangerously. They were all standing in quiet embarrassment now, for the father had got up from his chair. But Mary Jane started fussing with young Dermot to avoid further explanation; if you rapidly unpick your own argument it quickly becomes a nonsense. Her face had become thoughtful with bitterness and perspiration as she rushed to gather up a confusion of scattered clothing in readiness for the wash. She had got behind. Every household chore had been left with happy neglect in anticipation of the coronation party but were now returned to with greater vigour. In her present state of mind she was relieved when allowed to resume her normal household duties and was happy now that most of the children, as their memories of events had receded, had slipped away to resume their carefree games.

The parents felt unwilling to continue their conversation and to labour under the influence of mutual embarrassment. In fact they did not speak for fear of what might come out. Immigrants in a land of immigrants caught between lofty ideals and the hard realities. Since they could no longer blame their sins for making them expect damnation, Seán Docherty went out for a pint while his wife continued with her chores.

Now Michael had observed the conditions of their expulsion but, as he drew conclusions from it somewhat different than his mother, he asked why she did not tell father the real reason they were chucked out of the party. Mary Jane told him it would have only made him angry. Michael stared in silence. To Michael it seemed that the accusation had somehow debased his father's manhood, and his mother's failure to confront his father on the matter only added to his perplexity. As Michael continued to brood deeply in his chair, his mother, who was washing clothes in a bucket, began wringing out a napkin. The whole scullery was full of drying clothes. Suds ran from her arms as she wiped her swollen hands on her pinafore. Turning to look at her son, whose thoughts were often too complicated to follow, or else too clear, she remarked kindly, "What's wrong Michael?"

Loud noiseful capering came through the open door of the back yard where the other children were playing excitedly among themselves.

Mary Jane called to them to play more quietly but the brilliance of their game defied all caution so that, for a moment, she was not quite sure what Michael was saying in reply.

"All the other kids' dads fought. They faced the Prussian Cannon." Frustration came out in a painful, stilted awkwardness. A train in passing shook the house to its foundations, its mournful whistle echoing back through the alienating air so that the mother's thoughts began to stray among familiar objects. It saddened her, this woman, the mother of the children who would soon speak, though she might have struck out at something if her hands had not been so red and raw.

"The Prussian cannon," Mary Jane snorted disgustedly. Her voice became harsh and her whole face twisted up as the breath rasped against her taut throat. "That lot, they wouldn't face a maid with a duster in her hand. They'd do it in their pants if they ever set eyes on a gun, never mind had to use one. Most of them were hiding under the bed when the bombs were dropping and during the all-clear they were working the black market." (Though, the children's health might have suffered more without those commodities, which she herself had obtained from time to time, that were not available on ration coupons.) The memory began to plague her with little thrusts of guilt. The boy grew sullen again. He might have revealed too much of himself. But he knew that most of the other boys' fathers had served in the forces and he sensed that his mother knew this too and was only speaking as she was to console him. It was not within his power to say this to her so, his question, unanswered, settled at the back of his mind, slowly pricking his conscience. She plunged her hands to stir the articles which lay soaking in the bucket before attempting to persuade. "Why don't you go on out for a bit," she coaxed. But he made no answer and just sat there looking at his hands.

The war was not really that long over so perhaps the real fault lay with the times, these confused times where peace had not yet had time to harden into something good. There were many things to which she did not have the answers so that for a moment she was temporarily confused.

As the light filtering through the damp articles hanging in the scullery began to dissolve she shook her head as if she were awakening from a daze and sat down opposite him, settling her dress about her knees modestly, all indispensable factors in the drawing of a calm and even breath. Her voice was simple, matter of fact, and held nothing of the quivering undertone of emotion which she felt within herself as she spoke. "This is not your father's place, he was not born here, but you were so you have no need to worry about anyone. This is your country." But Michael was not so sure as he wandered out onto the street. The street where he was born, and, until a short time ago, felt reasonably secure.

The street was strangely quiet now. On summer evenings children usually played in the street and on the pavement, while their parents sat at open windows, watching the world go by. Then he remembered that everyone was at the party. A slight wind was blowing as Michael stood controlling his boredom, watching a coloured poster of the young queen stuck to a bombed house wall. Wind had already torn posters announcing events that had happened last year and the year before. She might have appeared to greater advantage, only a breeze had got behind the picture and in the process had upset the texture of the monarch's skin, so that her face shivered, and the circlet of gold upon her head wobbled. Though protected by her mail of jewels, the tattered picture had become unstable so that one good gust might rip it down. The silence of the afternoon began to insinuate upon the boy and he began to wonder, what was the difference between a queen and a saint, apart from the fact that both looked pale? Saints were also looked up to and people touched their pictures as if they might benefit from it. They did not do that to the queen's picture though. No, you did not touch. Instead they sighed like his mother had and said things like, "It will be different now." He looked away and for a moment was a bit lost as his mind recalled his father's words to his mother as they had left that morning for the celebrations.

"O, it will be different all right," he'd laughed in a jeering sort of way. "The crown has got clear blue eyes and a pretty nose now, waving her sceptre over a kingdom of bomb sites and bronchials and a few skinny kids and, along with her soldiers, she'll soon be spitting death from her soft pale cheeks." Death and suffering seemed to be the link-up as he recalled the pictures of saints that hung from the walls of the church, their bodies either motionless in prayer or writhing in torture and he wondered if his parents went so far as to will their own bodies into the physical pain the saints in some of the pictures were suffering.

After a while he squatted against a lamp post, his boredom returning, which made him yawn and flex his shoulder blades. For although the breeze was cold enough in his short pants upon his bare legs, he knew the breeze did not have the strength to pull the picture from its place upon the wall.

He peered at the monarch's picture intently. From her throne she returned her reluctant subject's stare. She did not seem that evil-looking although she had a kind of sharp importance, something more than a head teacher, that hinted that his father's words might hold some grain of truth. In this state he was possessed by an unhappiness, rather physical, not quite fear. She might be alright but he resented the indignity she had indirectly imposed on him and his family and he shivered for the wind to tear just once.

But the strange day was still unfolding.

He sat there thinking, wondering when he would be allowed to wear long trousers, while waiting for something to happen, as it did when a black van turned into the street and came to a halt outside Albie Adders' house. Michael stood idly watching as Mr Adders jumped out of the van and instead of shouting up at the windows that he was home, as he usually did, walked swiftly up and in through his open front door. Almost immediately he came running back out, accompanied by his twelve-year-old son, Albie. Suddenly as they approached the van it gave a loud groan, the back doors flew wide open and its contents began spilling out into the road. Michael stood transfixed as what appeared to be mostly women's brand new clothing, still in their cellophane wrapping, continued to fall from the van into the road. There were swagger coats, two-piece costumes and round beribboned hat boxes of many colours, scattered profusely all over the place. Michael began to feel apprehensive about Mr Adders' absence from the party. He wanted to walk away but did not like to move now for fear of being noticed. But unfortunately, he had already been spotted. Mr Adders, no fool, knew the makings of a bad situation when he saw it. The kid, he knew, had probably guessed by now what was occurring and if he spoke to anyone could make an awkward if not damning witness.

"Come on then, don't just stand there, you'll take root," he laughed, trying to make light of the situation. If the kid could be inveigled to help in some way he would be less likely to talk, since he would feel implicated, he reasoned. Though the boy's fear (aggravated now by a sense of not belonging) caused him to want to flee, the beautiful clothing and the elegant beribboned hat-boxes lying in the shabby street reminded him of a happy Christmas scene, rich and glorious and slightly unreal, a picture like the monarch's with her sceptre and her crown, artificial glory keeping reality at bay. His head began to be filled with splendours of his own. A warm glow was spreading through him at the prospect of being allowed to touch and feel the wonderfully rich and exotic garments.

Albie looked at him and not. His eyes denied Michael's presence. He resented the intrusion on the edges of his family and their newly acquired property, but the boy, although at first doubtful how he ought to behave, now went over and began helping to carry the stuff into the Adders' house, where Mrs Adders and her two teenage daughters were stacking the items in the middle of the front room floor. When the girls saw Michael, the eldest one, Elga, laughed and said "Every little helps," while her younger sister, started giggling and shook her head from side to side, as if these two functions, were all that she could manage, and in her haste, confused boxes with hands and hands with boxes. Gilt-trimmed and brightly coloured, the boxes were elegant and striking. The dresses and costumes with opulent restraint in their cut and colouring were, with the boxes they draped over, built up and arranged in patterns of size and shape so that an empire of demi-mode and cardboard began to arise.

Mr Adders talked too, while he worked, sometimes saying things that embarrassed his wife and daughters, but made his son Albie laugh. It made Michael laugh also but he hid his amusement, pretending to be preoccupied with the items he was stacking, in case Mrs Adders, unable to take her annoyance out on her husband, transferred it to him. Now that he had been accepted, he did not want to be rejected too quickly. It felt good to be involved in something positive. Many hands make light work and the van's contents were soon neatly stacked inside the Adders' front room. A monument of cardboard boxes draped in cloth, prosperity mounted on an altar of loveliness, they gazed at that in respectful awe. They began to walk round it, to view it from all sides. It had become the pivot of their existence and for a moment gave them contentment until Michael, rousing himself, began to wonder if he might be allowed some item to take home for his mum. But, Albie, perhaps sensing covetousness, had placed himself possessively before the booty, which put an end to Michael's speculation. He'd thought the possibility remote and anyway, he knew that his mum would not accept gifts, especially hats and coats off doubtful racks.

The noisy gaiety and loud laughter of the returning revellers suddenly coming from the street prompted Mrs Adders to remark that she had better start getting her family's tea. She had a mother's frown, the boy saw, as he made his way towards the door.

"O, are you off then?" said Mrs Adders, who spoke more to assert herself rather than with any great concern. "You've been such an angel. You daren't leave a thing lying around outside your own front door these days. They got a nasty habit of disappearing, so we've found it best to fetch all our stock in smartish." Her tone was significant. Her voice had begun to sound to Michael like someone's he had heard on the wireless that morning; perhaps it was the Queen's.

"It may not be much of a neighbourhood any more but we still try to maintain certain standards. Course, we shan't be here that long." She waited, to tempt her young listeners, curiosity, but she seemed to have forgotten that she had more than one listener, and when Elga asked, "Why not mum?" and her giddy sister tittered, replied abruptly, "Because we're not," and again waited for encouragement from her guest to reveal her reasons. But when none came, she went on without it.

"Because we're going to move back up 'Ampstead where we originally came from." The words were issued with a melancholy expression and an undertone of longing. She seemed to know by heart the desirable qualities of that Borough from which it appeared she had so recently and perhaps ruthlessly been ejected. Mrs Adders had been forced to move on more than once. Suddenly she seemed to brighten, like an actress assuming a different role.

"Whatever else we may lack in this country we've still got our royal family; there's nothing finer, nothing nobler," she was quite clear about that. The boy's opinion was not given a chance to develop, because Mrs Adders enquired quickly "Did you go to the party?" Michael nodded.

"With your family?"

"Yes," replied Michael evasively. Her expression became melancholy once more.

"I wish I could have gone only I had one of me turns, come on somefink awful it did. Had to lay down and seeing as how Mr Adams was at the warehouse collecting his stock for market tomorrow Elga and Violet stayed home to look after me and Albie bless 'em. O well a woman's work is never done." She sighed, then her head went up and she hesitated before looking directly into Michael's face.

"You shall have to come to Sowfend wiv us in August, won't he Fred?"

"Sure will," said Mr Adders, with a wink of complicity. He spoke with the air of a man who feared nothing and was totally at home in any environment. The warmth and spontaneity of it brought a tightness to Michael's throat. Southend beckoned, dangling like a jewel in Michael's mind as he ran all the way home. Mary Jane was in the scullery preparing the dinner when Michael burst in. She looked up at his flushed cheeks and smiled.

"Did you have a good time? Did you meet anyone nice to play with?" And he told her with a simple eagerness that he was working with Albie, helping him unload his father's building van, not mentioning what was in it, adding, to allay her fears, that they were going to repay him by taking him to Southend in August. She smiled amiably and remarked that August was a long time off but anyway it was all right with her. He watched her peeling potatoes.

"Do you want any help mum?" He asked, feeling guilty. He hated his deceit.

"No, sit there and rest yourself; sure you must be tired out running in and out all afternoon unloading that old van." There was such vast truthfulness in her voice that Michael looked away in embarrassment. Ignorant of the real reason, she was bemused rather than puzzled by the splendid strangeness of Mr Adders spontaneously inviting Michael to assist him, and stranger still inviting him into their home. Michael felt sure now that his mother had never been inside any Raglan Street home other than her own. Since she was avidly interested in everything, he could tell her about the Adders and their front room. Again and again, she would ask him what sort of furniture they had, was the floor carpeted or linoed, did they have an indoor toilet..? And because, in all the excitement of the moment, he hadn't really noticed, and also because he wanted to share something of his happiness with her, he started to make things up. Adjusting his descriptions of the Adders' house and furnishings to suit her mood, as she fastened with fascination on his words.

As he lay in bed that night he tried to keep out of his mind the sin he'd just committed but it kept coming back in. Yet in the morning he woke curiously refreshed. It was funny how sinfulness made glorious dreams.

The Adders called him by his first name now and he began once more to feel accepted, needed even. They had begun to patronise their down-at-heel neighbour's son, but when they asked for help now they asked as if he were obliged to give it. Their gratitude was brief, and only grudgingly given. He hardly noticed. Southend always beckoned with its promise of eternal sunshine, of sea, of sand, of candy floss, dodgem cars and lucky dips. Michael enjoyed having somewhere to hang out. It made him feel grown up to sit in the Adders' front room on rainy days and be included in the conversation of an adult other than that of his parents. He enjoyed listening to some of Mr Adders' war stories, especially the one in which he had won a medal for gallantry under enemy fire. But as time passed, one recurring story began to disturb him. A story about beating up a big Jamaican in a fight over a girl, a lively little thing who still had plenty of life left in her when Mr Adders walked her home to her bedsit afterwards, so much so in fact, that he outshone the big Jamaican even in that department too. Telling this story seemed to excite Mr Adders. He lit a cigarette and began coughing badly. Sitting in his chair retching, he suddenly seemed a worried little man and Michael began to have difficulty in matching the man in the chair to the Saturday night image of him, standing in the saloon bar of the King's Arms, dressed in his yellow Crombie, his trilby pushed jauntily back, wisecracking with fur-coated women and scantily clad barmaids, while knocking down big Jamaicans. Yet for some reason the image still disturbed him and gradually he began to experience an uncomfortable sensation as an image of his own father came to him. For the man in Mr Adders story differed every time he told it. Not in size, only in his nationality.

August came but none of the Adders seemed to remember that they were due to go on holiday, Michael mused. In fact there was no Southend or rather there was, but not for him, and even if there was, he wasn't sure, he wanted to be with people like the Adders anymore. It took him a long time to admit this and he suffered trying to hide his feelings.

His brother Danny never seemed to get the same aggravation as Michael did, but then he tended to mix less with the people of Raglan Street. The only contact Danny had with them was when he was sent on an errand for his mother to the small shop on the corner, next door to a bombed house. The place was crammed with cardboard boxes full of tinned food, beans mostly. Along with holding the tins, the boxes served a couple of other useful functions, since they formed a wall that partitioned the shop down the middle, and loaves of bread could be stacked on the top, along with a once a week tray of sticky buns.

Whenever Danny went in there, there were always a few women hanging around near the boxes. Mrs Cotter was a good-hearted old woman of seventy-five. Riddled with arthritis, she stood all day behind the counter in a long white starched apron which stood out vivid and luminous against the darker clothing of her customers, most of whom owed her something on the slate. These women waded in corsets, their hair done up in curlers under turbaned scarves, their knowing eyes peering out from pained and pointed faces, who liked to talk about the weather and minor ailments and sometimes sicknesses that led to sudden deaths, were just waiting for some youngster to come in so as to swipe some small article or other when Mrs Cotter's attention was distracted. If the kid happened to see one of them in the act, the others would start up a running banter to confuse the kid, by saying, "Ouu, what a big boy you're becoming Danny, it is Danny isn't it?"

"Yes," though it sounded silly their gravity did not ease.

"Are you the youngest?" At which point another would pretend to chide, saying, "Don't be silly Edith, course he's not." Then as Danny was about to leave with his purchase Edith might slide her skinny hand into a box for another lucky dip under the covering banter, "Ouu, But ain't he got lovely long eyelashes though, don't you wish you had eyelashes like that, Cott?" Whereupon Mrs Cotter, not preoccupied with eyelashes at that particular moment would just grunt. To which all the women would reply in chorus, "Ouuu!! I wish I had long eyelashes like that," in a tone that implied you got to be lacking not to want long eyelashes!

Danny liked to read and seemed happy to stay in the house with a good adventure yarn. He usually palled up with boys from his own school who lived in the less run-down areas. He had a good memory and somewhere not too far back in it he knew… he did not know the word, but sometimes, when he was coming and going from the house, the fear of it touched him. He did not want to be violated.

Danny had recently become a vegetarian. He'd read an article about it in a book about the Far East and he'd converted Michael too. No one except their mother had tried to advise them against it. They still ate what everyone else in the house ate. The only difference now was that their father got to eat the boy's untouched portion of meat. Danny was endlessly curious about the stuff he gleaned from books, some of it very strange such as incarnation. How people are born again and again in different bodies, sometimes as a king or a queen, rich or poor or even if really bad a dung beetle.

Seán Docherty sat alone, with the slightly forced confidence of his countrymen in this foreign land, in the King's Arms, with a pint of bitter on the table in front of him. Amid the bedlam of discordant noise in which 'Rule Britannia' (belted out by an enormous fat man at the piano) and the voices of the regulars competed for supremacy. Seán concentrated on the faces of the men about him, their vociferous loyalty quenched at last in a spluttering of best bitter and wondered at their weird inverted logic, their amazing capacity for self-deception. He smiled wryly. Most of them had mastered the art of getting a cigarette to stick to the lower lip without letting it fall out of the gob while talking, and all day long, surrounded by the odour of neglect and poor nutrition, they had only one theme; "We won the war!" recited in a voice that challenged the world to prove it otherwise, while their wives, grizzled women with eternal grievances concealed behind that peroxide blonde look with which they disguise themselves, swelled with virtuous indignation. As if afraid of some fearful stigma they would hug themselves in pity of their imagined or real condition as they pulled themselves back to nurse their paranoia inside the doorways of their squalor. Seán took a swig of his drink. Somehow, when they relaxed at night in the bars and pubs, their merriment was more difficult to stomach than their dedicated daytime aggressive jocularity and triumphant arrogance. He gritted his jaw and inhaled the boisterous air reluctantly.

When England screams, cannot she be comforted? Perhaps that's why each morning they religiously clean the stone step outside their front doors. The sacrificial stone, the first and most sacred step leading to the temple of the sun. No longer washed with virgins' blood, yet washed they are, and bathed and tended, and anointed with blood, just as reverently by the un-virginal ladies of Raglan Street, with ox-blood polish, sold for thruppence a tin by Mrs Cotter in the corner shop. Pale and glib, for an hour each morning they kneel at their appointed task with scrubbing brush and buckets of soap and water which they liberally apply to the step. But the step will not stay clean. The dirt has merged.

Seán Docherty finished his pint, fortifying himself against the difficulties to come and walked out. Raglan Street, he mused, was the end of the civilised universe.

HEROES AND COWARDS

On the street corner, Albie Adders leans up against his favourite piece of wall. He is twelve and a half now, a year older than the other kids. With this great advantage, he conceives the world of Raglan Street revolving around him. The other kids are slaves dedicated to his whims, and he demands respect from them all. But Michael respects people only as much as is good for them, and no more.

The gestures of Albie Adders had an air of experience so that everyone watched as he lit a fag. When he is satisfied that it was burning evenly he takes a long slow drag before turning casually toward Michael to ask him where he's been lately.

Michael is a bit put out by the question for, at times like these, he felt that it was degradation for one who aimed to be some vague hero or a soldier of fortune to be doing chores round the house for his mother. Goodness and helpfulness evoked amongst his peer group not admiration, but pity. So he replied that he's been busy.

"Busy," repeated Albie with a knowing smile. "What wiv, drying the dishes for your Granny?" Michael was speechless. He can feel his cheeks burning. The other kids look on seriously. They don't fully understand this line of talk, the meaning of it was too great for them to grasp and to avoid any involvement they start talking about the latest film starring Rita Hayworth. Someone says they like watching her cute walk. Albie dismisses this.

"Don't you know she's got a trick hip?"

"What about Jean Simmons? She's nice, though," offered Stanley timidly.

"She's just a tease," replied Albie glibly.

"Well Jane Russell's all right," insisted Charlie earnestly.

"How'd you know?" snorted Albie. "Go out with her regular do you?" All the other kids began to laugh. "Yeah, she's so all right," continued Albie thoughtfully, "that Hollywood's greatest doctors can't find a cure for what's wrong with her." And there the ailment waited unspoken, mysterious—too dreadful to name, while some of the younger kids stood looking down at their feet, others began scratching a grazed arm or peering at a scab on their elbow until Albie decided to brighten the mood. To cheer them up he shared a more realistic fantasy.

"You want to see some really nice birds you gotta go round Litcham Street offa Weedington Road around five o clock of an evening when the dress factory shuts." Albie's gestures were rich in unspoken hints of the primitive pleasures one might enjoy with a factory girl. They stood thinking on that for a while and could not marvel on it enough. Such incredible voluptuousness! Anticipation glistened on their sweaty faces, until a man walked past them, the front of his threadbare jacket covered with war ribbons, although it was not an official celebration. All the kids, who were flattered by the coloured ribbons, began to shout, "Good on yer Mr Jenkins." But the man did not reply.

"I've never heard him speak," said Michael.

"He don't need to speak, 'cos he's a hero." explained Albie, who did not appear to experience any difficulty in pronouncing that amazing word.

"Who says so?" asks Michael tersely. Albie's eyes narrowed dangerously. "My dad says so, said he's killed more Germans than your old man's had hot dinners." As the man continued on his way the kids started to holler after him. "Yeah! Brilliant, Mr J." The man with unconvinced bearing shuffling between the broken paving stones seemed unaware however of any possible splendour.

"He don't look like a hero," Michael could not resist.

"You what?"

Michael stays sullenly silent, but Albie won't allow this tremendous insult to pass. Screen goddesses will come and go but kids must have their heroes, whatever else might be in doubt.

"He's a fucking hero, all right."

"My dad's a hero too. He got injured at Dunkirk" a very small child added.

"That's nothing, my dad's killed hundreds of Germans with his bare hands," shouted another kid with a determined twist of his bunched fists, 'my dad's done a few like that too' laughed another forcing even wilder extravagances out of the rest of the gang. As the victorious chorus continued to rise Albie gave Michael a menacing look.

"How many's your old man done?"

"About as many as yours," replied Michael quietly.

"Here, you better stop talking that way," exploded Albie, "my dad had TB, they wouldn't let him fight."

Michael's whole body began to tingle with excitement at this remarkable revelation. He was so agreeably stunned by it that he lay back against the wall causing Albie to visibly stiffen at this encroachment on his patch, while at the same time he found himself forced back into a declivity where the bricks were sagging, struggling to maintain some passable shape in the devitalised masonry.

"He should have got 'noculated," said the small child whose father killed Germans with his bare hands.

"He did," replied Albie, calmly now in the wake of his distress, as if his father was intended for some higher dignity. But the group showed doubt at this. Contempt had begun to develop on their sulky mouths. Not only had they witnessed an indignity but the chain of command had also broken down. In the ominous silence Albie, (who in later life would become a barrow boy and something of a spiv) lit a cigarette and began combing back his sleek dark hair but his gestures were no longer distinctive. Comforted by this reassuring discovery but also to break the maudlin mood that it had struck, Michael, wriggling himself upright, suddenly announced,

"I'm going up Hampstead after some apples." And with that sentence, declared himself the leader of the Raglan Street militia in a bloodless coup. At this, everyone (except Albie) broke out into happy chatter about scrumping up Hampstead. Then they all moved off, including Albie who was jostled about a bit, though no one went so far as to shove him because it would have been worse to have got left behind, singing:

> "Hitler—he's only got one ball.
> The other is in the Albert Hall.
> Himmler is somewhat similar,
> And poor old Goebbels has no balls at all!"

Stanley, Charlie, Albie and Michael stood looking up at the top of the wall, beyond which lay the apple trees.

"Right then," said Charlie, with a show of bravado, "Who's going over?" But, since he'd developed a limp on the way up the hill, something told the others that it wouldn't be him. Stanley, Albie and Michael began to hum and haw, each cautious to make the first move.

"Come on," says Charlie contemptuously, secure within the knowledge of the wounded, "Hurry up, 'fore someone sees us standing here like spare pricks at a wedding."

"I'd rather fuck than fight," sniggered Stanley.

"Yeah, I know," said Charlie, peeved and indignant in the face of their common cowardice. As they began to walk away, Albie sneered with a sidelong glance at Michael, "So much for scrumping up Hampstead." Michael felt the others look at him and realised that the responsibility for the gang now lay with him

"Let's go back" he said, "I'll get over."

Under the wall Charlie and Stanley lock hands, making a step for Michael to spring upwards. Michael grasps the top of the wall, which, luckily, is not cemented with shards of broken glass. Turning swiftly, Michael lowers himself down to the extent of his outstretched body and arms, and drops the rest of the way to the lawn. He looks round quickly, then calls,

"Come on, it's all right, there's no one here." After some muffled grunts and groans, Albie's head appears.

"Is it safe?" he whispers.

"Course it is," scoffed Michael, "Come on down 'fore someone sees you up there."

"No, I got to stay here to take the apples from you and pull you back up—otherwise you could get caught," he said almost eagerly.

"No you ain't. We can help each other better down here. 'Sides we might be able to pull the bolt back on that gate over there," says Michael, pointing, but Albie won't have it and keeps calling down to Michael to break cover and retrieve what windfalls he can, while he stood on top of the wall like a cock about to crow. The others preferred to count the fruit on trees instead, so he went unobserved, while the apples continued to sparkle with mounting rapture. In the lazy sunlight the grass lay smooth and correct around the roots of trees. There was no apparent sign of disorder, though sometimes, consumed by some anxiety or perhaps decadence, the scene just failed to sparkle, yet it still obsessed. They craned their necks, separated by a wall of flint and stone. It was obvious that they were not gratified. Each apple trembled, fell, was gathered up in separate piles. Beneath a bower of strangled roses, in the still air the youths' hot blood tingled. Their teeth had already penetrated the tender flesh as they waited outside in the uninhabited undergrowth for something to happen to which they themselves would not contribute.

At last Michael sprinted forward, battle-sleek like a soldier in a war film, to reach the new cover of the first tree. The large glass doors at the back of the house are wide open. He looks back, worried, to where Albie sits safely straddling the wall. Someone is in that house, Michael just knew it. He wants to run straight back and fly over that wall. Then he spots the apples. They lie on the lawn just a few yards from the house between the trees, the juiciest Granny Smiths he has seen that season. Mouth dry, senses keyed up, he edged forward then pounced on those apples, stuffing the red ones into his pockets, ignoring the greens, watchful and wary, 'til his trouser pockets are full. On the way back he picks up one last juicy red, laughing greedily he bites into it with delight. A boy could fatten himself on apples. Though his mouth is full, he wants to bite into it again and again, stuff as much of that nectar down before he scales the wall.

Then he saw the maggot wriggling from the core, its black head wobbling on its slimy puckered body as if it was in pain. The boy spat and kept spitting quickly, throwing the apple to the ground. Then there was a great scramble, Michael heard the crackle of the undergrowth from which without hope of protection small birds flew.

"Hurry," whispered Albie, stretching down a hand from the top of the wall, "Watch out!" Michael starts tipping the rotten apples from his pockets, but by then it was too late.

"Got you!" a man's voice cries out behind Michael, as Albie drops to the ground on the safe side of the wall.

There were two of them, one well dressed, tall and straight, the other old and gnarled, scowling, sucking on an unlit pipe.

"Yes, we caught one this time Jack," said the tall well-spoken one, tremblingly, a big vein throbbing in his neck.

"Right, come along with me," he puffs, grabbing Michael's arm.

"I was only going to take the windfalls, mister, honest," cries Michael.

"Windfalls or otherwise, in this house we call things by their correct names. It's theft boy, no other word for it." At the mention of that word, Michael's stomach twists. This is getting serious. Michael starts pulling the remaining apples from his pocket with his free hand, dropping them back onto the lawn. To his surprise, the gardener stoops, carefully picking each one back up as he follows them to the house.

Inside, a woman and a girl about Michael's age, looking so alike you can tell they're mother and daughter, sat at a small, polished, ornate table. They look up, startled, from the game of chess they are playing. Michael stands in the centre of the room while the man tells them how he and the old gardener have caught Michael ruining the orchard. Michael stares at the chess board to avoid being intimidated by the man's hostility.

"It takes years to nurture a young tree." The man is addressing his remarks to Michael.

"I was only taking the windfalls, mister, I wasn't going to climb no trees, I'm frightened of heights anyway."

"Hmph," he grunts, "windfalls or otherwise, I'm going to phone the police." At this, his wife half rises from the table.

"Oh Winston," she cries. The man turns from her towards Michael.

"What's your name, boy?"

"Johnny Wivvers, sir."

"Where do you live?"

"South London, sir."

"Whereabouts in South London?"

Since Michael had never seen the sky over South London he racks his brains to think. He'd heard tell of it, but had no absolute conviction that anything existed beyond Camden Town or Hampstead Heath.

"Elephant and Castle," he blurts out.

"That's rather a long way to come to ruin my apple trees, how did you get over here."

"On the bus, sir."

"And what was the number of the bus you got on?"

"I never looked. It was a red double-decker, I just hopped straight on it."

"Yes, you seem to have a penchant for just hopping on or over things." There was a subtle, mocking inflection in his voice.

The man looked at Michael from under his bushy brows with the superiority of his class and rank, and felt suddenly the need to punish someone not of that class and rank. For that is an Englishman's prerogative, not even the Almighty could deny that. The two women attached to a situation over which they had no control, turned their gaze towards the chess board, casually trying to assess who had the superior position for whatever the final analysis might turn out to be. In this way, they were soothed to some extent at least, while the boy, listening to the man's lecture, did not fully comprehend the hot monotonously endless words, for he had taken refuge in his own aloneness, as protection from all worthiness. Besides, it was of more interest to look at what the women might be doing. As the stern man continued to draw parallels to various other incidents where children had scrumped apples from his orchard. Having read a bit about psychiatry, he was always looking for incidents that supported it.

After a while he stopped talking. He seemed to be debating what to do. The woman looked concerned. Michael is only a very small eleven year old, and he's thinking to himself that a little crying gag might be in order, but the man looks a bit military (in fact he was an ex-major) and instinct tells the boy that that type don't like to see fear.

"Oh, damn it, Elizabeth, it's not only the fruit, it's the trespassing!" he moans menacingly at his wife, "The sheer audacity of it. Traipsing all over one's private property, without a thought for the owners." He looks at everyone except Michael then lifts the phone and dials. It was no longer a child's game of apples, anything could happen and now the boy realised that it must. Perhaps he could fake one of Alfie Betts' fits. Where would that get him? Hospital. No good. If he made a run, it would have to be from the front of this place, where the gate must be. With his head turned on his upright shoulders the man is asking for the police. Michael suddenly wants the toilet.

"Please miss, I gotta go," he says bending and jiggling to emphasise the urgency.

"Come this way." The woman gave a quick, nervous smile as she led Michael out of the room and into the hallway. The front door at the far end is completely open. The woman turns to walk away but the gardener has followed them out and now stood behind Michael, his frayed jacket and trousers hanging from his raw boned body in a distrustful slouch.

"The bathroom's in there", she said softly over her shoulder.

Thus absolved the lady of the house returned to her chess game.

Once inside, Michael turns around quickly and silently locks the door. He looks about him. There's a window open slightly above the toilet. Michael steps up onto the top of the bowl and begins pushing the window up. It makes some noise. He grabs the lavatory chain and pulls. While it flushes he forces the window all the way up and tumbles out onto the gravel below. Picking himself up, he runs. He can't see the gate in front, just a load of trees. He veers left. No good. He swings right. Then he hears the men's shouts. He turns, running blindly now, among the pampered plants, beneath the apple-burdened trees through a grove of blue hyacinths.

A policeman stood beside Michael waiting for someone in the Docherty household to answer his knock. Finally, Michael's father, who freezes at the sight of the policeman, opens the door.

"Are you Mr Docherty?"

"I am, sir," replies Seán, his initial surprise now turning to shock. The Second World War was not long over, and criminals could still be birched or even strapped to a tripod and lashed with a cat-o-nine tails. More serious offences carried the death penalty, and anyone with an Irish passport could be deported. Indeed just two hundred years earlier, taking fruit from a tree without permission in someone's garden carried the death penalty.

"We had a devil of a job getting his right name and address out of him," said the officer. He did not mention that cunning hints inviting confidences had also been rebuffed with scorn.

"What are you doing with Michael?" cried Mary Jane, pushing past her husband, who was wedging the door.

"And you are?" inquired the policeman with considered calm.

"I'm his mother!" She had a reckless look, the policeman saw, as he began explaining how her son had been arrested for stealing apples in Hampstead and that he is bailed to appear before the magistrate the following morning at the local Juvenile Court.

Having divested himself of his troublesome duty to those who needed little persuasion that it was the truth (trouble was always in their thoughts) the policeman left.

Seán Docherty, unable to contain his fear and anger any longer, began shouting, though he did not know it, trembling with rage, his tautened nerves had given way. Shouting that Michael has brought trouble to them by bringing them to the attention of the British police, and furthermore, whatever his wife thinks, he himself has no intention, nor can he afford to take a day off work to appear in an English court of law.

"What in the name of all that's holy took you to Hampstead?" he roared. And then, as an afterthought—"Was there anyone else with you?" The silent boy was looking at his shoes. He felt his heart beating to think what was going to happen to him. He found himself looking up at his mother's face, but she was so absorbed in her own discontent she could hardly feel his. He stood there screwing all his courage up, it felt as though he was rehearsing an argument over and over in his head. His father was watching him, he could not grasp… it left him perplexed.

"I thought so. Them other latchkey roughs are too cute to stray too far from the street corner. Only this tinker here would do a thing like that. I'm going out for a packet of fags, mum," he said to Mary Jane as he walked from the room, still panting with something more like fear than anger.

To the layman's eye, the Juvenile court looks no different from the adult court. Three magistrates, grave and grey, sit behind a long mahogany bench looking sternly down on Michael, while the arresting officers stand either side of him. Further back, his mother sat silently, worrying and waiting to see how these grim interrogators will go about the task of correcting the faults in her delinquent son.

"The court is now in session," proclaims the clerk, pompously. "Will the arresting officers please present their case?" Whereupon one of the police officers begins to relate the events of the previous day. The other one stands by with his notebook at the ready to clear up any doubtful details. As the magistrates listen, they keep throwing glances at the accused, who must be deemed innocent until proven guilty. Though no one standing in the dock ever appears quite innocent enough even with all their sins deducted. The policeman finished his evidence, adding with a look of formal disapproval, "the boy was not alone your worships." For where there is more than one, somebody will betray.

The chief magistrate dressed in rigorous black, the dark weave a reminder of the dignity and responsibility of his office, begins to fiddle with his spectacles. When eventually he had realigned them to his satisfaction on the tip of his veined, liverish nose, he looked down at his desk, appearing to devote himself to the study of some manual in front of him. But instead of reading, he is really weighing up the accused. The boy wears an expression of extreme hostility, though it isn't at all clear what he is so hostile about.

"Stand up!" snaps the magistrate. Michael springs to his feet.

"How old are you?"

"Eleven sir."

"And where were you born?"

"Here in London, sir."

"Why did you steal so many apples?" The boy would have liked to explain to the magistrate that no one ever wrote a poem, commanded an army or married (in the slum he inhabited) Ava Gardner. And so he liked to escape every now and then to accomplish something with mystique even if it was only scrumping fruit from a tree in the orchards of Hampstead. But even if he had been able to explain in words his judge mightn't have allowed it. "I want you to answer each question. Say yes or no at least. If you can answer in more detail, do so. Do you understand?"

"Yes sir."

"Good. Now, who else was with you?" Michael remained silent.

"The court can show clemency if you are prepared to meet it

half way, if you tell us the names of any others that were with you," coaxed the old beak, his smile terrifying with gentleness.

"I can't, sir."

"Why? Are you frightened?"

"No, sir."

"Then why can't you tell us their names?"

"Because I was on my own, sir." This makes the magistrate's military moustache bristle a bit, and he goes into a whispering huddle with his two colleagues. After a long moment, he emerges, calling for Michael's parents. When Mary Jane stands up alone, he shouts, "Where is the boy's father?"

"At work, sir," replies Mary Jane. Her utterance seems to cause some genuine concern and has the effect of pushing the bench into another huddle, there were times when the reality of the lower classes eluded them, though a fine drawn sigh might have signified approval.

This time, when they lift up their heads it is to look at the clerk, who, with formal gestures, is indicating his watch. With the court lists so full, time is of the essence, not to be frittered away, least of all on compassionate caprices. It was after all a court of law, no one should expect to be given quarter. Though it might be an advantage to be innocent.

The main magistrate nods at the clerk, then turns his attention to the accused and commences in a reasonable voice, "I see here for example, it is right before my eyes, that you tried to evade arrest. Now that in itself is nothing very serious." He went on looking at the document. "But here is something extremely unpleasant. It seems that a latch on a lavatory window was broken, violently wrenched from its socket during your efforts to evade lawful capture."

"The window was..." The accused began to protest but was cut short by the magistrate's firm conviction.

"I cannot accept any excuses, for the wilful destruction of people's private property while in the furtherance of theft."

"But it was only an apple sir…" replied the boy who had by now repented of his impulse to visit Hampstead.

"I am reading what is in the policeman's report. One might even allow that it could have been an accident, certainly such things do happen and sometimes perhaps for the most innocent of reasons, but there are other factors to consider in this case. For instance, where are your colleagues? What part did they play in this unfortunate affair? Perhaps you would like to take time now since we can allow that you have been unfortunate in the choice of your acquaintances, to reconsider your answer and inform the court of their names and their role." The magistrate looked down on the accused knowingly. Many a culprit had wilted under that piercing gaze. After a while the boy did begin to fidget and even started to shuffle his feet, clench and unclench his hands. But eventually the old beak was forced to admit to himself that in all that time (even though the youth had turned his head once or twice) he never once seemed like a boy who was looking around for someone to tell something to.

With a hint of conspiracy, the three members of the bench continued watching to see the wrong thing done. The accused would have liked to look but might have given himself away. Instead, he gazed up at a shield that was fixed to the walnut panelling above their heads; like statues in a church, it appeared to be sculpted for eternity. Upon it, a lion and a unicorn were fighting for a crown, and in the hostile radiance his eyes grew sharp with attention for above it again was a large portrait of the queen. The crown sat in its nest of purple velvet upon her proud, permed housewife's head while the light slicing through a window splintered on her claret gown, its crimson reflected upward onto her white throat and mottled her pale cheeks. The genteel composure intended had been lost in the glare of the sun, so that the face took on a look of aloof and grim indifference, while the fragile cheekbones glittered with blood in this display of light. The accused shifted uncomfortably, rocking back and forth on his feet seeking the true axis of his being, looking for an identity he had also lost. In the violence of the crucifixion Christ gave his life for man, even saints give their blood for man but here, it seemed, man must give his blood for the queen, certainly this morning, when even the sun seemed unable to rise above her paper crown. Thus the boy pondered while awaiting his fate. The police were engaged in studying righteous, square fingernails on their thick-fingered hands. While the usher leaned across to place a note (perhaps it was a transcript) before the court typist. The arm did not immediately withdraw but slithered around for a while, brushing at intervals against an occupied arm which was pursuing a course of its own. But now the sleeve of the usher's gown slid back to reveal a bare limb, matted with curling black hairs. The somewhat obscene exposure prompted in the prim typist a sudden desire to adjust the neck of her pretty pink blouse to prevent any downblousing. Both actions however, did not go undetected. They caused the clerk to clear his throat so violently he made the depositions shudder in their metal trays and a naked arm abruptly slithered away from one that was too tightly bound.

Justice hung in the balance now as the bench conferred. The air was drowsy, the crime, some might consider too minor to necessitate prolonged speculation. Nonetheless, it seemed an eternity before the magistrate addressed the young felon once more.

"We find you guilty of trespass in the furtherance of theft." At these words Mary Jane's heart gave a sudden leap of fear, though her son seemed to take the utterance quite calmly as he waited for the judge to lay down the law.

"However," continued the chief magistrate, "In view of your age, and the fact that you have not been in trouble before, we are going to give you a twelve month conditional discharge. Of course, should you come before this court, or any other within that period we will have no option but to consider you for a borstal report." He looked down at the accused once more as he pondered what had not been solved though it no longer seemed of much importance.

"Dismiss."

The sun had regained its dominance. Its golden light dazzled the beholder as it climbed above the royal crest. The boy turned slowly to find his mother waiting patiently for him. She was not smiling, but her face looked very happy, even so she could not resist a note of injury creeping into her voice as she spoke.

"You can thank almighty god and his holy mother that you are not behind bars tonight." The newly convicted remained silent. "Come on," she said to the dawdling boy who was just getting used to his freedom. "I have to get something for the dinner." And they walked out of the court to catch a bus headed in the direction of Queen's Crescent Market.

As they were walking between the vegetable stalls Michael asked his mother if he could go in search of his mates.

Her face hardened, the tips of her cheek bones turned deep red, worry made her cross. She tried to make every word she uttered sound like an accusation, every word was shaped to sting. After a while she grew silent. It was now the boy's turn to speak but instead he hung his head and looked appropriately chastened because he knew from experience that they would soon be friends again. She was only trying to show how seriously life should be taken, since her husband has warned her not to let Michael go near the local kids any more, for fear they will get him into further trouble. In fact, she feels the same way herself. Along with that, her religion, her faith dominated her every waking hour, but from time to time, other more primitive forces would override it. For above all else her Viking forefathers had valued courage.

"Well I suppose, as your father might say, 'It's no lie to lie to the servants of the crown.'" Her face softens. "Go on. But be back before your father comes home from work." She stood watching his back as he disappeared among the crowd. Only the crown is capable of stealing an apple or even slicing a whole orchard in half and expecting the rightful owners to share. She gave a small sigh and went into the butchers' and came back out with a piece of stewing

steak because sometimes the only consolation for the sorrows of
this world and to staunch the wound from which anger flows, is a
good pot of Irish stew.

Mary Jane knelt down by the hearth and with a small piece of
cardboard began scooping out the ashes from under the grate. She
wafted the dust carefully up the chimney. She shovelled all the
ashes into a sieve with the same care for the dust and began gently
sieving them. When she had finished this, she went out to the yard,
came back with a bucket, and shovelled the remainder of the ashes
into it. She worked with careful consideration, though her mind
was split. One part strong, uncomplaining, labouring at her tasks,
the other fretful and anxious to establish a life for herself and her
family beyond Raglan Street. She picked up yesterday's paper and
sat down in Seán's chair by the fireplace. An advertisement offering
money for clean rags caught her eye. She tore the piece out carefully
and put it in her pocket. She tore the rest of the paper in half, then
quartered it. She got up, went out to the scullery, and with the
corkscrew, bored a hole through the corner of the paper squares.
Then she threaded string through, knotted the lot together, went
out, and hung it up in the lavatory.

   She looked at the lines of washing strung out across her
neighbour's back yard, then at the slate grey sky. There was rain in
the air. She thought of her dream. In it, she had worn a beautiful
new swagger coat. She dearly wanted one, though her beliefs, her
religion, prevented her from expecting too much in the waking
state, because she knew, with the sad philosophy of the poor, that
one does not receive worldly treasures freely without being baked
a thousand times on the dreadful coals of hell. Yet, she could
dream as extravagantly as anyone else could. Because now at
night the skies were clear and through the days there were signs
of hopefulness, a pot of spuds, a lick of paint to brighten a damp
patch on a crumbling wall to drool over while dipping your bread
and marge in strong sweet tea.

A car turning into the street coughed in a backfire that was like a gunshot. Flocks of startled pigeons rose, flapping their wings noisily in the air, from their bombed-house roosts. Mary Jane stood watching, for a while, the birds' reluctant aerial display, then she went back inside and up the stairs to the children's rooms. Then came back down, carrying their pots to the lavatory. England had won the war, and the new Queen had been crowned, but for some it was still the age of paraffin heaters, chamber pots and rationing, such are the fortunes of war. Things would change they said, but not yet.

When Dermot reached the age of five, Mary Jane took him along to the local Roman Catholic School and enrolled him in the infants. The hall was crammed with children, many of them trembling with fear and dislike of this strange new battleground. Shy and bewildered, they clung to their mother's hands, mothers who, very near to tears themselves, told them kindly but firmly to be good little boys and girls, to say their prayers and learn their lessons, and if they did all these things properly they would go to heaven; to which most of them replied, "I don't want to go to heaven, I want to go home."

Amid these sounds of anguish, a large, vast-bosomed woman appeared. Formidable in black to those young and innocent eyes, suddenly she clapped her hands sharply.

"Good morning, children. I'm Miss Maitland. Welcome to Saint Dominic's Priory." At this point, she made a sign to the mothers that this was their cue to leave. As they begun the sad exodus she continued, "Come, come, we don't want any crybabies! We don't want any little sillies here on such a lovely Monday morning." And although the skies were grey and it was spilling down with rain outside, she continued to cover their parents' sad withdrawal with such jolly banter.

Dermot stood in a pair of tough corduroy shorts and a large grey jacket which were not his own. Certainly, they had belonged to a child, but not him. Possibly a rich one, for his mother had acquired the clothes (and his shoes) as a bargain from some second hand shop in a better area. Dermot was beginning now to feel the weight of this solemn place, yet he waved bravely to his mother as she left.

"Now I am going to call all your names out from my register." The teacher was talking again. "And you must answer your own name loudly and clearly when you hear it, is that understood?" The kiddies nodded obediently; without their mothers' backing they were already under the thumb. "And after that we will do some exercises, which we call, P.T." This didn't sound particularly comforting. But comforting sounds weren't really what one expected coming from the direction of head teachers. Miss Maitland began to call the roll and the children answered her. When they next looked round their mothers had all gone. It was a nervous experience, but the nervousness itself was exciting. Then teacher closed the register, and Morning Prayers begun.

"Holy Mary, Mother of God," their voices chanted. The kiddies were attentive and obedient on their first day, but the naughty ones were only biding their time.

THE WASH HOUSE

At first sight, it looked like a prison or maybe a workhouse. St. Pancras baths was a colossus of Victorian power. The main entrance was situated in the Prince of Wales Road, where huge, gold embossed, wrought iron gates led into a baronial hall. But only the first and second-class male bathers used that entrance. Entrance to the women's washhouse was through a more humble edifice, a side door in Grafton Road.

Mary Jane manoeuvred her laden pushchair inside, down a long corridor full of old prams and battered pushchairs parked the length of the inside wall. Halfway along, finding a space, she parked her own pram. Then, after purchasing a ticket from reception, she began to carry her wash into the main building. The place was humming with noise-full women arguing, shouting, their voices carrying across the steaming room, their bodies drenched with running sweat. As they worked away the air was a blizzard of flying suds which melted against their hot skin. By dint of perseverance and two strong arms Mary Jane made a passage through the crowd and managed to bustle herself into the very centre of the washing area where, locating an empty tub, she threw her wash into it, glad to be rid of it, while she loosened the waist band of her frock for greater ease and, after sloshing about for a bit, she soon began to scrub in earnest, rubbing sudsy clothes against the ridges of the board, working herself into a lather of acceptance under her patterned pinafore.

Some time later she put a hand up to her head; without a net steam had caught in her hair and dragged it about. She straightened up to relieve her back; her washing board clattered discordantly as Mary Jane noticed a group of cockney mothers hanging around a top corner table, jawing and smoking: the aproned Mafia, full bosomed, rigidly corseted, their skirts held up with safety pins. They never said, "Please," or "Thank you," but, blunt and noisy, always got their own way through strength of limb, if not character. Among them, her quick glance showed, were women who had been felon setting at the Coronation party. A large fan whirred above that corner. Under it, in this cauldron of heat and noise, in this streaming world of water and steam was the most pleasant place to be as they rested for a while amid the cooler currents, reconstructing their hair and peering through the suds of white indifference at their new black neighbours.

Young females, sleek girls only recently initiated into the mysteries of the wash house, steam laving their hot cheeks, breasts nuzzled inside their moist blouses, were continually interrupted in their labour by the strap or ribbon of some private garment that kept falling in a loop upon their upper arm as they bent their heads above their scrubbing boards. Other more experienced girls, some of whom were not that long married, had removed as much as was decently possible from under their flowered pinafores to avoid any such bothersome distractions. Yet the sweat still ran from their temples and beads of perspiration formed over the vivid crimson lipstick, with which they would from time to time boldly anoint themselves, as they sulked over what they were about to endure amid the sprawling entanglements of so much Irish linen. Then they daintily stooped to accomplish some final more intricate uncoupling, while their faces proclaimed that nobody would take advantage of them, as they straightened once more, to submerge their hands in the clothes-filled troughs, and scrubbed away with their nylons coolly bunched now round their still shapely ankles. Detergents floated to the surface to mingle with the swirling waves of foam as they pounded and thrashed their dirty washing against the tub's blunt edge. After which, with feet splayed against the squelching motion of the floor, they wrung the water from the clothing, effort plainly visible on their sweating faces as the sodden articles dangled from their wrinkled hands, while the grey water began to lap and slop in puddles round their shoes. Dreams had lost their power, their lives were too plain, their heads thumped with the monotony, even their dependable corsets were against them. Yet they persisted in the threatening damp and even began to rinse with some tenderness, in the soft dissolving soap-flakes, their slithery smalls. But when a stubborn stain would sometimes drive them to distraction then some would get quite reckless with the bleach as they rubbed and scrubbed, plunged and churned the foaming water to an anxious froth.

Bewildered by the sudden shape of things amid the smell of soapy garments still waiting to be rinsed, eyes watery from the fumes of rising bleach, they frowned, while the sides of the tubs palpitated as the turbulent water rose up in bubbles of silky suds, the perspiration oozed from their faces and trickled down their bodies plastering their dresses to their stomachs and their breasts. Jumpers and cardigans sank or floated in the swirling water together with the blouses and used handkerchiefs.

Then their supple backs would grow rigid as they struggled in their labour against the possessive motion of their wash, so that they would be forced to stop and straighten and loosen the buttons on their dress, while trying to equate marriage with success.

As the water continued streaming out pouring from the taps bobbing and eddying around their wrists they flung their weight against the metal tubs, plunging down and pulling up the soggy articles in ugly handfuls.

But their high heels no longer gave them adequate support and, in the natural confusion of things, as they tottered beside the shuddering tubs, there was such a tangling of blankets, sheets and household linen. Scullery skirts bumping, humping and forever re-grouping, then bending and straightening until eventually wilting from the waist down over the churning grey water amid the straggling ruins of their hair. Where the foam swelled highest one woman dropped her wedding ring; it rolled towards the drain, it made a soft plop, ripples formed on the circling water, she stooped to grab it, it was just there but the drain gulped and it was gone. Then she began to cry. The tears were streaming down her cheeks not only for the ring but for all her former losses and her recent perm that was coming down.

Old women, seasoned skirmishers, veterans of many a wash house campaign, rising from the scum of water the top of their chemise or brassiere daringly exposed, waddling on their swollen ankles between drying horse and washing troughs, gasping under the weight of excess flesh their whalebone corsets were striving to contain, joked, smoked and scavenged cunningly as they meandered among the groves of heavy wet linen, swaying in the steam of sheets waiting to be starched stiff and ironed flat, before being folded together with their own cleanliness. They patted the hairnets with which their perms were set tight for Saturday night, while clutching things so tightly to their chests. The noise of the machines reached every corner of that unearthly inferno along with the harsh gurgle of water as it escaped down the drains and only when it was absolutely necessary did Harry the janitor descend from his rooftop office to take part in some mechanical capacity, which still demanded a male's presence in this cauldron of hell, while Doris Day began singing from the communal radio "that her dreams are getting better all the time…"

Mary Jane had nearly finished the washing when Michael arrived. He'd come straight from school to help his mother arrange the wet clothes in the drying closets, with both hands gripping it tightly. Mary Jane took hold of the iron bar on the front of the rack, and heaved with all her might, dragging the rack out with a tremendous noise from its place in the hollow of the wall. Michael jumped. He didn't like this place of shattering heat; the drying closets, the huge cast iron mangles in the mangling rooms, the white and brown glazed tiled walls. The tattered bits and bobs of laundry hanging on lines, the maze of shirts and sheets and blouses, long underwear, skirts, dresses and night clothes that had their original colours washed out, overalls and pinafores marred with patches. The poverty of the area hung up for all to see. Watching his mother toil, her face pouring with sweat, teeth clenched from exertion, her frock sticking to her back from squeezing water out of sheets. It reminded him of some medieval torture chamber. He wanted to say something, but his mother was busy again, folding clothes in readiness for ironing, working with impassive indifference.

The heat came up at him in suffocating waves as Michael carried the bundle of intimate washing into the ironing room where half a dozen ironing boards, with large irons standing up-ended on them, lay scattered about. Heat from the irons had scorched the surface of the boards leaving them patterned with brown and yellow patches. Only one person was in the room, a tall middle aged woman with straight, short dark hair, and grey eyes.

She wore a black high-heeled shoe on her right foot and on the other a big black boot. She gave no sign that she noticed the boy. As Michael moved further into the room he saw that the boot was built up by a metal structure that raised it about six inches or more off the floor, and metal callipers attached to the boot, ran up the woman's leg and disappeared somewhere under her dress. Michael contemplated the deformity with fear and awe. Though he had never seen the woman before he had heard of her. She was well known in the neighbourhood and had, it was said, been a great beauty once until she was struck by lightning. It run like electricity up the iron on her leg leaving her with a snow white streak running like some weird parting down the middle of her hair and destroying her beauty on one side of her face forever.

Some could not look at her face now but the boy stood watching with fascination as the woman, her slim, bare arms exposed, fingers crooked round the iron—deftly spread a pink transparent garment on the board, flicked a sprinkling of water onto it from a mug at her side, flattened it with the iron, flipped the clothing over, and repeated the process, all in one easy, fluid motion. She worked with a fierce, tireless energy, with a kind of elaborate reverence, as if detached somehow from her deformity, as if perhaps she was unaware the boy was watching her.

As Michael stood there with the underthings still clutched to his chest, the distinct, sharp snarl of steam as water hit the scalding base of the iron startled him, wrenching him out of his trance. The woman, still holding the hissing iron, was staring at him now with a look of devastating scorn. Half nervous, half affronted, Michael stood for a moment, enveloped in a cloud of steam. Hesitant, not knowing what to do or what to say, his face growing hot and red by the second.

"Do you intend to stand there all day?" Are your knickers clean? Do you want an iron?"

"Yes. No. I'm sorry," Michael mumbled.

"Why don't you speak up?"

Michael tried to explain that he was waiting for his mother. His confusion was turning into panic, the air had altered the texture of his skin. In the middle of his confusion, the woman spoke again about the underthings Michael held tightly in his hands. She did not refer to knickers as simple items of laundry like his mother did, but by inference and jocular euphemisms. Female underclothing became vaguely improper; somehow, every other word the woman uttered fired Michael with adolescent unease. He wished with all his heart that he hadn't come into the room now, as the woman, with slow deliberation, laid the iron down on the side of the board and with a hopping shuffle, placed herself in front of him. He could see the tiny flecks of green on the grey irises of the woman's eyes, and the tiny black beauty spot on her good cheek. Michael was transfixed. It seemed an age before the woman spoke again. When she did, it was to ask the child if he would be an angel. Would he?

"Would you do something for me?"

Michael got a whiff of peppermint, or maybe gin, as the woman gave him a thin slash of a smile. Then she seemed to balance for a moment on the deformed foot as she lifted her dress, rucking it over from the side. Michael glimpsed again the short brutal iron callipers attached to her otherwise long elegant leg and gave a curious shudder as the woman pulled her purse out from somewhere inside the pleated folds of her dress.

"Here we are then sweetheart," she said, proffering Michael a coin. "Run over the road and get me five loose Woodbines. I ain't had a puff all day." As Michael took the money in his free hand. The woman raised her eyes, "You taking those along with you too?" she laughed. With one swift motion, Michael put the underclothing down on an ironing table. "There's a dear. I'll treat you when you get back," shouted the woman after him.

Michael went over to the washing area to let his mother know where he was going, but Mary Jane was nowhere to be seen. Then he remembered the drying horse, but his mother was not there either. Michael hesitated to ask a black woman whose arms were white with suds, using another horse close by, he had never spoken to a Jamaican. The swaying motion of drying garments began to confuse him, wet folds of linen were impeding too. As he stood studying the implications the woman turned and smiled down through the distances of sheets that separated them. Michael felt her round warm smile; it glittered on her flattish nose and lit her purple cheeks. Her teeth were perfect pearls of laughter. As she swirled around those islands of steaming sheets, fanning her hot face with her hand she told Michael that his mother had gone to the lavatory, but she would keep an eye on things till she came back. There were some who could not contain their ironic smiles as sheets flecked the Jamaican's skin while steam evaporated in rising clouds on her generous breasts. Michael did not think it would be fair to burden this friendly black woman any further by asking her to pass on a message, and since he would be back in a moment, he simply thanked the woman and stooped to negotiate some article's wet folds, skipping the puddles of grey water beneath the airless avenues of drying clothes.

"What are you doing with my things?" asked Mary Jane coldly as she stood in the doorway of the ironing room, watching the crippled woman putting the clothes Michael had left on the table into an empty basket.

"Your things?" replied the woman, stopping in the act as she saw the resemblance of the boy in the woman.

"Yes, mine," replied Mary Jane, moving over and picking up the basket.

"I was looking after them for the boy. Lovely child who don't give saucy answers. Is he your son?"

"Yes!" said Mary Jane curtly, and then relented as her annoyance dissolved on realising that the woman had only been trying to help. "He shouldn't have left them unattended."

"Youngsters!" sighed the woman, as if that explained it all. She began placing her own few light articles in another basket in readiness to leave. "You wouldn't have a cigarette on you duck? I'm afraid I've left mine in me other pocket at home", she asked, sweat dribbling from the pores of her opened skin

"I don't smoke," said Mary Jane as she continued ironing carefully.

"And I don't blame you either," said the woman, "What wiv the price of 'em nowadays, and then I'm up half the blessed night coughing like a lunger."

Mary Jane folded the slip she'd been ironing and placed it neatly alongside the rest of the pressed articles. As she laid a fresh article on top of the ironing board, she glanced in the woman's direction, "Yes, coughing's the worry." The woman looked seriously at her.

"My husband's the same," continued Mary Jane, "Last night I thought he was going to bring up a lung." She stopped her work and looked into the woman's face. "That's why I won't let him send out any of the kids for them."

"Oh, that's very thoughtful," said the woman, "Yes, indeed, kindness is your cruelty, I can see that… limiting the amount he can smoke… I…"

"Oh, not at all," said Mary Jane, cutting in abruptly, "It's just that I don't want the children getting into the habit of buying them. Anyone who sends kids for fags deserves shooting."

"Well I wouldn't go as far as that, dear," gulped the woman, twitching her apron. Then suddenly brisk and busy, she gathered her belongings crackling with fresh starch and, in spite of her callipers, was out of the door with a speed and nimbleness that a woman half her age would have envied. She was just in time to catch Michael coming back through the main wash area. "Oh dear, what a pity," she said, all in a fluster, as she took the cigarettes from Michael. "They'll be the death of me yet. Now I said I'd treat you, didn't I love?" But look sweetheart, I ain't got no change," she said as she took the change from the fags out of Michael's hand, "Not a copper. Tell you what darling, you remind me next time you see me, eh?" she shouted back, as she swung out the door with her curiously nautical gait. But the boy's fascination overcame any need for reward.

BRIDGET ARRIVES IN LONDON

It was Friday evening, tea time in the Docherty house. They were about to begin their meal. Mary Jane was heaping potatoes on Seán's plate. "Ah, you can't beat a good feed of spuds," he said. The kids looked on, none too sure. Mary Jane sat down and Seán said grace, then they all blessed themselves and began eating. They had not got too far into their meal when Mary Jane announced. "There is someone coming to visit us," as if she had just read it in one of the empty tea cups.

The kids looked at her; there was a period of suspense as the utterance, pleasantly mysterious, hovered above their heads in the warm air.

"When?" they asked.

"Soon."

"Are they nice, mum?"

"Everyone is nice if they're not pestered by bold children." She said this with the greatest possible naturalness, as if she had no personal connection with the matter.

"Do we know them?" asked the children looking at their mother with a sort of curiosity that was both amused and distrustful.

"No, so you will all have to pull your socks up from now on and say 'please' and 'thank you' and watch your table manners and get up in the morning when you are called and not be always late leaving the house for school. And that includes you too," she laughed, putting her hand out to pat Dermot who was looking at her with an expression of utmost solemnity. Then she went on to list each of their little faults. They were their mother's usual, silly, unintentional cruelties and the children were used to them. Even so, a stranger was coming who might turn out to be nice but for the moment must be viewed with a certain apprehension, yet it was exciting after all.

"Eat up, and don't let your dinner get cold," said their father, bored now by his wife's naïve teasing, as he tried to dislodge a turnip stump from between his teeth with his fork.

"Do you want me to tell you who's coming?" asked Mary Jane with one of her ambiguous smiles. They all gazed at her, demanding not to be deceived.

"It's your Auntie Bridget Ann, that's who it is, and if you all behave yourselves properly she may stay here with us for a while." She assisted Dermot with his food before continuing thoughtfully, "Someone will have to be at Euston station to meet her tomorrow because I have to take Dermot to the clinic." The kids, their mouths open, lips glistening with cooking fat and cabbage shreds stared at her, looking for something to show in her face, some clue as to who might be picked for that exciting adventure. But though it appeared that there was going to be an element of chance in the choosing, everyone knew who it was she would choose.

"Michael," she began without any preamble. "You will have to be up bright and early tomorrow," she said, trying to make meeting the boat train from Holyhead seem like penance, so that the others would not feel that they had been left out. Residual nostalgia made the evening light glitter more perilously so that her face, which had become whiter, took on a rather serious expression as she gave instructions to Michael for meeting his young Auntie at the station.

She was thinking, of the clubs—usually run by Greek Cypriots swarthy, dark eyed looking individuals, strange foreign men known for their sinister preference for innocent Irish girls, for use in their clubs. A source of rich pickings she knew for them was to meet the boat train each morning as it pulled into Euston after its long and weary journey from Holyhead. She thought every Greek Cypriot was a white slaver and so, in an effort to evaporate the worry of tomorrow, she began sifting among the potato skins mumbling. "Be there at the barrier before the train arrives, and watch out for them auld Cypriots." For she could see their dark eyes over their fierce moustaches glinting terribly.

"I won't let anyone touch her case, mum," said Michael seriously.

"Good boy," said Mary Jane, but the smile she bestowed on her son was a little perplexed. She looked towards her husband for support. If his expression seemed to convey something of the same distress, he disguised his concern by gouging the eyes out of a large round potato he had been deliberately saving till the last. She sighed and continued, "It's not just the case, Michael. A case can be replaced. Just don't let her accept anyone's help. She doesn't need anyone's help." Now Michael's bewilderment was complete. "How do you mean?" he asked quietly.

Faced by the question, along with the uncomprehending look on her son's face, Mary Jane could not put her thoughts into plain words—plain enough, that is, for her adolescent son to understand. It should have been easy, but there were certain crudities... as she sat looking at him, Michael grew impatient waiting for an explanation. He looked down at his plate and began frowning, more from the realisation that he would now have to start skinning a spud than for his mother's obscure warning. She watched as he ate, noting his childish hips and knees, his short trousers. Somehow they seemed to lend him an air of profound modesty and shyness and she could not find the right words to convey her sinister fears to him. Indeed the gristle on the boiled pig's trotters would have curdled before Mary Jane would be so indiscreet. Since he had his head down eating, Michael did not see the expression on his mother's face. It was a mixture of love and a resigned acceptance of her son's innocence.

Next morning, Michael stood waiting at the barriers as the minutes jerked away on the big station clock. A short wait at the barrier made it easier for him to resist glancing in whatever direction help or gifts, Greek or otherwise, might be offered. Soon, amid clouds of smoke and steam, the boat train from Holyhead pulled into Euston station. The passengers passed through the barriers, among them a composed eighteen year old redhead dressed in inexpensive clothes.

She had long, slender legs, a small waist and a bit of a bust. Michael approached her hesitantly. The look, which she bestowed on him, seemed somewhat stern; it startled the distracted boy. But she was beautiful, he saw.

"Are you Bridget Ann," he asked. The young colleen gazed at this boy who had grown too long for short pants and the sleeves of his coat.

Like her sister, Mary Jane, she had the same resolute frankness in her glance, a blend of determination and strength while her features had the celibate beauty of unsullied innocence and the serenity that comes from the discipline of a certain self-denial.

"I am indeed," Bridget replied. "And you must be Michael?" Michael was struck dumb. It was too strange. She looked like Rita Hayworth.

"Am I a mess?" she said, running a hand through her hair, as he continued to stare at her openly. "The wind got a few licks at me as I got off the train." She gave him a spontaneous hug. The boy was surprised by the warmth of her embrace, and to assert himself he went to take her case. Bridget asked him if he was sure it was not too heavy. Michael, heaving it, assured her it was not. Her clear oval shaped green eyes suddenly fixed him with exacting softness as they moved off, heads bent against the wind to another local overland platform where they caught the little suburban train which seemed to have been waiting just to take them on to Kentish Town. Their first sensation was of pleasure as they pulled open the compartment door and felt the warm air of the carriage vibrate against their cheeks. Then there was some fumbling for possession of the handle of the case because there was such a considerable gap between the platform and the carriage floor. The boy had not the strength or it could be that he was short of breath. Then she looked real standing there lifting up her luggage. He grudged her this triumph until she sat with her pretty knees together once more, perpetually untouchable, while in the smooth pane of the opposite carriage window the boy watched her pretty form flickering gently in the still clear glass. Then the boy, who had the gift of seeing while not actually looking, noticed his own reflection offering itself for approval beside this girl who was his aunt, while the little train rocked and shook and gently swayed as it rolled along whistling sometimes under a plume of grey blue smoke. They were lulled and might have slept, at least the girl, she did almost, her eyelids closed and once or twice she seemed to doze. At one point she lurched against him, gave a start then smiled and straightened. He could not be too close.

At the next stop, four young, scruffily dressed kids got on. They knew Michael, and he became self-conscious. Two of them were the ones who had smiled maliciously at his expulsion from the Coronation Party.

And they blushed and wondered at the strange and pretty girl who sat so close and still beside him now, as if she held the secret of all things in her calm green eyes.

They had become a little jealous perhaps, and became animated by her stillness. They certainly had no intention of looking, though each hoped she would take special note of them, but they could not compel her. They would have liked to show how brave they were and cast about for ways to demonstrate, but they could not find anything just then. So they asked him if he wanted to come with them to try and bunk into the pictures. *King Arthur* was on at the Forum. He declined their offer which drove them on to further recklessness.

The faces of the doubtful began to talk excitedly about the film, to make the red-haired girl respect them for their knowledge. They started to perform, throwing their arms and legs around to emphasise the method of using axe or lance in ancient mortal combat on the moving stage. The girl seemed more amused than awed by their frenetic joust. Yet in the end they did compel as the train pulled into Kentish Town West. One of them fell against and broke the carriage window.

The four kids sprang from the carriage, and the guard chased after them, but they easily outran him, jumping over the tracks and running off down the line. The guard returned and approached the two travellers. His brow beneath his greasy cap rippling with responsibility.

"You were with them," he said to Michael eagerly.

"No, I wasn't," cried the harassed boy.

Bridget bit her lip, a faint blue vein throbbed in her pale smooth forehead just below the milk white skin. They had only come three stops yet they had been involved in a play for which they had not been prepared.

"I seen you talking to them," insisted the guard.

He was breathless with anticipation, in the hiss and fizz of steam as the train creaked and strained at its couplings. The situation that contained them all had begun to stifle, not to say menace, as the boy suddenly remembered the magistrate's warning. It was approaching the hour when many would travel, passengers' faces stared out from the train windows motionless with curiosity, yet eager to resume their journey for nobody cared to speculate where this might lead. The Station Master appeared on the scene. He was a young, dark-haired, regular featured individual who stood calmly listening while the flustered guard explained the situation to him.

The station master handled this like any other situation.

Moments later, the two suspects were standing before him in his office. The transition which had been so swiftly accomplished might have intimidated if the will to establish some truth had not prevailed. So the girl pushed the hair out of her face while her young escort squared his broad shoulders and prepared to resist that which had begun to develop. They were very close now, now the wreckers had gone. The station master cleared his throat and gave an authoritative pull to his cap, which was not quite military nor yet overly casual.

"But the guard was of the opinion that you knew the boys," he said to Michael. "And if you just give me the names, you can go." He continued from his formal attitude beside the table.

The boy hesitated an instant; he was conscious that he must choose between two risks, since his aunt was aware that he knew the boys and if pressed might tell. On the other hand if he admitted any knowledge of the boys, he would have to give names. But would that satisfy the station master enough, enough that is, to let him go or would he still hold onto him? He stood in the everlasting moment that was waiting to enmesh him, while his young aunt, frowning from some anxiety, watched the walls of the strange room, which the station master took for granted, close in. Outside in the cool spring air, anonymous figures wandered along the platform of the little station or walked more purposefully up and down the entrance steps. Others of less vigorous disposition—ladies of refinement wrapped in their furs—sat expectant (for the timetable had proclaimed), shuddering with anticipation in a wooden shed, above which a tastefully painted sign declared:

FIRST CLASS

LADIES ONLY

The astringent smell of soot and smoke seeping from forlorn paint assailed the woman's nostrils so that she suddenly felt compelled to assert, "Michael was not involved with it sir, he's a good boy, and was only helping me." The station master, whose name was Alan Marshall, replied, "That's a lovely brogue you've got. Not from round these parts, are you, Miss?" He spoke not with authority but a kind of intimate familiarity. Before Bridget could reply Michael butted in with frightful daring. "She's got nothing to do with all this. She's just come over from Ireland."

"Indeed," replied the station master somewhat seriously, "and already she's acquired a brave stalwart." Michael felt a proud little thrill run through him. "However," the station master continued, directing his attention to Bridget, now, as he explained that damaging railway property was a very serious offence and that if she could throw any light on the boys who done it, he'd let them go. He leaned forward, hands tense against the tabletop; the better to accuse it might have seemed. The girl tossed back her red hair, which would flame at times.

"Oh, I see, the typical English ploy. Turn informer and we'll free you. Well to hell with your little train," she cried, pulling out a couple of notes from her pocket. "That's all I've got!" she said, placing the money on the desk. Although the action could have damaged the dignity of his position, the station master looked bemused.

"Ah, the Irish." He laughed and began rearranging some official looking documents on his desk, as he told the immigrant girl that anything to do with railway property was never such a simple matter. So they continued to stand, the two suspects in that dusty office, hemmed in by walls of implied judgement before Mr Marshall the station master who liked working for the rail company because it gave him a sense of security, of being dutiful and correct. But now, after giving the matter in hand a sufficient amount of thought, he could no longer lay claim to such lofty virtues if the dramatization of this minor incident continued. Consequently as he had already testified Michael could go, he informed Bridget, but she might have to make a statement. Nothing serious. He smiled to show her not to take his statement as an accusation—just a formality— adding that he would drop her home. The whole exchange was suddenly, familiarly, pleasantly low key. She was genuinely touched by this friendly Englishman. Yet continued to feel apprehensive, although each knew the necessity had passed. The boy was not too comfortable though, with this, as he recalled his mother's warning. He glanced quickly at his Aunt's face, but it had become concealed beneath a falling mass of burnished copper hair. In that thin light he felt confused but at least it would prevent anyone accusing her. The man and the woman were all awkwardness as they stood in the light and shade of the confined office waiting for the boy, who was not making any sign to leave. Then Bridget assured him that it would be all right and that she herself would be along as soon as she'd completed the statement, though, even as she spoke she felt a pang of guilt at falling in with the handsome station master's inspired deception. He went of course but not obediently, for he had suddenly interpreted a mystery.

"So!" said Alan, with provocative good humour, when they were alone at last, "Your first day on English soil and already you're involved in sabotaging a train." Bridget joining in with the humour of the moment replied, "Isn't it a good job I never arrived any sooner, or I might have put the Germans out of a job."

Alan liked the sound of her voice—the soft, throaty lilt of her brogue. And there were the extraordinary emerald green eyes that fixed him with passionate unrest so that he kept asking her mundane questions just to hear her reply. But after a while his voice seemed to acquire a curious air of repetitive flatness. It suddenly struck him that the girl was not really listening— something about her eyes made them seem veiled. It also seemed (though she stood erect) that she was trying not to yawn. Then he remembered that she must have been travelling for the best part of a day now, and the whole of last night. He smiled guiltily at the girl, whose clothes had been creased by that journey, then he bent down and picked up her case. "Come on," he said, "Let's get you out of here before you put me out of a job."

BRIDGET ARRIVES AT THE DOCHERTY HOUSE AND LATER LOOKS FOR A ROOM

An old Ford pulled up outside the Docherty house. A man and a woman got out, then the man dragged a suitcase from the back seat and left the young woman standing beside it as he got back in the car and drove away. Left alone on the pavement, Bridget contemplated her guilt; had she been selfish? Perhaps. Certainly she had acted irresponsibly. The girl accepted it as she stood awaiting an answer to her knock. Fortunately, it allowed her to escape her thoughts. Anticipation might have made her nervous. "Bridget!" cried Mary Jane as she flung the door back, grabbing and hugging her sister tightly, as if she were the vulnerable one. Speech was difficult in that state of excitement which long separation had intensified. Then Michael's face appeared, smiling over his mother's shoulder and somehow it absolved her.

Over a pot of tea, Bridget poured out the latest news from home, whilst her sister listened with rapt attention to her every word, lost in a kind of blissful nostalgia. A quite different atmosphere from the usually dull and ordinary life seemed somehow to have enlivened the little front room, and so the children, awed and curious, listened also. But after a while, even this warm, exotic-looking person could not keep them from being bored and they began to wander from the room. "Will you have a few hours sleep now," asked Mary Jane when Bridget had finished her tea. But Bridget felt too excited to go to bed, saying that she'd love to see Piccadilly Circus and walk along Oxford Street to view all the latest fashions in the shop windows. Bridget felt sure she was bursting into new life, a life that would be free, blossoming and adventurous. And she didn't want to waste a minute before beginning it.

Mary Jane laughed at her younger sister's eagerness. She knew that feeling—had once been full of it herself; still was, perhaps, to a lesser degree. She went to get her coat but when she returned, she had to smile. Bridget was stretched flat out asleep on the settee.

On Monday, Mary Jane allowed Michael to take the day off school so that he might accompany Bridget in her search for a room. They stopped by a house that displayed a sign on a small piece of cardboard on the front door—Room to Let. They smiled at each other and climbed the stairs. They stood surveying the front door seriously for a second or two. Then turned, deceived, accepting their guilt; even though the young woman kept telling herself it was unnecessary whatever the accusations, as they walked back down the steps, that solid Victorian stone stairway, for beneath the bright capitals of 'ROOM TO LET', dark lettering proclaimed: 'No Blacks no Irish no dogs.' And for that reason Monday became Tuesday, Tuesday became Wednesday and still they had not found a room. (On one quiet road there were no signs in the windows except for an advertisement for washing powder and a poster proclaiming KEEP BRITAIN WHITE on the wall of a pub.) Their jaws growing leaner from expectation, they walked along another street with many houses displaying 'No Vacancy' signs, or 'Room to let, would suit cultured, refined, genteel person.' It takes a lifetime to unravel such hypocrisy and the girl had only arrived by last week's train. Another house displayed a sign, 'No Irish no Darkies no dogs.' Eventually they approached a large Victorian house, its brickwork coloured by permanence. A big clear sign hung in the window:

ROOM TO LET

As they were about to mount the steps, a black dog of mixed breed startled them as it began barking furiously behind the garden gate. Bridget was the first to recover her composure and, mounting

the steps, remarked cheerily, "A dog! well we're half way there!"
Because these words covered their shame, the boy grinned and
sprang up the stairs in front of her, playfully jostling her aside in the
process. As he put out a hand to press the bell the door miraculously
opened to reveal an old woman and the dog that had previously
been in the garden. Now it bounded out welcoming the boy with
a flurry of affection. He was a huge hairy creature and his fine coat
showed that he had a good home. The old woman was laughingly
trying to control him but the dog, crazy with excitement, avoided
all her attempts by dodging in and out and around about herself
and Michael. No one could be heard above the dog's hysterical
barking, so the game had to be played until its mistress managed to
get a firm grip on its collar. At last, the great shaggy animal calmed
down and yawning massively it gave a long luxurious stretch, which
rippled the length of its muscular body, and flopped to the ground
by the front door, looking up at its mistress's face.

"So what are you after, eh?" said the landlady, who was in a mood
for kindness.

"A room," replied the boy too loudly, flattered into thinking that
the question had been addressed to him instead of the sloppy dog.

"Indeed," smiled the old lady, who had been pleased to lose herself
for a while in the play of the dog and had enjoyed the conversation
purely for the pleasure of speaking to the friendly boy. But now the
owner of the house began to feel the weight of her responsibilities
once more, while at the same time she tried to avoid any slight to
the grown-up attitude of the child.

"I do believe," she commenced. "That I have a nice top floor
vacancy, well perhaps a little higher, but I hope you will not consider
it unmannerly if I now turn to your good sister. What a lovely girl,
so nimble looking and lithe of limb, a few stairs more or less will
be of no great consequence to her. Let's see what she thinks," she
smiled, coming to the end of her consoling pleasantries by ruffling
Michael's hair. He was on the point of correcting her mistake,
but some cunning forced him to silence, so that Bridget became

cautious in turn, allowing the likely but erroneous assumption also. "Would that suit or did you have something larger in mind, dear?" prompted the landlady, hands folded patiently beneath her ample bosom. Bridget would have liked to stay in the warmth of the previous moment but the moment of truth had arrived, she could no longer avoid it. She could no longer conceal herself behind her young nephew's accent and was racked by the fresh embarrassment to which she had submitted herself. Why she had allowed it is difficult to say, except that it had been the same yesterday and the day before yesterday, and it might be the same today and tomorrow and forever. She glanced at Michael but accents did not bother the boy, he was looking happily at the dog, while the landlady waited with a sweet smile upon her face for the girl to state her intention. For a moment, the younger woman was intensely conscious of some nervousness inside her so that her voice when she spoke was not convincing to her.

"The attic will suit me fine," said the flushed girl. The landlady began to tremble for the discovery she had made.

"That's a lovely Welsh accent you have." Whether this was so or not the woman claimed it, and seemed to believe it. Bridget was about to admit what suddenly she could not, since she was filled with a melancholy longing for permanence. After a few moments of hesitation, the old women chatting cheerfully throughout, motioned with a plump benevolent hand for the lean girl to step inside. "I'm not prejudiced myself but most of my other tenants would leave if I started to cater to Irish and darkies." Her lowered tone suggested that she could have revealed more, only discretion would not allow. "Scotch and Welsh are fine," she continued brightly "in fact I've had one or two Welsh people staying before." She smiled, giving Bridget a broad, conspiratorial wink which dared her to assert herself, so Bridget smiled back to put an end to speculation. She might have thanked the woman, (this girl whose worn down shoes were hurting her feet) if she knew what voice to use. Instead, images of shame began to present themselves to the young colleen for the step she was about to take, while the boy, whose own future was still obscure, watched as her tongue flicked to moisten her lips. It seemed an almost insignificant act, this gesture which allowed the mouth to settle back into its original shape. She tensed her shapely calves in her old shoes that still showed signs of their decent origin, and stood firmly on both legs. And now her voice was her own. There was no reason why it should not have been.

"I'm not from Wales," she said looking at the woman with the sudden realisation that she would forever be an alien in this land— great and wondrous though it be.

"Of course you're not," said the landlady glittering with sweetness after disguise has been abandoned. There was a tremor in her lip as it curled round her teeth which in anyone less prejudiced and benevolent would have been a sneer. And calling the dog to her side she closed the door in their faces. The closed door emphasised the silence of the afternoon and increased a sense of isolation as they both stood staring at the polished knocker.

Bridget looked at Michael. He burned with shame. Jolted out of her own unhappiness by the nakedness of his emotion, she started to fuss with the collar of his shirt to purge herself for incriminating him in her disgrace. And putting a comforting arm around him, she steered him away from the door down the mopped steps and out of that respectable street. The girl's spirit still walked erect. Only her sagging shoulders betrayed her own private humiliation. But the boy's body had become awkward for some need that couldn't accept her shared pity. As they continued along the pavement he was aware of strangers pointing fingers at him from inside curtained rooms. The youth's isolation was made no less terrible by his white skin. His own guilt was bending him as he remembered the songs his father often sang of those men and women who had not submitted to the tyranny of the crown. Each day after that she set out alone determined not to allow the stunning misery of the previous day's racial knockbacks to become dead weights upon her own spirits. For along with a room she was also seeking a job.

One day Bridget enters an old building and hurriedly enquires but is made to wait while the receptionist attends to some adjustment of her costume jacket. This takes up all her concentration. Finally, the older woman; after brushing something, dust or dandruff perhaps, from a sharp lapel, looked up at the country girl with excessive casualness then waved her away. "First left then right," in the tone of voice she kept for foreigners. The applicant, with all her shortcomings of speech and dress, did not forget to smile back her thanks at the superior woman who ignored even the mechanical gestures of her own directions. Bridget rushed around the corners, then began to step more cautiously on finding that many other women had arrived before her and were already waiting outside the Interview Room. The girl was stunned but managed to control her gasping breath. She was quite exhausted; there was a desperate longing in her eyes. Troubled at not being able to express herself in the ways of her adopted country and in her dowdy clothes, she had begun to feel her inexperience of life. Though there were already one or two other competitors for the job, the slim girl felt she had the strength and ability below the surface if they could be gathered. The sophisticated women, shifting reluctantly to make room for her on the waiting bench, seemed to have a subtler longing in their eyes, as if they had already transcended such mundane virtues.

Bridget entered another building... the offices of a law firm. She sat in a room near a desk and waited for the elderly man behind it to finish reading her references. She had waited in this or another office for how long she could not tell. In all those other places, women with taut cheekbones and a hope for the future had also waited, facing the reality of a hard chair in front of the grand inquisitor, who sat behind his mahogany altar impassively. They smiled, these girls, showing their perfect teeth terribly, for most knew they would not survive his judgement but were only just tolerated by the sceptical eye. Yet still they came, passing each other like ships in the night, to sit there, legs crossed with a whisper of nylon, bottoms tightly wedged to an unyielding chair with hopes intensified to a point that was unwise.

"You see," said the severe looking man, though not unkindly, "along with your normal secretarial qualifications, one also needs a diploma in legal administration." Bridget quietly rises to leave. "I'm sorry, miss." Bridget nodded politely. They were honest humiliations at least.

The young woman stepped off the train at Kentish Town West and began walking along the platform close to the scuffed whitewashed edge. Suddenly a voice called out

"What's happened to our little saboteur?" The passenger looked up to find the station master standing in front of her looking strong—heroic even. But it was unconvincing, she could barely muster a smile. "I never thought our trains were that bad." To greet passengers cheerfully was an official act, but now inwardly the man quivered with some private emotion. The girl's face brightened slightly.

"That's better," quipped the enthusiastic man. "Come and have a cup of tea?" Bridget hesitated. "It will cheer you up", he entreated but the forlorn woman was not so sure. "I know it does whenever I'm feeling down," said Alan the station master guiding her towards his office. "Take the weight off your feet," he continued when they were inside, "While I make a cuppa." He turned towards the gas stove where a kettle sat, its spout raised.

"Do you live here?" she was naïve enough to ask.

"No" said Alan, I've got a room at Mrs Watson's, a nice old lady who keeps a lodging house at Hampstead. But on seeing her looking at the bed, exclaimed: "That's for when the gangs are working on the line. Then I have to stay nights." He filled the kettle, placed it on a small stove, lit the gas and turned to his guest. They gazed at each other for a moment. Alan is sensitive to the fact that she must be feeling lonely and vulnerable in a strange land. He is about to say something when the kettle's shrill whistle startles them. They both laugh, then Alan brews the tea. He hands her a big mug. She takes a sip.

"Not too hot is it?"

"No" …She smiled.

"Been out sight seeing?"

"Chance would be a fine thing," replied the girl almost irritably. "I've been looking for work."

"Any luck?" She shook her head.

"Something will come along," quipped the confident man. The woman sighed as she sat there, mercilessly exposed in the still light of the dispassionate room. But the young station master, staring at the cup in his hand, could not help her. He began to stir his tea again while he looked at her lips, which were all awkwardness and had changed colour. He picked up a roster. He was glad he had the timetable in his hand and was employed in this way among signals and levers, capable of guiding to their destinations trains full of people, while averting with a touch of the hand accidents and catastrophes and quite often death. While the girl, unable to free herself from some constraint, continued to sit, sipping guiltily at her tea in this room, amid the smell of clean oiled metal where only essentials were given any space. For a long time they were silent as the man attended to his various duties, while trains hurtled through the small station whistling on one note, so that the young woman began to feel apprehensive as she listened for sounds of their approach. Something had made them strangers or it could have been that they were embarrassed by proximity. The woman watched the man's assured hands. He was sufficient in himself. It was no consolation to remember her own inspired dreams which were now much reduced.

Suddenly a tear stole down her cheek as a sob shook her body. He turned and in his bewilderment put his arm, which was more familiar with the motion of levers and trains, round her shoulders. He was full of concern "There, there," he murmured, and went so far as to squeeze a shoulder. In the devastating silence that followed the young woman started to wipe her hand across her eyes trying bravely to smile. Embarrassed now she began to straighten herself up. "I think I'd better go," she said, because something was expected of her.

"Stay; have some more tea," said the man, because he felt his own awkwardness.

"No, I think I've made enough of a nuisance of myself for one day."

"I'd like to see you again," he said, barely offering the words.

"For sure you will," replied the girl with some bravado. "I'm nearly always on that train." But he could hear the breath trembling in her words, he put his hands on her shoulders and looked into her eyes.

"Not as a passenger."

Mary Jane was patching a collar on her husband's shirt while he was sitting in the armchair reading the paper. Dermot was playing on the floor using one of his father's boots as a train. Michael and Danny were flicking cigarette cards up against the front room wall. When Bridget, who was ironing clothes on the table, suddenly made a little sound in her throat that was difficult to interpret, then asked of no one in particular, "Would you mind very much if someone were to call round here for me on Saturday night?" Seán Docherty blinked in surprise at the unfamiliar request, while Mary Jane and the children, suddenly alert, anticipating an event with some enjoyable surprise, waited to see how he would respond. But he had been stunned into silence by a mixture of shock and uncertainty, and for the moment did not have the wit to reply. Bridget lowered her head and guiding the iron carefully, she continued pressing gently to avoid singeing the inside shoulder of her blouse. Resentment and irritation finally forced Seán Docherty out of himself.

"Who is it?" he asked gruffly.

"Just a friend I met at the station," replied the laundress, her hand steady, as she negotiated the heavy metal around the buttons of the blouse. Seán Doherty's brow wrinkled with uncertainty.

"I know him, I know him!" blurted Michael. Everyone including young Dermot turned to stare at him. "He's got gold and red stripes down the sides of his trousers and a great big silver badge on the front of his cap," continued the messenger unabashed. To the boy, the station master's splendour could not be denied. So if he perceived a golden tassel shimmering brightly where only a brass button glinted dully, or a furled signal flag for a sword then he was only investing his image with those benefits and wonders we all hope to find at the heart of our mirage.

Seán Docherty lit a cigarette and took a long thoughtful drag, then spat the smoke from his lungs into the fireplace. He watched his sister-in-law's supple body as she bent over her makeshift ironing board. Lulled by the movement of the iron, his thoughts slowly drifted as she passed it with a flourish over the strips of fresh steaming cloth, nudging the tip inside and around the pink puckered brassiere cup, delicately gliding along the slim suspender belt, so unlike his wife's boned corsets and other things of firmer armature.

Suddenly Bridget lifted the iron, tilting it towards her face, she pursed her lips and primly spat (to test its heat) upon its metal base. An act which some might have considered coarse, he found intriguing and it roused in him an urge to rub a lipstick holder's crimson tip (which stood upon the mantelpiece) into the secrecy of that murmurous iron's metal base where heat could be felt without touching, where spittle curdles on contact to disappear in a hiss of steam. As she continued to make smooth the awkward wrinkled shapes of her laundry, the occupants of the room turned their gaze to stare at the laundresses' hands, dazzled by the transparent unprotected skin, their eyes glazed with an indefinite anxiety.

It might have stayed that way forever except that Bridget's laundry included a colourful cardigan, which served to provoke her young nephew's recollection. So that he began to intrude upon the silence with further, even more glorious descriptions and embellishment of his auntie's beau's attire. His father had lost interest; he lowered his eyes, and withdrew his gaze. His gaunt face was veiled in brooding, while the boy blushed excitedly in his eagerness to get it all said. For Mr Docherty sinister prospects were opening in his own house. As he listened to the sound of his son's voice he was torn between trying to take in Bridget's request, his son's outburst and the noise of the rest of the children as they started to resume their games. He solved this dilemma quickly enough, however, by suddenly ordering all the children upstairs to bed. Bridget feeling terribly guilty at being responsible for their imminent departure looked on with affectionate despair. As Mary Jane picked up Dermot and began ushering the rest of her brood from the room, she asked if they wanted to kiss their auntie goodnight. But the children, even the youngest of them, had developed a wary reticence and did not avail themselves of the offer as they continued their reluctant departure, though one or two of them did bestow on her marvellous imitation smiles.

Now the silence in the room became immense. They were both awkward for a while trying to observe the common forms of courtesy. The man looked over at his sister-in-law hoping, perhaps, to avoid some indelicacy, but his strength was not up to it and so he demanded, rather than asked. "Is he a military man, or what?" But Bridget was prevented from answering just then, because Mary Jane, shuttled between bedding her children and monitoring a situation, had come back into the room and, having overheard her husband's blunt question, began scolding him to be quiet. But he ignored her request, continuing unabashed,

"I won't have any bloody British soldiers under my roof." The girl looked up at him with a little frown of pained anxiety.

"He's not a soldier," she said quietly. "He works for the railway."

Later that same night, with his hand under the bedclothes, Seán Docherty placed it between his wife's thighs. At the same time, he tried to kiss her, aiming for her mouth, but hitting mostly cheek. She pushed him away, annoyed but the hand insisted.

"Ah musha will you quit that auld nonsense?" She turned her annoyance into a mild sigh. Completely frustrated by her carnal indifference, he gave a low moan.

"If only you were as quick at saying your prayers," sighed Mary Jane. Seán looked up at the ceiling before replying, with resignation, "When the Buffalo dance hall is full to the brim every weekend with young Irish men, why in the name of all that's holy did she have to take up with an Englishman?"

"Now, there's no cause to fret," said Mary Jane, (here at least she could console) "Because she can't marry him unless he becomes a Catholic."

"Are you sure about that?"

"Well, I suppose she couldn't be stopped if she was set on it… but I think he would have to agree to let their children be brought up as Catholics. Still, children are the least of their worries at the moment."

"Are they?"

"Of course."

"Are you certain ?"

"What are you saying?"

"Nothing, nothing at all. But…"

"Are you codding, or what? Sure they've not known each other five minutes." In the pause that followed Mary Jane closed her eyes to offer up a few prayers.

"Ah," whispered the husband, from out of the silence he pounced and laughed a conniving laugh, "many a job can be finished before that."

"Will you quit being so daft? Bridget's a fine girl and not thinking of marriage at all," grumbled Mary Jane from a tangle of disarranged bedclothes, her attempts at pious serenity wracked by menstrual torments.

"But wouldn't it suit you just fine," said Seán, (not so much for defence as taking revenge for some neglect) turning away from her and wrenching the covers over and tighter about himself. "If she were—two in one go. A husband for Bridget and a convert for the Church."

But now the exposed woman had found contentment in prayer along with a warm cosy burrow between two hillocks in the lumpy mattress, and chose not to hear as she mumbled herself to a sleep as virtuous as the man she had married probably felt.

On Saturday afternoon there was a lot of bustle in the Docherty household, in preparation for the stranger's visit. Mary Jane had sent the children to the public baths for their weekly scrub, while she had cleaned the house and generally busied herself in the activities of poverty. At around six o'clock, Seán lit the gas lamp in the front room and all the family were herded in there to await the railway worker's coming.

So few and far between were the visitors that called at No 14, that, when the knock on the front door sounded, they all tensed. Then Michael sprang to his feet. "I'll answer it!" he shouted. An event in any way out of the ordinary became an emotional disruption.

"Sit down you," hissed his father angrily. "Your mother will answer it."

She returned with Bridget and Alan and, after everyone had shaken hands, a strange game of musical chairs began, in an effort to accommodate the courting couple within the crowded little room. When eventually all were seated, an awkward, embarrassed silence followed. Alan smiled over at Seán in an effort to break the ice. "Have you been here long, Mr Docherty?" he asked politely. But, since it wasn't clear whether he meant in that house, Seán Docherty began to feel his confidence ebbing, he was conscious of this himself; perhaps a bit too conscious even—he felt that he had to be just that little bit aggressive and facetious to prove that he was at ease with this Englishman. He began talking and, since he spoke rapidly, it seemed he was speaking spontaneously. "Too long," he laughed, mirthlessly. "And I'm thinking of going back one of these days," he continued, launching into a speech about the wonders of Ireland, where on another plane of reality he belonged.

Alan listened attentively, but Mary Jane knew he was only repeating outdated sentiments—old stories and jokes. The country he was describing no longer existed. But her husband, too firmly launched now on a wave of sentimental excess to care about details, pulled a photograph from his shirt pocket and offered it to his guest. It was a picture of himself as a young man with his arm across a horse beside a plough. Alan noticed it was discoloured and dog-eared.

"Jeez, Seán," said Bridget, in an effort to rescue Alan. "You paint a wonderful picture. You'll have Alan packing up his job and going back with you too!"

Everyone laughed, and Alan now turned to Mary Jane. "What about you, Mrs Docherty?" Mary Jane, jolted from her reverie, looked up at him, unprotected. She did not respond, she sat quietly, seemingly unmoved, though she felt guilty each time she betrayed the past. Where could she go? Uninvited, she has promised herself to this place; she can no longer imagine herself anywhere else, and there is no pleasure in remembering her life before she came here. Time lay like gentle mists across its stones.

"How do you feel about it?"

"Aren't I as happy here as anywhere else?" she smiled. But Bridget knew she was only pretending—putting the best face on it for the sake of her children. After that it fell silent. In the thin light Seán Docherty rubbed a flat hand across his anti-British eyes. The children were bored but had to endure this for the sake of the guest, though pimples or a wart if they could find one were more interesting. Meanwhile they cast imploring glances in the direction of their mum until eventually she revived everyone by offering to make tea. Her husband was too absorbed to more than mumble his approval, the courting couple smiled wistfully while the children who, by this time, were bashing their heels against the old settee so vigorously they were knocking bits off it, jumped up and followed her out of the room, not to assist but to prevent rigour settling in their youthful limbs.

As she opened the cupboard in the scullery Mary Jane Docherty frowned at the sight of the chipped crockery, though after her initial disappointment she stood staring like old women who gaze with rapture at the dregs in a cup. Romance and courtship were softening her. It was impossible to escape what might, after all, turn out to be an unofficial engagement party. Mary Jane had embraced her dream at last. "Michael, she called gently, "run over to Mrs Cotter's and get me a sliced white loaf, a block of vanilla ice cream, two bottles of Tizer, a large fruit cake and a small packet of serviettes." Electrified by the festive air which had suddenly filled the scullery the children brightened. Michael snatched the money from his mother's hand and rushed towards the front door. While Mary Jane began to set out her table, too entranced with her vision now to notice the shortcomings in her crockery.

Later that night after Bridget and Alan had gone and Mary Jane had seen the children to bed, she gathered up some of the kids' clothing that she had intended earlier for mending, and sat down at the table, now to begin, while her husband continued sitting quietly at the grate. Comfortably and contentedly occupied with her sewing, Mary Jane should have felt protected; but she was not. Some uneasiness kept nudging at the back of her mind. On closer examination, she noticed that Seán was, perhaps, not sitting so contented as he first appeared. Then she remembered that he had not gone out for his usual pint the night before. This break with routine was what disturbed her, so she asked,

"Aren't you going out for a pint tonight?"

"Ah, I won't bother," he replied.

"Is anything wrong, Seán?" she asked softly. When he failed to reply she went on "Sure, wouldn't you be better off going out for an hour or two than to be sitting there staring into the grate?" He made no answer, and did not look up, and now she was certain there was something very wrong. Forced to broach a subject he seemed determined to avoid, Mary Jane threw aside her mending and moved over towards him. She was most anxious to touch again the things she knew.

"What is it, Seán? What's wrong?" She felt a fear creeping over her, she insisted though, because it is better finally to know.

At that moment he might have been persuaded to reveal, but his contemplation of the grate appeared too grave to be interrupted, so she was forced to probe a little deeper, as the white flames shimmered and danced behind the grate's warped unequal bars.

"Seán" she called softly, as she watched the spitting sparks. He closed his eyes, he was becoming hypnotised by the grate, obsessed by it. Now at last he roused himself and turned finally to face what he could no longer avoid.

"Ah 'tis this—this is what's wrong." He said as he pulled a piece of paper from his pocket.

She took the letter from him nervously. She did not wish to see, but must while he continued to look into the fire, she frowned or squinted to read the precise and deliberate words aloud:

"Some Utility Company's interpreting the wishes of their customers who have voiced concern over immigrant workers entering their homes will in future limit the amount of Black and Irish workers they employ." Mary Jane broke off, whispering "God in Heaven!" At such times she began most grievously to feel her own vulnerability. Then, steeling herself, she put her hand into her pinafore pocket, pulled out her purse, and took from it a ten-shilling note.

"Any man that's worked hard all week deserves a few pints on a Saturday night," she said firmly. He looked up at her. "Go on," she coaxed gently. And, looking at her now, he remembered the time when he had first held her in love at a dance in Ballymote.

Seán Docherty sat very still now, as other thoughts of Ballymote came to his mind... Then his body gave an almost imperceptible quiver as the penance of memory began to unfold.

It was a time of hardship and heavy taxes. And when deer from the local Lords' estates would stray onto one of the farms, then poachers would snare and kill it, and hide the animal's body under a blanket of green rushes, where it would lie until nightfall, when it would be loaded on a donkey cart by the farmer and taken to an outhouse to await collection by the poachers who would allocate a hefty chunk of venison to the farmer before taking it away to sell in town. When, one cold grey November day, a great fallow buck happened to stray onto Seamus Docherty's wet land, it was duly snared and killed and lay under its mantle of rushes until nightfall, when, at around midnight, big Seamus set out with his ass and cart towards the boggy field to collect it.

Snow began to fall as he led the ass further up the hill. Away in the distance he could make out the lights of the barracks in the town, and knew that the patrols would soon be about. But it was safe enough. The Tans were keeping strictly to the roads now, since there had been a hanging in the town a week before. A boy of sixteen was accused of hiding arms under hedgerows along the road for the rebels; and, since the area was under martial law, he was tried for it, standing before a court martial in the square. Drummers of the Royal Dragoons beat him bravely to the gallows and he was hanged there at the barracks in order that the people of Ballymote might learn loyalty and obedience to the British Crown. Big Seamus pushed on, dragging his mind away from the thought. Far off, a cur howled chillingly in the darkness, and the grey ass listened with quivering nostrils.

As the night increased, the wind rose, driving the snow ever thicker, in great gusts. The soldiers drew their greatcoats more firmly about them and, cursing the night and weather, slouched along somewhat reluctantly behind the tall, trim figure of their Officer. They were hard-featured individuals; their ferocity was well-known and their reluctance stemmed in no small measure from the fact they were not subject like regular soldiers to strict discipline. The brainchild of Sir Winston Churchill, they were offered pardons for their sins—provided they joined the Black and Tans, to police Ireland. Suddenly, in a moment of weakness, which his men took for kindness, the Officer decided to take shelter and, turning off at the first house they came to, marched up to the door and rapped with his stick on the shutters.

They were polite enough. "The night is long and the weather cruel, ma'am," said the Officer, poetically, tapping his boot with his stick as Agnes Docherty still stood, blocking the doorway, surveying them without pleasure. The Tan Officer was carelessly unanxious. His father was a Baronet, his mother a Lady, and they had brought him up to have respect for women. Anyway, entry was assured, since he carried a King's Warrant and, more importantly, the means to enforce it. As he stood deciding on this, a sound reached them. The unmistakable sound of a creaking cartwheel. The soldiers stiffened and turned to meet the Officer's nod; then, with unslung rifles, they stealthily crept away.

Not a word was spoken as the Officer retreated to the shadows away from the lighted doorway where Agnes Doherty stood. Suddenly, a shot rang out in the crisp night air. Agnes crossed herself and gazed appalled. The officer saw this and smiled with sour contempt. The sound of shouting, coupled with the noise of the trundling cart, woke young Seán and, springing from his bed, he ran out to the yard to stare with childish wonder at his mother's tearful face. Suddenly, vividly, with an intensity that wrung his heart, he saw his father's lifeless body lying where the soldiers had placed it on the freezing ground.

In after years, Seán Docherty could not remember with any great clarity, the night of the Tans' visit to his parent's house. In his memories of what happened, there was only an animal—a great dark furry beast with horns, sprawled, bleeding on the ground, turning great patches of snow into crimson slush, and a soldier standing over it, tapping his boot with his stick. Somehow the awful arrogance of that habit had impressed itself on the young child's mind.

Then the drumbeat came echoing across the fields and down along the road as the government line split and then reformed and Seán Docherty got up, for it had started pounding in his head.

The days were full of shaken emotions and ravished landscapes dotted all over with bomb sites. In a country that had frequently put the rope around the wrong neck, the noose was tightening, though most immigrants still had expectations. Trusting to instinct that somehow things would eventually be restored to balance, allowed to settle back naturally into their original easy-going shape: viewed thus the situation appeared more tolerable. So, men rose while it was still dark and wandered about in search of civilised employment but somehow there was a problem with their timing. They always seemed to arrive a little too early or perhaps it was a little too late, the assured receptionists were kind enough to inform them, but in the end even by the full light of day they could not tell the appropriate hour. If here and there a body became exhausted by the weight of it as it took root in those orderly English suburbs then that was to be expected.

Though nobody believed there would ever come a time when justice was not to be had in the lives of the despised, even if the writing on the walls of the public urinals declared otherwise. The wall chalkers it seemed would never have enough room to proclaim their opinion.

Though you could avoid seeing by not looking it was somehow always in the line of the eye. Hovering above the brown stain on the white urinal. So that even the pure and the innocent who might otherwise have misinterpreted the usual signs were left in no doubt:

PADDY FUCK OFF BACK TO THE BOG

Faced with the prospects of making a life amongst this, an idea of going away would sometimes lift and lighten their hearts. Until on reflection, in a moment of complete loss or clarity, they would remember that exile meant staying forever.

THE SHAPE UP

The men stand (some cursing to themselves to stiffen their resolve), row upon row of Irish immigrants, a quarter of a mile long and six deep from Camden Town Tube Station, right up along both sides of Kentish Town Road. They are dressed in the uniform of the navvy—a short jacket (or "donkey"), an old pair of trousers (many with thick patches sewn roughly over the knees) and a pair of hob-nailed boots. Some have digging irons in their coat pockets: a flat metal plate to strap onto the instep of the boot, which will help drive the shovel's blade into the ground with greater ease. "A man should always have a good pair of boots and a good bed, because if he isn't in one, he should be in the other," was the ganger's pithy philosophy. Yet very rarely are both these basic necessities achieved. Certainly, everyone has boots, but not all have rooms or beds—and so many of these workers are forced to sleep rough. But now their hard hands began to take shape as they whistled a tune that had stuck in their head and stamped their blood to life.

Some of these men are legends amongst their navvy brethren. Their fame as fighters, workers and even drinkers is known to almost every Irish labourer up and down the country, and varied incidents about their lives are common gossip amongst the work gangs. They are men on the lowest rung of the social order, yet their work is vital in building the infrastructure that will bring about a modern Britain. Through the toil of Irish navvies, Empires have sprung up around the globe.

As the dawn dusk is just lifting, a raw wind thickening with rain begins blowing through their ranks. The men turn their faces away from the rain but it is hard upon their necks.

"I'd as soon be cutting turf with a broken loy on our bog," remarked a Mayo lad standing next to Seán Docherty.

A fleet of trucks stand, parked at the kerb's edge. Some green, others grey, their colour denoting which section of country they work on. Some of these men will travel as far as Canterbury or Eastbourne today; others even further. Depending on their route, they will either dig trenches out from virgin chalk or shovel shingle and running sand. For this, they will receive four pounds and they will earn every penny of it. When they finish at nightfall, they will be tired out, wet through and muddied to the thigh.

Now the lorries start revving and their racking fills the air. At a signal from the agent, the regular men move forward and begin clambering aboard the waiting trucks, while a gang boss walks up and down the line taking the measure of all the new men left in the shape-up, the street resounding with the ringing beat of his hob-nailed boots. Every so often, he stops before a man.

"What's your name?" he demands curtly.

"Docherty." The interview is over. "Jump up on the back of that truck." The transaction is completed. A man is hired. Cold words on a cold morning, but the walking ganger's harsh manner gives pulse to sluggish blood.

It is still dark as the last truck pulls out of Camden Town. The new men are tightly packed, sitting on the floor of the lorry. Cigarettes are rolled and smoked as they speed along, heading for the open country. After about two hours, the truck pulls off the highway into a side road. Seán Docherty yawns and stretches out his leg in order to relieve a cramp. The men are starting to get edgy, their hobnails scraping on the metal floor as they are jolted and swayed. Eventually, the truck comes to a stop by a wooden hut in the middle of a field. The Ganger gets out of the cab and walks round to open the tailgate. The men climb down. The Ganger unlocks the door of the hut and begins handing out shovels and picks. There's a trench to be dug, a hundred yards long, six feet deep and three feet wide. Soon, the air is filled with the ring of pick and spade on flint and stone along that sunless furlong.

Seán Docherty is stiff and clumsy at first, but gradually, he loosens up as he gets into the rhythm of the work. Kicking down on the shovel's blade, bending the handle over the knee, swinging back and letting fly in a fury of labour. After half-an-hour, he is streaked with mud and sweat. The rest of the gang are spread out along the trench about ten yards apart, working their section, tearing it up and throwing it out, the lumps of earth and clay spinning through the air to land at the side of the swiftly deepening trench. And so they work their way through the morning with an hour break for dinner: tea and sandwiches, which they ordered from the Ganger, who wrote down their choices on a slip of paper which he handed to the driver to fetch. During the afternoon, it starts to rain. The trench was quite deep now.

The rain stopped and suddenly the sun shone through the clouds. They were well below the brown topsoil, yet the going had become harder since they'd struck a tighter packed layer of red clay. They became spattered with it as they struck with their picks. Seán Docherty's hands were a mass of calluses and blisters. He sweated and swore. In the late afternoon haze, the fading sunlight was ruddy upon them. The Ganger walked along the side of the trench, his craggy face giving no sign of his thoughts or mood; perhaps watching everybody and then again, perhaps not. At the far end of the trench he paused, rolled a smoke, took a drag then slowly sauntered back again. The men were becoming impatient, stealing glances at the Ganger, waiting for his shout that would end their day.

ST PATRICK'S NIGHT DANCE

Though it would always remain the work of younger men, within a few days Seán Docherty became more accustomed to the heavier labour, and, except for a twinge in his ankle that from time to time caused a slight limp, he had more or less taken to his new job, and with more energy to spare found himself (in theory anyway) taking part in the wild humour and sudden bursts of horseplay of the younger navvies, so that when it was suggested that their older workmate might join them for a pint at the forthcoming St Patrick's night dance he readily agreed, because he liked them. So on the following Saturday night Seán was found by his workmates sitting at the bar in the Buffalo dance hall in Camden Town, while the girls waiting to be asked to dance were standing around in huddles, pretty and provoking, with intriguing little sprigs of shamrock pinned above their firm busts. Though many were only recently arrived immigrants whom everything surprised, some native cunning prompted those (whose nature was to run to greet) to put a little reserve into all their dealings and expressions. And though their eyes might be averted with virginal modesty, each new cavalier was noted and appraised. Low on their forehead bounced Celtic curls as the men approached with a consciously virile swagger the colleen of their choice, but their earthy excitement was soon curbed by some of the girls nonchalant reserve. Though pleased at first by the request, accepting an invitation to dance is never a simple matter in a place so big with fate. To show a bit of reluctance gave more edge too, however certain a girl's acceptance might eventually be. Two young girls, who were sitting at a corner table would nudge each other. Any man who approached made them giggle with virginal hesitancy. The willing—the not so willing wilting wall-flowers, all were approached by the young cavaliers until eventually everybody (even those who it seemed would refuse every would-be suitor's advance) was dancing, swirling round the floor, heads up, flaunting their bold happiness. Some of the men held their partners so far at arms' length, that if they wished to speak they had to shout. While others clutched theirs so tight many a poor girl was close to fainting from lack of air. Over by the bar voices roared with laughter at some tale that was certainly indecent. Now and then a girl would pull her chaste cheek back from a partner who was moulded to her bosom, their heads full of cautionary horrors about what kissing a man could lead to. Ground gained one moment seemed to be lost the next as each suffered the other's feet. They were, from time to time, humiliated by the clumsy lunging and plunging that passed for dancing in some of the older men and for these the women had nothing but scowls and pouts and a longing for the dance to end, while more tender sentiments were aroused in a colleen's heart for those with fresh skin and impeccable feet. But soon, like the music, everybody began to fall into their own natural rhythm. So the evening progressed with gaiety and laughter until finally the band stopped between two notes. There was a roll of drums from the stage as the band leader encouraged the ladies and gentlemen to take their partners for the last dance. Couples moved out onto the dance floor.

As the band struck up for *The Siege of Ennis* the floor was thronged with swaying dancers. While some of the men watched from the sides others including Seán Docherty stood finishing their drinks at the bar. The noise became intolerable as cheers and shouts were added to the tune. As the music ceased the crowd began to whistle and clap. The evening had come to an end; women were putting on their coats while men were making one last visit to the cloakroom. Though the dimming lights lent to the atmosphere a touch of melancholy, it was not a scene of sad partings; most would see one another the next day at mass. Then the lights went out completely, so they did not know where they stood. They might have remained clinging to the walls, or their own inadequacies, if they had not evolved during the evening to a world of trust. Some lips were open to be kissed. Others after so many hours of intimacy intended to be touched (in an appropriate place) but fumblings in the dark reduced the girls to giggles, some put out a hand and there was nothing while others were thrown against a thigh so that there was laughter and many a sniggering jest as male and female bodies closer than they needed jostled amid smoke and human stuffiness towards the exit.

A few moments later they emerged from the depths of the darkened dance-hall into the cool night air. They might have felt cosseted except for the fact that whatever harmony they had experienced in the early part of the evening a discordant note had been struck for the latter. They moderated their step and huddled close, disturbed by the vagaries of a world they had been forced too quickly to re-enter. It was the natural outcome of limbs that have learnt to co-operate together, as they spotted the motionless apparitions lining the road which slabs of dark shadow were helping to dramatise into formalised poses of figures about to begin some sinister tango. The moon's meagre light broke through a space in the clouds while the dancers continued hemmed in by the tall motionless forms, who still stood with a certain poise evidently gained from prolonged balance on the ball of the foot, not quite military nor yet were they auxiliaries, perhaps they were tango artists. They certainly seemed capable of breaking speedily from the rigid formations they had adopted into a quick step. By this time everybody was deceived, since most things had become disguised by so much proximity no one believed in them and yet suddenly their uniforms, their imperial helmets with the silver spike jutting from the crown, their arrogant faces expressive of triumph aroused in the dancers the base fear of foreign authority that centuries of subjugation had engraved upon their soul. All that had hitherto been happy and joyful in the dance-hall had disappeared and what was now visible was only calculated to awake fear or provoke anger, which indeed it did as some tried to suppress their sense of injustice while others where all for having a go. Their indecision produced other more complex motives of hesitation, for few doubted the possibility that the encounter would end well for the dancers, and as if to confirm that sentiment, a police superintendent began ordering the Irish men and women to 'Move along, clear the pavement'. He shouted, menacing with suitable penalties those who should be disobedient to his authority. The people who had gathered on the pavement, talking in groups now, began to give each other courage by asserting from time to time that they'd soon have to be going anyway. But not until they began to advance preparatory to making their way homeward did the crowd allow themselves to contemplate fully the danger with which they might be faced. For the borough councils in areas where Irish pubs and dance halls were situated were quick to latch onto a scam that greatly helped to enhance their revenues: fine heavily Irish drunks. And the police were only too happy to apply the law, except that very often they found that the Irish monopoly on drunkenness turned out to be a myth, but they were not too dismayed. The British bobby is nothing if not inventive. Simply arrest anyone with an Irish accent drunk or sober.

Now, with their backs to the contoured doorway of the dance hall, they felt shapeless with a fear they were not yet prepared to admit by a difference which they had been made to feel, not knowing to what extent they were at the mercy of anarchy.

Then something amazing occurred, the more improbable because the man could hardly stand up straight. The two opposing groups watched quietly and in the prevailing silence he might have seemed invisible. Thus lulled, he continued his dubious journey with footsteps that were no longer familiar to him, though the sense of weightlessness which was so exhilarating in free swinging limbs, made him sure of completing his journey by direct means and approaches. Somewhere a room, a bed, that recurring promise, was doubtless beckoning, waiting for the weary, which strengthened his resolve. Teetering sideways with little drunken steps he continued on his way, clinging to whatever was offered him by way of support, stretching the body from the tip of the toes to the top of the head. He seemed to find the sensation pleasant for he was shaking his head and smiling, the smile of the upright running a gauntlet of cripples, cripples whose lopsided figures loomed on either side and did in fact guide as he progressed according to some law of motion between their serried ranks, until suddenly and savagely the sequence of events was wrenched out of his control and he perceived that the legs of the cripples were long and straight. It was only their large heads that conveyed an impression of deformity. With an expression that was almost touching in its helplessness he looked up to see one of them staring down at him from an odd angle. Nice and extremely polite, the policeman asked him where he was going. Relieved after his sudden twinge of fear, here was a friendly face, a friendly soul.

"Sir," he began, he felt grateful for the chance to explain himself, "I'm going home." In fact he was so convinced he repeated himself a couple of times.

"Ah," said the policeman as if it were of hardly any interest to him. But as the home lover made to walk or stagger off, hands grabbed him roughly. He was aware of confused shouting, and he fought against the hands that held him, shouting, "Let me go. Let go of me," but they didn't let him go, his squirming body was dragged towards a Black Maria and powerful hands lifted him up off the ground and fired him head first into the back of it. Angered by his countryman's treatment a young Galway man pushed himself as far forward as he could and challenged the policemen to put up their fists and fight fair.

"Come on then Pat," a voice hailed from the police ranks, "I'll give you a go," and to his surprise one of the coppers stepped forward with his fists raised and his body crouched in perfect imitation of a pugilist's stance. The young Galway lad stood there among the crowd bewildered for a moment by the prompt acceptance of his challenge. "Come on then" sneered the copper provocatively. Which indeed the young lad did. It was a fatal error, for no sooner had he emerged from the anonymity of the crowd than half a dozen of the policeman's colleagues sprang forward, grabbed him and swiftly reunited him with his comrade in the police van. While these dramas were being played out, the shadows had enshrouded every building. Now the shadows assumed ever more vicious shapes. In the boisterous night the two parties were perhaps unaware of the play of shade and light, though it did seem to place them in the same mould but the uniformed men rejected that esoteric theory, moving towards the Irish dancers with an anger that had only been suspended. They drew their truncheons, to put them on equal footing. The levelling influence of a lump of hickory, without which they would be no match for an honest pair of work-hardened fists. And they who had been reared among the green fields waited, their backs against a concrete arcade, their hands raised less from reason than by instinct, and waited for the foe to try and breach their human wall. For the field whether it be intended for ploughing or battle is the natural habitat of the Celts.

But in all, especially the women, the over-riding impulse was to get away. For the moons meagre light had magnified the objects on which it was lingering. Faced by the dark demon that was threatening them, its persecuting presence undulating in and out of time, obscured a freedom which they had somehow never fully attained.

In the ensuing confusion, Seán Docherty slipped away. Limping into a side street that led out near Camden Town church, whether through fear or some nobler emotion it was not the moment to consider, for the police snatch squads were now laying into the crowd with such a ferocity it evinced indifference to the safety and dignity of the women, some of who now began fearing more for their unborn children than for themselves or their husbands. The police, their faces white under the formal helmet, might have been surprised by the bravery of these bog trotters whom they had expected to grovel in keeping with their lowly station and in view of the superior weapons and tactics of their assailants. Nothing daunted, the Battle of Camden Town continued unabated as the unarmed men strove to hold their own. If they sustained physical wounds from arching truncheons, they neither flinched nor cried, but countered instead with vigorous kicks and punches, cursing and grunting from the effort to defend themselves. There was no time for more, the police were closing on them, the place was in uproar, the crowd roaring, shouting and pressing forward. But the police were in tight formation, shoulder to shoulder, pushing their way ruthlessly through the dancers. Their charge seemed irresistible until, a storming fury, strength pouring from his gushing veins, a giant, red faced, red haired, swinging his huge fists cleaved a breach in the police ranks. The bobbies were thrown aside, and were trampled as the dancing Irish filled the breach that their comrade had made. Their ordered ranks now broken, the battle bloody, the policemen wavered to and fro. And now the inferiority of their truncheons became apparent, deprived of leverage in the tightly packed mêlée they were unable to swing them. Almost sobbing with rage they were thrown forward with only their fists left for the bloody struggle. The sweat had turned to an unprepossessing hue upon their rugged features, adding a hostile radiance to their skin. Yet evidence of a nobler countenance emerging was being coaxed out of the moon's uncertain light. Seán Docherty had returned with the priest.

In the hostile night the priest walked dauntlessly to the police ranks. He did not try to force his way but silently walked through the police lines which spontaneously opened for him. They could be courteous, those uniformed men who would not hesitate to risk life and limb in helping old ladies across the road in rush hour traffic as if they were their own dear mums. So they stood and watched as the priest walked nobly towards them. Though they were not so sure about the avatar's companion whose approach lacked resoluteness, his status was unclear. Suddenly the silence that had descended conveyed itself to the commander. He turned abruptly, the gleam of fanaticism fading from his eyes as he looked into the austere face of the old priest. The police snatch squads, as if obeying a single will, ceased their obscene onslaught and turned their gaze towards their commander, who stood somewhat awkwardly facing the cleric, who showed no sign of preparing to put him at his ease. Instead he launched into a withering rebuke.

"As guardian, like myself, of morality, decency and justice, sir," said the priest firmly, "you will understand the deep distress I should feel were I forced to make out a report to your superiors and the press about the actions that have taken place tonight under your command."

The dance-hall crowd stood waiting expectantly; the silence hypnotised there was not even a cough or the sound of a sigh. With an effort the police chief's mouth opened and it seemed he was going to reply but the priest gave him no time. While his less precise attendant, unused to assisting at such ceremonies, stood clenching his clumsy hands to control his emotions, perhaps dreading more the priest's abrupt utterances than the policeman's threatening attitude. Seán Docherty would have liked to push his reluctant arms into his trouser pockets but refrained at the last moment out of deference for his new office. 'We can discuss this together later, sir," continued the cleric, "but for now, as I am sure you'll appreciate, these people need to be up early for their work in the morning along with those who may have been detained by mistake in your vans."

The police chief, who had earlier turned amidst his men to face the priest, to deliver an ultimatum, a brutal one if necessary, was now reduced to taking refuge inside his thick blue serge. Though his eyes, which glanced once or twice, no more than formally, never out of interest at Seán Docherty, now appeared expressive of a state of anticipation rather than fear. His expression continued to menace but the cleric's higher self remained untarnished by the layman's heavy presence, even the new acolyte seemed to have benefited from his short association with the good Father and stood erect with something of the monastic about him now. Certainly Seán Docherty's face had grown leaner as both parties stood staring at one another, trying to decide who had the better of it. Of course the police officer knew that his authority as guardian of the Queen's highway was beyond dispute. He had never failed to deliver prisoners to their proper destination in his long and illustrious career, but his encounter with this priest might yet place some doubt on that. Suspecting this, while avoiding confirmation, he waited to hear what the priest was going to say next. Perhaps he might commit himself in some gross or subtle way?

The dark robed priest looked solemnly over at the Black Marias. He might have been summoning subtler energies before continuing sadly. "Though it is doubtful now whether normal relationships can ever be established," he made the words linger, "the best one can hope for is that, after a night's rest, not too many will press charges in the morning for assault." His tone was one of resignation and acceptance of a fact. It was a bluff but excellently done. After this prediction the seer fell silent, while the superfluous assistant's limbs began trembling, audibly thrilled by the master's daring. As the vans were being opened up the humiliated police chief (not yet entirely vanquished) recovering some of his self importance (though mentally the knighthood was receding), straightened up his braided shoulders and commenced to blather. But the priest would not be shaken. Though dressed in humble black, he was destined for the crimson.

Then the crowd were saluting and waving. Their 'God bless you father' ricocheting off the Black Marias as they made their way home.

THE BUTCHER BOYS

Michael was eleven and a half when he got a job as a butcher's boy. The shop was situated in Hampstead High Street. There was this sort of Head mistressy looking woman with glasses behind the till and doing the accounts. The boss, Mr Liekmann, was a big old Jewish guy, never got any blood on his apron, even when gutting a goose, whilst Sid, his half-brother, would be wading in it if he only halved a pork pie. An old black and white tomcat made up the rest of the staff.

On his first day, Michael stood at the back door pinching his cheeks till they were both hot and red, to make himself look older. The effect obtained was more of bruised innocence than ruddy-faced old age. Then, pushing open the door, he walked in to receive his instructions from Sid.

"The wages are five shillings and sixpence for the day, and you can have a lump of steak free while you're here," said Sid, taking in Michael's slight frame. "You'll soon fill out," he continued.

"I don't think so," said Michael.

"Course you will. We've had lots of slim lads started here, but they soon filled out when they got a few pounds of that good English prime down 'em." Convinced by his theory of enlargement he gave Michael a playful punch on the arm. "You'll see."

"Yeah, but I can't eat no meat," says Michael.

"You what?" said Sid. "Here—you ain't a poofter, are you?"

"I just don't like meat." Sid gave him a dubious look.

"You like girls though, don't you?"

"Course I do," says Michael, getting a little perplexed. And since Sid kept staring at him silently, added, "I've seen some things, don't worry."

"You have eh? Well, see that bike?" says Sid, pointing to a big black pedal cycle with a basket as big as a car boot on the front. "Start loading it with today's deliveries."

After the basket was loaded, Michael began to push the bicycle forward, ready to go—when suddenly Sid shouted after him: "When you've finished, come straight back here. Don't get larking about with them idle buggers over East Heath." Michael assured him that he wouldn't, and until that very moment, had never heard of East Heath. But now, nothing in the world would keep him away from it. After he'd finished the deliveries, he determined to check it out.

Although Hampstead was a borough of wide horizons, his route often took him up tiny cul-de-sacs and narrow lanes, mountainous hilltops and low valleys. He would be in transports of ecstasy as he launched himself from the top of one of these steep inclines, the thick handlebars smooth against his hands, his face like some wild charioteer, full of joy as the bike, gathering speed, flew down to his port of call below. But his joy soon evaporated when, after completing a delivery, he turned the bike around to come back, for it was far too heavy to be ridden back up. And, at these times, the winged charioteer became a humble beast of burden, dull and heavy, schlepping along beside the bike.

By the time Michael had made his last delivery, his face was covered in sweat, and lifting his hand, he stopped for a moment to wipe his brow with the back of his sleeve. On a bench at the corner of Hampstead High Street and Heath Street, he thought about taking a rest; but instead, he turned north and, in turning, it seemed that new strength flowed into his body as he made his way to East Heath.

It was a fresh spring afternoon with a light wind blowing from the fields, the smell of the awakened earth. At the top of the hill, he shaded his eyes with his hand and looked into the bright quiet of the Heath. Against it was a glitter of metal where a group of youths were sprawled with their bikes amongst the thick red and purple heather. Slim elms cast frail shadows over the coarse grass. Nearby, a giant chestnut tree had fallen and lay half buried under bracken, where all around daffodils and red nettles flourished in abundance. But most surprising of the plants that grew about this leafy glade were the profusions of white and green flowered shrubs of box holly. Since olden times, butchers used to suspend this plant about their shops to keep the flies at bay, and used the stem as a broom for sweeping down their chopping block. Michael shouted a greeting, and got for reply a flurry of frantic leaping, plunges, struggles and dives; but on spotting him clearly, they ceased their erratic behaviour and gazed back at him calmly with tremendous disdain. There were five or six of them and one of them was a girl. The boys all looked heavily built with raw red throats and even redder cheeks: their faces were pictures of sturdy health. They stood, solid limbs straddling their bikes now, the big baskets in the iron cradles on the front looking like anti-personnel weapons, as they gazed with hostile eyes. The fixed sneers on their faces suggested that nothing in the world could appal them—certainly not in Hampstead at least, where they menaced mankind from the top of East Heath and shouted sexual innuendoes at unobtainable middle-class girls. Michael gave a few exaggerated puffs of exasperation, then said "I'm knackered looking for my tribe." No one answered. They weren't ready for a truce yet. But behind the hard faces of the boys, Michael detected a mutual agreement. They were not openly smiling, but there was a grudging recognition that he might be one of them. One of the boys at the front of the group suddenly let his bike fall flat on the grass. The others, taking this is a signal that the immediate crisis was over, followed suit and began to relax. The kid came forward towards Michael slowly. He was a lot shorter than Michael, but he was built like a tank. And though he was the leader of the butcher boys, he sported a large baker's boy cap on the side of his head.

"How did you know we was up here?" he said, coming to a halt directly in front of Michael.

"Highest hill in Hampstead! Where else would you be?" The kid nodded understandingly. Over his features played an eager desire to state the full amount of his valour. Instead, he waved his hand with enticing nonchalance.

"It ain't really the highest," he said, "but it's the steepest. And definitely the most turny and twistiest."

"Yeah," replied Michael, looking at the long, winding road with a cyclist's respect. The kid shrugged his shoulders as he gazed down on it, as if East Heath Road wasn't fit to hold his dignity.

"You ready for it then?"

"What?" The kid looked into Michael's face. His cap was tipped, with an air of challenge, over one eye. "You reckon you could free-wheel to the bottom without touching your brakes?"

"What brakes? I got a fixed wheel." The kid acknowledged the bravado in Michael's retort with a wry smile.

"But could you go down it with a bird in your basket?" he said quietly.

"Of course," said Michael, slightly puzzled, "I delivered three chickens and a pheasant to the bottom of West Hill today." This brought the others out in fits of maniacal laughter. Michael felt humiliated. Then, almost immediately, as if their laughter had put it into words, he suddenly sensed the image of the girl sitting in the basket on the front of one of the bikes, like a figurehead on the prow of a Viking warship. Michael made a sign of disbelief, and turned to look at the girl, as if seeing her now for the first time. She returned his look with strange, wicked, ironic amusement.

"That's Vicky," said the kid proudly. "We're supposed to be racing against the Golders Green boys today." "What time?" said Michael.

"Three o'clock." "It's nearly that now." "All right, let's get your bike ready quick," said the kid, pulling from one of the other boys' baskets a large sheet of white wrapping paper. Folding it carefully down the middle, he placed it over the crossbar of Michael's bike. From the same basket, he took a handful of goose fat and, lifting first one side of the paper then the other, he smeared it all over the metal plate that advertised the shop's ware, address and telephone number.

"Not all publicity is good," he grinned at Michael. "This stops you getting any nasty surprises when you get back to your shop."

"Sounds like a good idea," offered Michael.

"It is," said the other, "and now I just gotta mask my own. Then Vicky and I will be ready to rock 'n' roll."

As he went to attend to his own bike's camouflage, Michael noticed that the rest of the gang had already masked theirs, and were exchanging tales descriptive of their prowess; it appeared they were invincible in bicycle races. Michael kept glancing at Vicky as he waited in holy wonder for that which was about to happen, while the girl stood, chewing bubble-gum, cool and poised, regarding Michael's admiration with aloof indifference.

As the church clock began to strike the hour, the Hampstead Butcher Boys stood ready and waiting at the top of the hill for their opponents to arrive; and dead on the stroke of three, released from the tension of the preliminaries, since their opponents hadn't turned up, they burst into wild shouts of victory. The kid who was straddling his bike said something to Vicky, then beckoned to Michael and said, "Give her a lift up." Michael looked at them both with astonishment.

"We're going to do a lap of honour," smiled Vicky. The rest of the gang greeted this pronouncement with a cheer, as Michael lifted Vicky's slim figure into the basket on the front of the kid's bike.

"It's very high. Will you be all right?" asked Michael, as Vicky wriggled herself into a more comfortable position.

"'Course she'll be all-right' scoffed the kid, "she lives on the top of a mountain, a metal mountain. "Really" said Michael but the girl merely nodded, a set smile of nervousness on her dry lips. In the late afternoon sun she could see *The Freemason Arms* and the steeple of St. John's church far below. But in front of her lay the snaking, treacherous hill, which might afford vast thrills to the sensible cyclist, but could exact remorseless penalties from the heedless. "Be careful," she said to the kid—a warning he took with a shrug of the shoulders as he swung gallantly into the saddle.

They began to freewheel slowly at first, down the hill, the kid's bike in the lead. As they veered round a bend they began to pick up speed. Now Vicky's extra weight began to hamper the necessary equilibrium, so that they became dangerously angled as they sped round a curve, narrowly missing a horse trough. But now they were riding into the sun, its dazzling rays half-blinding them. They fought to keep their bikes upright, while the baskets shook and juddered. They rode as if into the glare of a floodlight. Suddenly the kid's bike began to wobble dangerously, as Vicky tried to pull her legs inside the basket. But this was by no means easy to achieve. The kid shouted something that sounded like "Abandon ship!" But at that moment, a lucky cloud obscured the sun, rescinding that order, if such it had been.

As they began to pick up speed, the wind froze tears to the girl's eyes, whipping her long hair back from her head, while oncoming drivers' mouths were agape at the sight of her in a basket with her legs dangling over the dented side.

Michael soon got used to his round and every Saturday all through the summer he worked making his deliveries as swiftly as he could so he could hang out on East Heath, where he soon gave up being a vegetarian when he saw all the other boys cooking their free meat ration over an open fire at lunch time on the hill. "Easy meat," said the kid as he stuck a stick through a piece of steak and held it over the flames. Michael smiled. There was a feeling of permanence about it all.

Michael had been working for about six months when Mr Liekmann called him to his office one Saturday evening just as he was about to finish for the day.

"Sid tells me you're such a good worker," he began "and if you were a bit older we'd have liked to keep you with us but in the circumstances we need an older full-time boy now for the winter."

Michael could only stare. He had thought he was their permanent boy, which in fact he had never been. Though very disappointed, Michael had to accept the fact that he was still at school.

As he was walking home he seen a man chalking something on a wall. The man turned as Michael approached. "I don't like having to do this son but you know what the Irish are eh?" He winked conspiratorially, "Fucking bog-trotters." Michael flinched the word bog-trotter fell on him like pain. More painful still, it drew attention to the words upon the wall.

FILTHY IRISH PIGS GO HOME

Astonishment made him catch his breath. He was bewildered by these words, they seemed to mock him but there was no way of expressing himself about these feelings, they had forced their way into his mind. He stood poised between anger and embarrassment; the gap that separated him had become wider still. It gave him an acute sense of his own worthlessness. He felt that to be called or related in any way to foreignness was a shameful failing. He had to escape and saved himself by remembering the butcher boys, who told about a place where half tamed wolves roamed at night at the base of a metal mountain. Their youthful exaggerations added further to the effect of these descriptions upon the boy. The mountain became a solitary comfort to him, it deepened his fascination, it made him regard the wharf where the mountain stood as a source of wonder, a fabulous, fathomless place. As he continued listening to these stories each week he was carried to the furthest rim of the universe. He saw himself become buoyant, it drove away the ominous foreboding, his feeling that he was worthless; it gave him a new stature, it occurred to him suddenly that he might project himself still further beyond the mountain where no one in the world could threaten or insult him any more.

When he got home that evening, he never mentioned anything about what he had seen; he began to doubt the reality of words, he had begun to alter. Instead he explained to his mother the reason he had been let go from his job. She replied—'God works in mysterious ways' and, since the butchers wanted an older full-time boy she would send Danny, who had just left school, along to apply for the job first thing Monday morning.

At around five o'clock one evening, a policeman entered Raglan Street. As he continued walking along the pavement, the children playing hopscotch in the road stopped their game to watch—to see which house he would stop at. When eventually he located the correct address from the slip of paper in his hand, he knocked loudly on the door.

Mary Jane was scrubbing out the toilet in the back yard. She scooped up Dermot in her arms and rushed to answer the door, her face a cross between query and challenge. The Policeman was curt and brief. Seán Docherty had an accident at work that afternoon. He is now in Hampstead General Hospital.

"Is he badly hurt?" The Policeman could not answer. He simply did not know. He left. She shut the door, turned swiftly and went back inside. She saw the room she stood in plainly with faded yellow paper on its walls and the shine on the nails from hanging the children's coats. And now there was her youngest child Dermot standing by the table looking at her dubiously. It was not his first glimpse of life and she smiled, or at least tried, in so far as her mood was capable of.

"Are you sick mum?" asked the child, looking at her thinly stretched pale lips.

"I don't feel anything in particular," said the mother from her daydream state. But then, as happens when one awakes to the full implications of a situation, she found herself without answers.

'What if I should have an accident?' She looked toward the open window. Terrible possibilities began to confront her (though there to protect somebody), they were intensified by the narrow doorways of the houses in the street outside. The little room was in no way shameful except when exposed suddenly to those it had been hidden from. The woman sighed. She would have drawn the curtain if her many failures had not deterred her. But it soon became unnecessary; the neighbours had turned away, the plight of immigrants was too complicated to follow.

Yet there were those who believed that ignorance could be avoided but Mary Jane Docherty knew that it was something more than just a struggle for dignity. She knew that there was no escape except by living through it. She could not start out for the hospital just then. Hopefully the children would soon be back from school. In the meantime she was sitting, waiting, listening, until she thought she heard their footsteps in the hall but it was only wind running through the passage way. The war years had been worrying times; yet people had seemed much more decent then. Life was not taken for granted, some faith was needed, some prayer, some awe. Memory could be dreadful but anticipation was more awful.

The mother was powerless now but the child to whom none of this was fatal began playing with some boxes on the floor. It was her children that filled her thoughts so that she was compelled to get up. She looked at her young son. She touched him once or twice to console or reassure but he did not look up, he was too protected by his game.

Then she heard the key and a moment later Michael came through the door. Now she could get going to the hospital, to see her husband, to find out whatever it was intended she should find.

She was sick with worry by the time she got there. Mostly brought on by the unknown, by her imagination running riot. So that it was something of a relief when she entered the ward at last to see Seán laying flat in bed.

"Are you all right, Seán? What happened?" asked Mary Jane, as she reached the bed since the details were not apparent.

"Trench collapsed," he replied in a subdued tone.

"Are you in any pain?"

"A bit. The old back's playing me up—they think it's a slipped disc." Mary Jane's face relaxed at this.

"Thank God you weren't hurt worse." Seán nodded in agreement. Mary Jane rummaged in her bag.

"I brought half an ounce of Old Holborn and some red papers. I couldn't remember whether you used red or green."

"They're fine," said Seán. "The blasted trouble is, they go berserk if they catch a man having a smoke in here." Mary Jane smiled sympathetically. He was strong of course; he had always worked hard and could stand a bit of knocking about.

"When do you think they will let you come home?" She asked as she handed over the papers and tobacco.

"I haven't a clue—maybe next week, I hope. Are the kids all right? Jazus how will you manage in this man's bloody land?" Suddenly with the calm indifference of the already informed, her anger at her situation began to evaporate; the disgust she felt for the filthy street and the squalid old house and the nagging horror of spending her life there without change or escape. The feeling of misery produced by Seán's accident and the further reduction to her family's circumstances, was all but forgotten in the realisation that she and the children would be eligible for state welfare relief in this land. Welfare officials were not the worst in the world. If sometimes they raised their voice to a shout or a scream it was only because they were dealing with foreigners. Her husband stared up at her. Worry had twisted his face into a tortured grimace of anticipation. Her foot shifted nervously or it might have been to ease a corn. She swallowed rapidly. Her voice sounded ugly and was almost too ashamed for what it was about to disclose. For in that high arched ward under the full glare of the dedicated light all words might sound deceitful, as the man's wife who was also a mother began to reveal herself in another role.

"I'm going to apply," she began, "first thing tomorrow for government assistance."

"I see," said Seán Docherty making his utterance sound unpleasantly significant. He gave the impression he was taking part in a conspiracy.

Mary Jane looked down at her handbag, allowing him to preserve a vulgar dignity. She simply did not want to burden herself with ancient woes and began searching the bag vaguely, to deflect the wave of contempt that was directed at her, while allowing time for that to be accepted which would rather have been refused.

"You won't get a lot from the Crown," he remarked with malicious complacency. "Well it will be better than nothing," she said and hoped it would be left at that. She accepted the painful rebuke as something that her mind in the end must suffer. The silence thickened around them and might have congealed if the Matron had not soon appeared to extricate them from it in a swish of starched skirts, hectoring with her mantra those visitors, or intruders to her domain, that it was time for them to leave.

Lips pressed against dull cheeks while chairs scraped against gleaming linoleum and in the atmosphere of departure figures retreated with contrite steps, as Matron bore down on the tardy, among whom she began to rove and amble, which declared the seriousness of her intention, together with her agitation towards those wilful stragglers, forced to run the gauntlet of her scorn. As she sailed off amid a swell of expulsed visitors, Seán Docherty began to build himself a smoke.

On the way home, Mary Jane considered calling in at the Church, but the doors would probably be shut now—there would be no one there, except the statues standing in the shadows of quenched radiance, spattered with cold candle droppings draped with cobwebs in the illuminated dust.

After Mass on Sunday was the best time to meet other Irish people. The Church was full every Sunday. Sometimes there was an overspill, with the women going in and the men remaining outside, kneeling on one knee on the pavement. The Church was important not only for its services, but it also served as a point of continuity for her life in the homeland.

She enjoyed going to church and confession too, after which she could endure most things. She gave one last glance up at the darkened windows of the chapel, whose deepening shadows guided her eyes towards the sky, where, on that altar at least, the candles still burnt brightly to the glory of God.

So the resilient housewife, who was also a mother, lulled by her spiritual body, made her way homewards. Her feet led deliberately, though she thought of calling in at the corner shop on the way—she might need a shilling for the meter in the morning, but something intervened between the intention and the act, her features had become honed by experience. She would always expect to be victimised afresh, by acquaintances and neighbours who were always on the lookout for disasters and mistakes.

There were never enough incidents, nothing really stimulated since the war. It appeared that she would soon reach the correct degree of humbleness—or fatigue. She could also have lost interest, though she had often been inspired to attempts at winning her neighbours' approval. The murmuring voices coming from the corner shop might have created an illusion of warmth and friendliness for anyone less experienced in listening for it. Suspicion has a way of overcoming trust, doubt leaves no immediate trace but lingers in the atmosphere so that her guilt remained even after she had prepared something nice and tasty for the children's supper. That night after she had removed her corset and taken down her rosary, she knelt in her slip by the bed lost in some higher form of discomfort.

BRIDGET GETS A JOB

Formidable and grand on a hilltop in Kentish Town the massive building of St Dominic's priory dominated the approach to Hampstead. Thrusting up from the priory roof, its spire rose into the clouds. People coming from any direction can see this colossus of religious grandeur which, reflected in the impoverished area that surrounds it, exhibits a quality of excess. Nonetheless one cannot help being seized by its spirit of splendour and Bridget Kelly, seeing it now for the first time was no exception as she blessed herself and sighed, 'Isn't it grand?' She was fond of the source of her reassurance; it was essential to cling to that. And gilded by the moon and glazed by their respective crosses, the two sisters ploughed on in the direction of miracles and martyrs. As for the statues, sheer audacity gave them a status and importance, which made worshippers unnecessary, yet Mary Jane smiled at her sister as their faith drove them on, for it was with a sinking heart that Bridget had put on her coat earlier to accompany her to mass. Adjusting their head scarves, which had become alarmingly lopsided, the two sisters climbed the steps and entered the nave and after blessing themselves with holy water from a font (over which a saint presided whose ear was broken off at the lobe, presumably while the sculptor had been hammering out the ego) genuflected in the direction of the high altar and proceeded down the middle aisle. As the rest of the congregation were settling in to their pews, two lay brothers clad in black robes, whose faces beneath the cowls showed they had surrendered their sufferings, glided to and fro, lighting candles and distributing prayer sheets with funeral pace. All knelt with bowed heads as the Mass began. Though Bridget's head seemed bent perhaps more from worry than devotion, since kindness can suffocate in the close confinement of a scullery.

Sensitive to every variation of the Docherty household's financial troubles she had offered many a time to leave. While her sister Mary Jane had become sentimentally reproachful at any such suggestion looking into her face, her hands resting firmly on her young sister's shoulders, expressing an intimacy of persuasion it was impossible to resist. Soon the whisper of the passing prayer sheets notified her of the progress the lay brothers were making in their rounds. They would come to her in turn. Though by then it might be unnecessary since she had already said her prayers after a fashion and in her own way. Asking God to bless everyone before putting in her own petition for the following day…

'Begging or worship?' She wondered which, until the distraction of a more immediate pain caused her to take a hanky from her pocket and place it between her knees and the floor. Though it would take more than a handkerchief to ease the ache of foreignness out of the bones from which she suffered, she tried within the confines of that space (her long legs and flat shoes protruding at an angle) to rearrange the flimsy article into a more tolerant shape. She might have kept to her intention of trying to control events except that her stooped fumblings were beginning to cause some distraction to her immediate neighbours, so that she was forced to resettle herself swiftly in the prescribed attitude, with appropriate gravity, back into her pew, where she began to take part in the service with faithful simplicity, yet was sufficient in doubt so that her gaze kept wandering every now and then towards the statues, who with stern ascetic rigour guarded the entrances to the collection boxes situated in front of the gates of the numerous side chapels that ornamented the long aisles. Her eyes returned to the pulpit where the priest intoned his office in grave archaic Latin but, despite her desire to worship, she was not consoled. The words seemed to have become an illusion of his own importance. Above him St Agnes sat serenely on a white marble throne, her bosom carefully veiled by the wings of cherubims, their chubby cheeks and quirky smiles nourished by mischief, hovered about her Gothic breasts like naughty schoolboys but found themselves compelled at the last moment to change their erotic intent by the stern gaze of St Dominic whose stone arm was raised in a posture of anger, though Agnes herself seemed undisturbed by any dishonesty which might have lurked behind an object.

As Bridget watched the priest's hands making the familiar though mystic passes over the utensils of his office, lulled by the spiritual vibrations that filled the church, the communicants began going down, heads held humbly while arranging themselves gravely at the altar rail, where they gulped so greedily at the proffered host that the priest was compelled to withdraw his fingers swiftly from their straining mouths, so they no more than brushed their lips on the blessed bread but were none the less consoled for the forgiveness so easily conferred.

Bridget tried desperately to find some comfort in the priest's words but drifted instead away for a while in the mesmeric melancholy sounds of the organ. As the voices of the choir began mounting, her future no longer seemed relevant, while the strains rose, then hung, in a moment of pause before bursting, erupting to consume and exalt. As light and music began to reverberate from nave and chancel she felt the notes float around her, then the fingers no longer moved on the beads. The tongue no longer uttered the letters, for prayer is contained by temporary words and bears its meaning on its face, as opposed to the eternal sound of the incoming and outgoing breath. She might have became transported to the plane on which miracles take place and other fantastic things and was almost persuaded by something deeper in herself, but returned with her mind to the present as the service drew to an end. Whether distressed or elated, Bridget Kelly would have jumped up if her fellow worshippers had not forestalled her. After floating on the surface for most of the service, they now seemed lost in prayer. She decided to risk their displeasure again by stooping to retrieve her belongings. "God is good," whispered Mary Jane encouragingly as they began to make their way out of the church, though, as the rain began to fall outside and the congregation started to split up, and the slippery steps confronted, that sentiment did not seem so certain. They began the slow descent. It was an uneasy journey. Mary Jane was aiming for somewhere that now eluded her, so that she could only seek solace in her faith, because there was nothing else she could do. Bridget turned, offering up her unsatisfied face. The right position is to have both feet on the ground while contemplating the skies, but as always occurs when light wrestles with darkness, you took the evidence of an infinite world on trust. There were certainly one or two questions, but of course Mary Jane could not explain because faith is a notoriously nebulous word which had already fulfilled its purpose.

You can put out your hand and touch only so much. So that the two sisters, sensing they had sullied what they had been brought up to respect, hastened to join the unconvincing figures on the damp street who rushed and darted to avoid the rain. But their deliverer was not deterred and as they knotted their scarves more firmly around their unworthy heads a voice from out of the darkness hailed them.

"Is it yourself that's in it?" said a fairly well dressed, chubby little woman, who was standing before Mary Jane.

"Oh, hello Mrs Hart," replied Mary Jane pleasantly; rain glistened on their foreheads which almost touched. Eileen Hart was around the same age as Mary Jane and had come over to England some years earlier. Her husband was a plumber and always in good work and although they lived in the same borough as Mary Jane, the area they dwelt in was considerably posher. This comparatively cocooned lifestyle enabled Mrs Hart to devote a considerable amount of her time to helping the Church.

"'Tis terrible times we're living in," said Mrs Hart, involuntarily placing a hand on her stomach as her corset swivelled alarmingly.

Mary Jane fully agreed and then replied flatly to her sister that they'd better be going.

"I'm just going to hand in the keys to Sister Veronica over at the priest's house and I'll be off home me self," said Mrs Hart. As both parties turned to go, Mrs Hart suddenly called over her elegantly padded shoulder. "The nuns are looking for a girl to work in the sacristy. If you know anyone, will you let us know?" Mary Jane and Bridget looked at each other. It was an immense moment. In the dank air they had become revived.

The Domina of St Dominic's Priory was not surprised when she opened the door of the Sacristy to find three people waiting there instead of one. Many people called at odd times throughout the evenings and even late in to the night to discuss their business at the priest's house, so she suffered their intrusion almost with ceremonial grace. As they stepped in shyly onto the polished wooden floor a frown bent the seams of her face when first she heard and then looked, at the two thin women standing head and shoulders above such an ample donative as Mrs Hart, waiting (she could tell by the angle at which they held their heads) not to give but to receive. Though tonight there might be room for both in this house of renunciation and possession.

"We would never have anyone but a good Catholic girl," said the nun, who did not care for visitors except officially. "And written references I shall dispense with, since Mrs Hart has so generously vouched for you," she added, smiling primly at this girl whom she was most anxious to impress with the strictness and the regularity of her house.

Sister Veronica did not have a kind face, a sad omission in a nun. In fact her yellow jaw was rather long and somewhat bitter, but if this daughter of the church lacked the allurements, she was complete with every other instinct proper to her sex and any girl that could stand still, and look you in the eye, would certainly be capable of saying irritating things. Indeed, reasoned the Domina, were this creature a dumb mute her comely features and aggressive hair would be enough to antagonise a saint. The keenest torments were the most private. So Sister Veronica blew her nose into her handkerchief with savage efficiency and looked away to hide her guilt, for the good woman suffered terribly from the sin of pride.

The rain was coming down heavier as the nun opened the front door to allow them to leave, and since none of the three women had an umbrella, the nun offered to lend Mrs Hart the priest's one, and Mary Jane and Bridget her own. "You can fetch it back with you tomorrow," she told Bridget. Though the wind had risen, blowing rain into their breathless mouths and wrenching at their borrowed umbrella in forceful gusts, they did find (as they walked briskly home) time to discuss and even exalt in their apparent good luck.

"Well!" said Mary Jane happily, "That's you fixed up in one stroke. And you will be able to come and visit us every Thursday on your afternoon off."

"I will, to be sure," replied Bridget joyfully, "and I'll be able to pay you something back too, Mary Jane, for helping me along."

"Oh, not at all," said Mary Jane, putting her arm fondly round Bridget. "You just make sure you look after yourself now. The wages aren't that great there, but you'll have your keep, and didn't Sister Veronica say that, as House Parlour Maid, she would teach you to wait on table herself?"

"Ah sure, it's as good as a trade."

"Oh, but won't you be the grand girl," said Mary Jane, giving her younger sister a hug. "We won't know you at all." Bridget smiled with delight.

Early next morning, Bridget left to take up her job at the priest's house. Everyone, especially the children, felt very sad, since all had become so attached to her during her stay, it amounted to an emigration.

BRIDGET BEGINS WORK AT THE PRIEST'S HOUSE

Bridget was led upstairs by an austere-looking Sister Veronica, to a room at the end of the passage. "This is where you will sleep," said the nun, hitching up the rosary, which she wore round her waist, the shiny brown beads big as conkers. Bridget was thrilled to see an oval-shaped enamelled wall basin with two taps above. She had never before slept in a room with running water, never mind a house that had a bathroom and an indoor toilet as well. The walls were painted a light blue; the ceiling was white, as were the borders and the skirting boards. There were pink drapes hanging on the window and a thick mauve carpet covered most of the floor. Above the bed hung a crucifix and the Virgin and Child looked over from a frieze on the opposite wall. Against another wall stood a huge, ornate mahogany wardrobe, with gleaming gold-coloured metal handles on its beautifully carved wooden doors.

"You can hang your things in there," said the nun, regarding the scene without interest. Her attitude affected Bridget deeply.

"Yes, Reverend Mother," she replied respectfully as she had been taught. Anyone who could regard such a room with indifference must be accustomed to very great things.

"On holy days and holidays of obligation, the house follows certain rules," continued the nun. Bridget was standing almost at attention. The nun's voice softened. "But if one observed all its austerities, one would hardly survive… However—" she looked meaningfully at Bridget. "This is a very good position for any young girl, never mind one who's just over from Ireland, without any housekeeping experience at all. Now sort your things out," said the nun turning in a swish of robes, "and I'll give you your instructions downstairs."

But, after her first week in this place she had chosen to do her penance in, the girl wished she was back home (as she had begun to think of it), living in her sister's place.

Bridget shook her head, trying to clear her thoughts, and knelt back on her heels to continue her work, rinsing out the rag in the bucket by her side. The floor around the gas stove was thick with ingrained dirt and grease. In her efforts to dislodge it, she took a firmer tuck of her rag and began sprinkling the bleach straight from the bottle onto the floor.

"No, no, no! You'll have us all in the workhouse," cried the voice of the nun, berating her without tact. Bridget was startled—she hadn't heard her approach. "You mustn't waste cleaning materials like that," continued the Prioress with her eye sternly fixed on the imprudent maid. Bridget tried to explain. But the brute Templar was bent on administering one of her homilies on the theme of wilful waste, staring down into Bridget's face to see that she got it and ending (as she usually did) with:

"Your sister's a very good Catholic and a hard worker too. You mustn't let her down now." Sister Veronica was ruthless about it, and Bridget submitted because she had to.

For an hour or two, the girl slept deeply, in utter exhaustion, but when something roused her, she could not drop off again. Her mind was suddenly active with thoughts of the previous day. And then she did not want to sleep, since it would too quickly bring the morning and another day like the one that had been. There was moonlight in the room and she lay in its soft, soothing glow, contemplating what she should do. She was desperate to establish an identity that was stable, that others could believe in. But her mind, groping after explanations, found only more bewilderment. The emptiness of the room made the shadows seem more gigantic. Along with a certain unease when she recalled the last time she had seen Alan. He was walking her home from the cinema when he enquired about the Dochertys. She had told him that Seán, along with many others, had been sacked simply because they were Immigrants. She was angry at this yet Alan seemed to be able to summon an indifference to it. She felt disturbed, distracted and betrayed. They were within a few yards of her door when she pulled away.

"I've got to go," she said.

"Wait, will I see you on Saturday night?" he called after her.

Bridget whirled round; she was being sucked back by dreadful undercurrents of the past.

"I don't want to see any more of the people of this country." She cried, the hurt inside making her lash out.

"That's fine by me," he replied, the shock of her actions sharpening his voice to an anger matching her own. Her eyes stung in the intolerable shadows. The sweetness of love had vanished as if it had never been.

As dawn was breaking, she got up, put on her clothes, pulled on her stockings and knelt down by her bed to offer a few prayers. Then she went downstairs and the day's work began.

BRIDGET GETS ACQUAINTED WITH THE BOMB-HAPPY BRIGADE

Harry Jenkins' days and nights were a blur of mumbling, hallucinatory existence. He had no home, no family, no possessions other than the ragged clothes that hung from his narrow frame. His life was simply a minute-to-minute foraging for a tasty scrap from a back street dustbin—perhaps a half-eaten cheese roll, a rotten apple, or maybe even a half of chicken that someone had discarded because it had turned blue-moulded. Harry didn't mind the blue bits. You just ate round the sides or, if you were hungry, you ate them too. His mind had stopped functioning on January 14th 1942 when a German stun-grenade had exploded in the trench he was occupying at El Alamein. That he had once been a school teacher in Norfolk, a father of three daughters, a fine husband, and won a medal for gallantry under enemy fire was no longer part of his memory banks. And he stood, staring now, at the hair of the young girl who had opened the door to his knock because it was so red. Redder than a fire engine.

"Can I help you, sir?" enquired Bridget tactfully.

"Can I have a cup of tea and a slice of bread?" said Harry, stepping in the door, for he knew the drill. And he made for the small room on the right that was used for administering alms (in the form of food) to the poor.

"Were you in the War?" asked Bridget gently when Harry had finished his tea. He nodded merely, not looking at her. Then he gave her a frightened glance, and saw her warm smile, and he smiled slowly back.

Over the next few months, Bridget was to meet many more men like Harry Jenkins. Their stories differed, but the essential core was always the same. They were victorious fighters returned from the Second World War; but in the process of winning, they had also become its shell-shocked victims; so, instead of glory, laud and honour from a supposedly grateful populace, they were shunned— frequently pelted by children with stones in the street, to cries of: "You bomb-happy bastard!"

In their deranged state, they were often short-changed by shopkeepers, robbed outright by publicans and finally thrown into a cell by the police. If they were beyond pardon it was their own innocence that had condemned them. Because in the end they had no voice except that of drunkenness. So she tried to use whatever means she could to help while Sister Veronica, if she had dared to think about such things, might have benefited too.

Bridget bent her head to check her seams. She was at her most inadequate though she would not grow bitter, like some from the disciplines of religion, daring sometimes even in the presence of the nun who passed her now, to hum a tune and even to indulge a song while pushing back her thick heavy hair. So that in time the strong spirit of the girl began to cut the nun's stern consistency to the point where she would often unbend, making less harsh demands upon the servant, who could, merely by breathing, personify sin.

It began in small ways. A man might have trouble remembering his National Insurance number, or his army number, or perhaps he needed some official form or other to accomplish some aim or to make a claim. Then Bridget, whilst out doing the shopping for Sister Veronica, would call in at the post office and pick up a form. At other times, she would check for information at the local library. She also wrote and typed (when she could) innumerable letters using the officially-headed Church notepaper to lend extra credence to the correspondence on the men's behalf; and numerous enquiries were made and a lot of legwork saved by using the Sacristy 'phone. To minimise the risk of detection, she would say to those who might need to 'phone back: "I have to go out for a while now, but I shall be here at such-and-such a time. And she would make sure she was, conscientiously dusting and cleaning in the vicinity of the 'phone at the appointed time. She was very resourceful. In fact, all her activities became very subtle to avoid censorship by the nun.

Everything went well for a time but eventually, as was to be expected, Sister Veronica did find out, when, not busied by vigils and prayer, she answered the phone one morning to a Major Bamford calling from the pensions department of the War Office. But, after she had listened for a while, Sister Veronica simply replied: "I'll get the young lady for you," which she did, and stood a little way off listening while Bridget dealt with the caller. When she had replaced the receiver and turned apprehensively to face Sister Veronica, Bridget was surprised to find that the nun was not annoyed at all about her secret Welfare activities. In fact, quite the reverse, probably relieved to rediscover a mission in life, she was touched and laying aside her habitual severity, said she would speak to Father Ignatius about the possibility of allowing Bridget more time to devote to the work.

That same afternoon, there was a rap at the door. Bridget went to answer. She thought it might be Harry Jenkins. On drawing back the door, she gave a sudden exclamation and put a hand to her throat. "Is it really you?" she gasped. Her shock was laced with delight.

"It's me all right," grinned Alan. They clutched each other.

"It's so good to see you," whispered Bridget. For a moment, they clung together. "How did you know where to find me? I might have gone back home. God, I'm glad I didn't do that now!"

"Oh, I knew you wouldn't do that." She looked up at him, questioningly. "Not after we'd been to the pictures together," he continued, mischievously.

"How could you be so certain?"

"Because you stood for the National Anthem!" Bridget laughed out loud, then heard movement above which could only be the clergy coming to interrupt their reunion. She put out her hand and gave him a little shove.

"Will you get going quick," she giggled, "Before you have my reputation ruined."

Alan turned to wave back at her as she gently closed the door. Sister Veronica, mumbling a novena came slowly down the stairs. From an upstairs window she had seen Alan leaving.

"What did that fellow want?" she asked suspiciously.

"Oh, just a bit of attention," replied Bridget breathlessly.

"Really, he didn't look that needy to me. Well—I suppose you know how to deal with them, but you'll have to be careful," she added with prim severity. "Scrounging has become an art form, and some live very well off it, their imaginations are extraordinary." Though they were both standing motionless she contrived an exaggerated shudder, then paused, absorbed momentarily in picking at a piece of candle grease that had congealed into a puckered grey scab on the sleeve of her black habit.

"Oh, well," she laughed, on a high single note of scorn. "If only someone would invent waxless candles."

"Ah," said the flushed girl looking inwards. She was more interested in her own immediate inventiveness. She phoned Alan at the station next day and they went dancing in the evening. Afterwards he drove her home. Stopping outside the priest's house and switching off the lights, coming up against each other unexpectedly made her breath catch while he, who might have taken part in scenes like this before, draped his arm over the back seat until finally it came to rest on her shoulders, hand hovering somewhere in the region of her breast, while she remained impassive trying to suppress a vital stirring she was not yet prepared to admit.

The priest's house had taken on a mellow core. The days seemed to sigh their satisfaction as the girl, awaiting the results of her exams, went about her work. While the Domina strode less forcefully, all sorts of people came and went until eventually a messenger strode forth.

The news which Sister Veronica had to give was as brief as it was astounding. By consent of the Church administrators, Bridget was to be given an annual grant to allow her to engage in full-time study of Law. She would be allowed to continue to live rent free at the priest's house, and on completion of her studies would represent the church in all matters legal. Bridget seemed dazed. The nun blushed, she who had so recently been the holy tyrant was now attempting to perform acts of kindness. The girl trembled with embarrassment for this new person or emotion which was beginning to dominate the whole room. "I think this calls for a celebration. What about a cup of tea?"

"Oh, yes," said Bridget, turning towards the kitchen.

Sister Veronica put her hand out, stopping Bridget short. "You're no longer a maid of all work", she said, gently pressing Bridget down on a chair, "allow me." The Domina had, it seemed, donned completely the veils of tenderness.

Bridget's free time now became extremely limited. She began reading all the relevant law books she could get hold of. Masses of homework was given; sometimes she couldn't complete it on time. She might have regretted her decision now since it was hard at first in the world of Latin documents, affidavits, depositions, deeds and waivers, habeas corpus… then worse. If the statutes had double meanings in them they were simple when compared to the words that made them legible and enabled their insolent utterance and pompous pronunciation in high and county courts around the country. Stiff and formal, it was a tough business to ease into, though sometimes her laughter destroyed the authority latent in that world. But she was endlessly curious about her subject. She was also fully determined that she would succeed, and when she sat for her exams it came as no surprise three years later when the results arrived that she had passed. Sister Veronica, a woman so used to the comings and goings of the clergy, from Novitiates to Bishops that she could no longer be excited by anything or anyone, hugged Bridget tightly to her, her disciplined arrogance evaporating. "I always knew you would do it," she said.

BRIDGET AND SEÁN

The Docherty kids were happy it was Thursday, because they knew that when they got home from school Bridget would be there. She always called on Thursday on her half-day off. Sometimes she brought an article of clothing—a jumper, or second-hand pair of shoes for one of the boys… and sweets: she always brought them sweets. They regarded her with awe, they spoke about her with humble pride—a pride full of wonder at the reassuring knowledge that their own aunt was as smart as a teacher. But they also knew that there was some problem with that between Bridget and their Dad over Bridget's work. Something in his words did not fit with Bridget's educated ideas. It made them terribly nervous and confused.

And so when, on reaching home, they found Bridget and their father in the front room together, Bridget writing at the table, their father reading the paper in his armchair by the hearth, they could not hold down their despair, and slowly drifted from the room. They had learnt that when Bridget and their father were alone in the same place it was better for them not to be there.

All this was bound up with things they didn't understand. Like the posh voice on the wireless that spoke of a place called Russia and an Iron Curtain that somebody called Stalin had made, and who their teachers told them had also tortured priests to make them suffer for their faith. And their father suddenly eloquent with rebellious folk tales between the fierce and saddening songs where you were expected to give more than you possessed. So with absorbed little faces tensed and wrinkled, they listened to the posh voice on those mornings when death became immanent in the little Raglan Street front room, fidgeting and fiddling with the porridge in their bowls.

But meantime they were ready, they were waiting. If only there were some clue. Would the murderer get a last minute reprieve? Did he have any children? It must be a terrible thing to be orphaned by the scaffold. Somehow they must learn to suffer, but possibilities to seduce the crown into relaxing its harshest law, slipped with the chiming of the clock. And when on the cold hard stroke of nine you knew with BBC certainty that he had not managed to gain her majesty the Queen's clemency, you jumped at the rattle of the trap opening beneath the man's bound feet, or perhaps it was the echo of the spoon against your empty porridge bowl. Catarrhal snifflings made their own emotional comment in the drawn back mucus of a runny nose, as they remembered their own sins.

Seán was reading an article in the paper about a Jamaican bus-driver who had been arrested on suspicion of murdering his landlord. He experienced a queer, distorted sense of triumph. He felt that it would somehow enhance Bridget's campaign if the Government were to be distracted by unrest elsewhere.

"Are the Blacks ever going to do anything?" he asked. Bridget carried on writing, ignoring the question. She didn't want to give him the satisfaction of an argument. When he got no answer, he gave a quite laugh. "Ah, the Blacks are tidy," he continued. "And why would they bother their auld heads when it might interfere with their chances of being accepted as British. Jasus, that's the last thing the Irish want." He shook his head at the thought. "It's the longest war in the world: we've been fighting for over eight hundred years against British rule." *The English have been as wolves rending and tearing all that fell into their merciless paws and grinding them with their teeth of iron.*

In the early evening light as the mind probed for old sorrows, it was good sometimes to sit, to feel the anger creep up from the soles of your boots. Acts of violence excited Seán Docherty. He began to savour, to deliberate some refinement of revenge from behind the kitchen dresser. He began to talk now more or less to himself.

"If one could only act without hesitation like the German

soldiers had at the Russian front entering hell the glorious way via the Iron Cross. But the English like everything else they put their hand to, have devalued it, arguing that only their bravery has merit."

Usually Bridget submitted with silent dignity to his frustrated outbursts; she endured his brooding anger. But at times she was goaded into comment. She looked up:

"Some of them have been fighting for centuries against the Crown, every one of their countries has been invaded by the British at some time too. As one great Black writer, Celestine Edwards, put it: 'Mass murders are permitted under the British flag. If the British nation stole no more, they have stolen enough; if the British nation has not murdered enough, no nation on God's earth has.' He worked himself to death—literally—trying to get Black people a better deal. To get them accepted here."

"That was well put," said Seán.

"Oh, they have their writers too."

"Cowards masquerading as heroes." He spat into the fireplace. The night of the Tan's visit to his house was enshrined upon his heart. The English were guilty of many things, but Seán Docherty blamed them for everything. He seemed to have lost something of himself long ago, and in a way he could not really understand. To him England was a place of hardships and insults and secretly he felt a grudging admiration for anyone who defied it. "You'll have to be careful you don't end up like that Black fellow you just mentioned, dying for the cause." He grinned, stirred to mirth by his own crude wit.

"I'm not anxious for martyrdom—just doing enough to satisfy a nagging conscience."

It was a waste of time, he thought, working for something that could never be. "Wouldn't you be better off if you used the auld education to teach the kids a bit about their own history?"

"I'm not sure about that."

"And why not?! Where else will they learn about it? Certainly not at school, where Irish history seems to be taboo." He pulled out his tobacco and papers and began rolling a smoke. "And that's not the only thing that's taboo. Did ya hear about that new English teacher that Michael has now? Oh, a queer hawk if ever there was one. On the first morning she was calling the register and when she came to young Seamus O'Brien's name, she called out James O'Brien instead. Of course, he didn't realise she was talking to him and when he didn't answer her she pointed at him, 'Are you deaf or daft, or what?' says she. Sure, wasn't the poor kid confused. So she calls him out to the front of the class and shows him the register. "There!" says she, pointing at his name and crossing out Seamus, as bold as you please, replacing it with James. "That's the way we pronounce words here in this school—in proper English," Seán took a pull on his fag before resuming. "But young Seamus had got a bit of his pluck back by this time and he said to her, 'That's not my name, Miss.'"

"Jase, the bitch must have been taken back, but cool as you please" she replied, "I'm amazed by this obstinacy in snubbing civilised language."

Some held that all Irish names sounded the same, O Kelly, O Leary, O Donnely, O this and O that, though they knew little of Ireland and cared less.

Seán shook his head at the memory of it, and straightened up in his chair. "Did you ever hear the like of it?" He gazed up at Bridget. "The Irish were sent as slaves to the colonies to work on the plantations long before the blacks."

"Do you mean as indentured servants?" asked Bridget.

"Some but most were field hands, Irish men, women and young children. They were sent in hundreds of thousands and at one time made up seventy per cent of the total population of the colonies. When the African slave trade began, Irish slaves, since they only cost five sterling compared to fifty sterling for a black slave, became totally expendable. If a planter beat an Irish slave to death it was never a crime. They had their tongues cut out for speaking their own language and this continued for over a century and has never been taught in schools or mentioned in the history books, unlike the African slave trade.* Why is this, why is it never discussed?"

In the ominous silence Seán looked at Bridget with an air of expectancy, but she did not speak, and very slowly she got up. As she began to gather her papers together the man began to mumble.

"Our poets are no more, our deeds are lost in those of another race, our language, our very voice, is hastening to decay." He took a suck on his disintegrating roll up. "Tis the curse of immigration," he hissed, "with these eejits trying to hustle us down the road to complete degradation."

Bridget couldn't help feeling a certain sadness for him. Even his own children spoke with Londoners' tongues in their heads now. They were no longer Irish. London colonises its children quickly; the last few years had made the conversation all but complete. They hardly ever slipped over to their Celtic selves any more. That part of them seemed to have gone forever. Expelled with sharp, quick, second generation voices. Specialists in pacification appearing kind and considerate having mastered the art of offering a cup of tea in place of an explanation of what they are doing in someone else's country. England makes an acceptable conqueror to some until they wake up one morning and realise it has all been a great big con and they have all been conquered by stealth.

"It's going to need careful negotiation, all right," she said quietly.

But Seán Docherty did not hear as he gazed into the fireplace, for the soldiers now stood erect until they heard the rattle of a single drum which beat out across the land and was taken up by other drums that set the soldiers' feet in motion, so that they began to march through the green fields of his homeland and all the while the drums continued to strike a regular remorseless beat inside his head producing a pain that was still too terrible to tell.

---

* Seán O'Callaghan *To Hell or Barbados* (Dublin: O'Brien Press, 2000);
Don Jordan and Michael Walsh *White Cargo* (New York: NYU Press, 2008).

END OF PART ONE

THE METAL MOUNTAIN

The sprawling, ugly, man-made mountain of mangled metal rose up over a hundred feet towards the sky, many times that in breadth it disappeared into a haze of distance. In summer, or even winter, in fact any day when the sun shone down, catching the sheen of the metal, it glittered on the tin and made those that looked at it screw up their eyes in pain. On rainy days the wet metal glistened and the sound of drops falling on that mass of metal echoed across the railway siding like a drum tattoo. But on foggy days it was at its most intimidating.

But now on this blazing hot afternoon, the huge cataract shimmering in the heat appeared bent and warped—curved by the relentless glaze of the August sun. This iron escarpment, streaked throughout with variegated coloured metal objects of every conceivable size and description, had provided the country with the munitions to fight the Second World War. And on this sunny day, it sparkled with almost heavenly lustre.

Facing arrogantly as it was in all directions, it announces its prerogative, by refusing to acknowledge other possible worlds, full of the knowledge of its own grandeur as if it were somehow self-effulgent, shining by its own light. Seen from afar with its isolating mystique, people suspected it of hiding a subtle secret instead of being a mere speck, a tiny black dot reflected in the orb of the sun.

In a clearing at the base of this freak landscape called 'the salvage pit', four lengths of iron railway track, driven vertically into the ground, acted as a stanchion for a small roof of corrugated iron; for even a washer falling from a considerable height becomes a dangerous missile. The sides were left open to the wind. Under this reinforced lean-to the Farrier plied his trade: a weather-beaten work-hardened old man whose hair stood out in grey shocks, as he worked the lever on a crude cutting machine. The work—as a couple of missing fingers from his left hand attested—was not without its hazards since metal sometimes had intentions of its own.

A jumble of loose metal lay around the floor of the lean-to, amongst which a bomb, presumably a dud one, lay angled, its nose sunk into the ground. The bomb's fin stuck up in the air menacingly like a shark's dorsal from the middle of the mottled cylinder on which someone, perhaps a child, had daubed a swastika. The lethal looking thing evoked in dealers amusement rather than fright, though most still gave it a wide berth. Here the Farrier worked. First, he would take hold of one of the pieces of metal, heft it onto the floor off the machine and slice it in two, manually working the lever in similar fashion to a guillotine. The cut-up metal was then thrown in a heap to the side of the shed to await collection by a lorry, which called once a week and took the waste metal to a foundry to be melted down and recycled. When metal was delivered to the wharf, old Pop the Farrier would get the superintendent to order the wharf's huge crane to lift the metal onto the mountain top.

The Farrier was in need of an apprentice to form and firm and spread the metal evenly around the mountain top and also drag chunks down from it to the machine in the lean-to below, since his last boy had been injured. In fact he had broken his back when he fell from the mountain. The local paper had reported the incident after the boy had died from his injuries the following day. Rust-flaked dust blew on small winds as he worked from one end of the salvage pit to the other, swirling around the lean-to until finally drifting to the ground, where they spread their ochre carpet a little thicker every day. At night the guard dogs' barks echoed around the mountain, by day they stood voiceless and cast their lupine shadows.

"Need any help, mister?"

The voice behind him made him turn his head. He devoted a full minute to inspection. "Naw," he drawled. He spoke with sneering annoyance. He believed that strength was a quality of bulk and brawn. The kid that stood before him now appeared to have neither.

"I'm looking for some work. Need a job, see," replied Michael, refusing to be fazed. The Farrier let go of the chunk of metal he was about to slice and turned round fully to face the lad, his feet giving rise as they shifted to little puffs of dust. It was not lost on him, as he took out his tobacco to make a smoke, that, size apart, the kid seemed to have an air of sternly controlled energy about him; as if he carried victory in both fists. He looked like he could cut iron with his teeth. The Farrier drew the smoke deep into his throat, considering. The kid was looking past him now, up at the metal mountain, as if seeing it fully for the first time, as if he had briefly forgotten the Farrier, in the process of assessing the size and scope and perhaps the monotony involved in the endless labour of slicing up the mountain into manageable pieces, Michael leant up against the battered remains of an old Victorian bath which had once been lavishly ornamented. He went to turn one of the taps, but the dreadful heat made it impossible to touch the metal with his bare hands. Michael's eyes suddenly focused on the old man's. "Pop," he said, "Ever thought of doing something else?"

The question was unexpected. For a second the Farrier lost his purpose. "There's something else?" he replied, opening his eyes wide in mock amazement.

"I hope so," said Michael, shaking his head in feigned concern.

Yet he could not overcome his wonder at the soaring Gothic structure, at the chunks of ore that had been split open by the sun. There was something magical about it, like the mystery that surrounds the obelisk, the labyrinth, the pyramid and the tomb. "I bet there's snow on the top of that bugger," he said with awe, looking directly at the summit where it towered black in the shadow of a sudden cloud. But it was not long before the sun's golden rays touched it once more. Then the light seemed to explode. It ricocheted off the mountain cascading down its metal flanks. The whole earth was flaming: all the colours in the world rushed together and reflected from a thousand twinkling points. Bits of tin caught it and winked while facets of innumerable prismatic edges picked it up and sparkled like uncut diamonds and from its jagged encrustations higher up many subtle coloured lights hopped and sparkled like a million blazing stars.

The Farrier smiled, and now Michael knew that the old man's sternness was feigned. "Yeah there's snow up there alright" he could see the flakes frosting on the rim. "Why don't you go up and see?" the farrier said.

"Yeah! I might just do that, Pop."

"Here—take these gloves, and if you manage to reach the top without breaking your neck, throw me down a few pieces to be getting on with here," he growled, turning back to his machine as the yellow light continued shifting over the surface of the metal.

Michael sprang forward to run the gauntlet of the sun, the one sun and its heat reflected in the metal many times. He jumped across a narrow chasm, landing on top of an old Ford 8. Zigzagging upwards he leaped another gap, came down on top of a lorry cab—wobbled—held—regained his balance and moved on, more cautious now because he could not be sure—not completely sure— when leaping, if his landing place would hold and not give way. But, face set in dreadful purpose, his confidence returned and he leaped unconcerned from car to rusted water-tank to mangled rail, lurched, righted himself, then he climbed or alternately descended, ridges of iron and steel which burned skin already burned past obtrusive elbows of corrugated tin which whipped and slashed, while ducking to avoid pricking beneath bowers of barbed wire that had become viciously entangled. Any suffering involved seemed to be intensified by a merciless sun. The world had begun to exist in oil, rust mould and glare in a rambling maze of metal torment with the iron eating into his shins, he sprang aside he feared he might be devoured by the teeth of iron. He looked up: a hamstrung engine block hung precariously from a ledge above him, the sun reflecting off its copper grill striking him full in the eyes. Two crows, dark shadows on a sheet of sweating zinc, watched disinterestedly until, goaded into a lurching run before taking to the sky, as he fell. A ridge of iron cut his fingers (slicing through his gloves) as a result of him using it for support. He threw the shredded gloves away, in his small boned hands his strength might now be questioned while he remained disguised within his slim-boned frame. Heat melted in deadly waves on metal buffed raw by time and elements, while any moisture that dropped from the summit was immediately consumed by the boiling tin. The hot air had begun to pulsate emphasizing the shape and intensifying the colours of the metal.

He was assailed by harsh smells where oil had mingled with battery acid and lay stagnating in pools of rain water distilling a sharp almost indecent scent. There was distaste on his twisted lips as he lay among the metal, iron eating into the rim of his jaw. The putrefying grunge working its way onto his distorted cheek while he listened to the reverberations of his laboured breath. All over the mountain the metal was bulging, heaving, undulating, tugging at its iron roots it had taken on grotesque forms. Challenging the sun, extinct volcanoes that might be attempting to erupt, rust flakes had taken the colour and texture of hot ash. His skin rejected the one substance: Iron. Failure flared up at him in this limbo, caught between the summit and the base. As his mind retreated from this thing it had so foolishly undertaken, torments of the flesh persisted as he tried to ease his galvanised limbs.

He ran his tongue over his scorched lips, and would have licked the gashes on his racked body from which the flesh was coming away but in his writhing might have toppled right back to the start of his ascent.

From where he lay the mountain rose in waves of steel. He was conscious of the vibrations. They were growing solider, heavier. He was weary and unsure he could go on; the dust of the metal was still in his throat but he would have to, he knew by now; because it had burnt its way into his flesh. He took a deep breath to rouse himself and began climbing, or stumbling over the blazing ridges which shone in a dazzling dance of light with the brilliant radiance of countless suns. From time to time his smouldering eyes glanced up from out of their charred sockets at the mountain's summit, heat seeming to increase the distances. Plumes of dust rose like smoke in purple bloom as he continued in the narrowing perspective his slithery journey, clambering over the bulbous metal's treacherous smoothness in a pair of worn boots shod with tremendous nails, while the mountain continued to rise, with all its colours and sharp corners increasing breathlessness, its steel claws tearing at ankles as he clambered around tangles of wire which threatened to enmesh him, their pointed barbs wreathing and intertwining made the mountain glitter more perilously, as he grappled with its unorthodox angles, clawing, hauling, groping frantically around the contorted corners of this vast tundra in the searing, vibrating light. Where paint had blistered on moss-encrusted aluminium, thorns sprang up beneath his fingers. His nails were tearing at the jagged tin. He bumped against iron. It clattered dangerously. As he fought for new footholds sparks shot out from beneath his boots, tangling with ganglions of wire: the mountain began shaking, lurching with a strange self destructive motion yet he could not, would not be rejected by this relentless mass of metal. The climb became steeper. Already so exhausted there was no time to weigh dangers, the sun was burning up what little strength he had left. As the youth fought harder to reach its formidable pinnacle his limbs trembled against iron and steel, against that which had not yet accepted. Many emotions flowed from his fingers, fear and hatred came by turns as he clambered around the body of a decapitated Morris Minor. The chipped edges were dreadful. The sun-blistered metal tore at his flesh but the youth finally reached the summit and was initiated into secrets he had never suspected. Because he had visualised it otherwise, his weary bitter face began to glow. The sky was a blaze of gold, lit with silver clouds manifold in their variety. The all pervasive light emanating from this radiant cluster poured in cascades of shimmering exaltation down the mountain sides, the sparks set off by the sun's rays striking a million little mirrors of tin, releasing a stream of ice-blue particles filtered sensually through the brutal imagery; all was light and nothing but light as it continued to shine; its brilliance increased to celestial radiance. In the burnished light the vulgar gloss became illuminated. Time is annihilated by such intimate glimpses.

As atoms danced, filling the air with delicate pinpricks of liquid blue, a shiver of recognition ran through the youth, and in that moment he experienced such enchantment at the vast silence, a peace so deep that anything that was not peace melted into it. The silence was immense. There is a moment when silence no longer resisted rushes into the mind and one lets go inch by inch of the desperate clutching. So that the moment seemed to last forever and the permanence of iron was a myth. It was mesmerizing, breathtaking in both its beauty and its enormity. From where he stood, he could see all the way to Raglan Street. When he turned right round, he could see the fields of Hampstead Heath. When he looked left he could see up Highgate Road. He smiled and squinted, his gaze following the twelve-foot high perimeter fence until his eyes finally settled on the area around the main gate, where a brick building stood, occupied by the Wharf Superintendent, whose job it was to check the weight of incoming and outgoing vehicles as they came to a halt on the weigh bridge outside his office. The building also housed a couple of railway coppers, one of whose duties it was (along with a dark grey German shepherd, a long, lean, hungry looking brute) to check anyone walking in or out of the railway sidings. Those that ran, he left to the dog. The other policeman's duty was to patrol the perimeter fence.

He ran, giddy-legged now, along the uneven metal crown, stopping in the middle erect and proud to survey his new domain.

Glancing forward into a region where possibility crystallised great clusters of ball bearings into precious stones, and out of this would grow the purpose of his being. He stood against a slab of shadow, remote and present too, eyes fixed on future pleasures among iron and steel that had turned to light and shadow, strangely silhouetted against the rim of the sky, in a smell of oil and battered tin.

The born observer is never self-conscious about his method. If you asked him, he would say that he merely makes as little fuss as possible and keeps his eyes open. Michael Docherty was such a one. Like the wolf, he moved now across the face of the metal landscape, soft and wary. He knew that this mountain contained infinite possibilities. He knew more by instinct than by cold, calculating reason that if he searched properly amongst the startling objects he would find gold, or (more precisely) precious metals.

Some held that all metals would be gold if they could but were prevented by the impurities of the earth.

Like some divine vastness, however far he saw, there was always more ahead. Such was the pervasiveness of the metal mountain.

The great thing loomed and brooded, at times dense and sullen, at others shimmeringly opalescent but always enticing. He was like an explorer walking into a landscape flickering in a shimmer of distance which might prove mirage. Nonetheless the youth was pretty sure that this landscape was an actual one which held beneath its enamelled armature many rare and varied treasures. Glittering images stirred inside him as he walked on the edge of the mountain and a breeze played subtle melodies among the twitching tin.

He began immediately, lured by a pleasure that was as hard as pain, into making sure that his boss never got a moment's break, because he would never leave old Pop without a surplus of metal to be cutting up, while he himself searched high and low from morn till night for precious scraps, not the obvious kind, such as bronze or gun metal, heavy stuff, which, quite apart from their weight, are far too bulky to transport. No. Michael found himself thinking more of certain types of screws; castors; electric cables of thin copper wire, others full of aluminium, their warped and twisted branches, lying amongst the rusting iron like coiled serpents; wooden doors with brass locks and hinges; and grey-blue lead pipes, sheets and panels of zinc which can be cut into small pieces quite easily. Nothing was too much trouble. He found some old ammunition boxes, and into these he placed his treasure, separated according to type. So the chips of metal mounted daily as they were carved out.

Like any mountain, this one had its sheer drops and jagged edges, the only difference being that injuries sustained here were caused by metal rather than rock. The whole mass was in a permanent state of flux. In his constant search for precious metals, Michael learned to avoid pretty patches of flowering shrubs and grass like quicksand. Wherever birds and wind had carried seeds, these treacherous oases sprung up, usually in hollows full of crushed and broken debris, red-rotten with rust, which the slightest pressure would turn to powered dust, plunging the unwary to the rusting depths below. Rainwater draining from the summit nourishes the flowers but these pretty places in summertime sometimes caught fire from the friction of iron striking iron as it falls or lightning which burns away the foliage.

Sometimes, in his struggle with gravity, missing his footing, he trod in a pool of stagnant rainwater that collected in the inverted bowls of upturned vehicles or their mudguards, until he learned from experience to feel first with the foot before putting weight on it. Nothing was overlooked. Finding himself wedged in holes and crevices that turned out to be too narrow, he had to crawl back feet first, using everything he could to get a hold: knees elbows, back or buttocks. Eventually he became as sure-footed as a mountain goat when clambering up and down and round about the metal mountain and as slippery as an eel when crawling into and out of the crevices beneath it. His was a slow labour, a matter of eye, time and tenacity.

This iron world with so little evidence of civilisation, did fit perfectly the shape of what he felt missing from his life. Total acceptance of the present moment, harmony with things as they happen, friendship with the inevitable. Viewed thus, the whole mountain took on a permanent grandeur. But sometimes even iron lost its substance; flowed, and whispered and took other forms.

He had prepared, groping over surfaces and rummaging in pockets for the secret act of toting. He bent to pick up a piece of gold or perhaps it was a bit of brass. The sun was low, its light ate at the ridges and wind blew under tremulous sheets of aluminium, the mountain was murmuring its eternal lament as the wind continued to skim over it. Here some of the metal was of a darker hue.

Long black tongues of wrinkled tin lolled and twanged among the debris of tinkling zinc. The hammer from long holding was warm in his hand. There was a menace of uncertainty in the air as he approached the thing that crouched beyond the shadows. The wind veered and slammed hard at the mountain's surface, the sun had become curiously veiled but allowed enough light to penetrate the entrance to the cavern to reveal the serpent—a twisted piece of copper tubing tensed like a cobra ready to strike.

At the bottom of the mountain about twenty yards from the lean-to where old Pop worked was another clearing with a metal shed which was always kept locked. This shed held the valuable acetylene equipment, gas cylinders and torches that were used for cutting the largest pieces of metal: war surplus on the sidings, such as car and lorry bodies. In the jargon of the trade, an iron monger's apprentice was known as a 'cradle rocker', on account of the fact that as rocks and roots and stones held the soil of a mountainside together, so too did the burnt-out shells of old cars and lorry cabs serve exactly the same function on the metal mountain. The test of a good cradle rocker was how to overcome the difficulties of extracting the cars and lorry cabs (which were usually wedged upside-down) from the entangling metal mass that held them together, without causing an avalanche. Great skill was needed, delicacy of movement, and of course, brute strength.

Michael soon realised that, like any mine, sooner or later he was going to have to go down deeper into the bowels of this one to locate the precious metal, where in summer, crawling beneath its iron crust would be like entering an airless oven, and in wintertime, an Arctic cave. So when one fine morning old Pop ordered him aloft to get him down one of the cradles with the admonishment "not to rock himself to sleep in it," Michael laughed. The big, black Buick lay wedged upside down on its roof with the ends of its chrome bumper turned outwards like the horns of a bull. Michael stepped back from it to establish the correct angle for levering. It was awkwardly wedged amongst the knotted tin. When he sunk the crowbar down on one side of the Buick there was an unmerciful shriek of metal grinding against metal. With every inch gained he had to judge precisely when to keep his feet flexible and when to keep them nailed. By probing and wrenching when his hold was good he managed to free the cradle; then he got his hands under the chassis, planted his feet and heaved it forward, causing the veins to stand out in his arms. When he'd got his breath back, he walked forward kicking any loose metal out of his path and stamping his makeshift runway flat with his foot.

For a while he stood, looking down at the railway sidings from the top of the mountain. He never tired of the view obtained from this spot. He watched the engineers working on the trains over at the marshalling sheds and then his gaze fell on the engineers' cottages nearby, their place of work, each with its own small garden where a variety of vegetables grew. Old Pop's house was situated at the furthest end, and could be distinguished quite easily by the many different flowers that had filled his front garden.

Michael continued to gaze on the comings and goings below. The Sergeant was talking to the Supervisor over at the main gate, while the Constable was making a leisurely tour of the perimeter fence, the grey, half-wolfish creature slinking along at his side. He pondered the scene, tight-mouthed, narrow-eyed and grim. It was going to be a bit of a problem getting his treasure out of this place all right. But he couldn't wait forever: he had plans for the money that the scrap would bring. He would have to make a move soon.

He stretched out his arms, took a deep breath and applied himself to the task in hand once more. Pushing shoving cursing groaning heaving and grunting the cradle rocker's lament he manoeuvred the Buick cradle along, every so often going from side to side to apply the bar, so that it zigzagged slowly forward, furrowing a ditch in the loose metal beneath. Eventually he reached the edge of the mountain. He angled the cradle into the tilting position, careful never to lose control until he was ready. Then, with the roar of a conquering lion, he shouted: "TIMBER!!!" and with one final push, sent the shell of the car, accompanied by the grim notes of clashing metal, plummeting downwards. For a moment, the noise was deafening, until the mangled mass came to rest at the bottom. Then there was a death-like quietness, until old Pop appeared in the middle of the salvage pit. "Hoi, hoi!" he shouted, "You might have killed someone wiv that effing car."

Michael laughed. "Why didn't you warn me the brakes were so bad?" he shouted back. The simplicity of it was making him enjoy himself. All day long he wrought at the iron until the sun plunged behind the metal mountain leaving a red afterglow on the earth around the salvage pit and the first star sparkled white in the coppery sky. The evening was basking in the soft edges of its purple light while all around metal, tortured and twisted as if tempered in hell, had settled into exaggerated shapes. Where heavier, cruder metal had gouged finer civilised pieces the sun had cauterised the flesh, for iron cannot know iron except in conflict.

Sometimes he couldn't tell where he was in this reckless mass of iron. The days were out of season, some days the sky was so low the clouds might have been stitched to the metal if they weren't already sewed up to the sky. At other times they would rise so high above him a light not of the sun or moon or stars shone down.

Throughout the following months, old Pop the Farrier, thorough, conscientious, unshakeable, his grey hair billowing like a prophet worked steadily on. Wherever the hammer struck and was skilfully parried by bucklers of solid steel, then the acetylene rod spat its tongue of thin blue flame which sliced a puckered gash right through the stubborn metal, while its deceptive gentle purr seemed to suggest some transcendental quality, especially when, on encountering an obstacle, the point of the flame would seethe up into a head of golden sparks and flicker with such glittering gobs of greenish iridescence that it did seem more a devotional act than a simple rendering process.

Sometimes the Farrier would look up, beyond where the bowed iron jutted like living ribs at the sky, as if preparing to receive revelations beneath the steepled tin and when he struck the pocked metal it sprang like a shadow, the hammer strokes echoing around the salvage pit with their distinctive ching, while the breeze rang prettily on the glistening metal. A supreme accolade of sound and form pulsed within time and space accompanied by the dry sighing of the wind swirling keenly around the pit in sallies of grit, while iron, under the influence of fire and hammer continually underwent a molecular cycle of birth and death.

His young apprentice kept him well supplied, fetching down from the mountain such huge, barbaric chunks that he had to use the bolt cutters on them before he could even attempt to put them under the guillotine. Michael was, without doubt, the best lad he had ever had: so accurate and precise at levering out cradles awkwardly wedged under upturned vehicles and he'd learnt how to use the cutting equipment and understood the electrical side of things very fast. And yet old Pop couldn't help feeling a little guilty sometimes when he thought about it, but he couldn't dismiss a suspicion. He shook his head as he placed a piece of metal on the ground. He could not understand the almost desperate savagery with which the young lad went about his work and suddenly he was reminded of The Bible: "He rageth and again he rageth, for he knoweth his time is short." He sighed as he remembered asking. "What was the rush?"

and the boy had replied "I don't want to waste time." But the old Farrier could only smile because here time did not exist. You may watch the clock tick or the sun rise and set but that is not time. That is simply movement.

There had been a beginning, mused the Farrier, after the government had declared war on Germany. "Bring us metal," they had cried "and we will accomplish the task." But when the task had been completed the order had not been rescinded and so every week truckloads of scrap metal are still delivered to the wharf while an equal amount is carted away, so that everything keeps moving according to its nature, every action creating a reaction, which balances and neutralises the action. Everything happens, but there is a continuous cancelling out, and in the end it is as if nothing happened. Each is the cause of the other. Each is the other, in truth. For the mountain, like the present moment, is always there, standing in the timeless now.

Yet whenever strangers look at the mountain they find only a structure of unbelievable chaotic pattern. Perhaps it is thinking oneself to be separate from it that creates the illusion of disorder, of death and decay. And yet the only way to renewal lies through destruction. The mountain must be melted down into formless iron before it can be moulded into new shapes. He gazed down thoughtfully. The future balanced on such fragile foundations and a past clotted with angry blood. With these sombre thoughts the Farrier with steady hand and hopeful eye resumed his work, striking the metal with his hammer so that it chimed and sang and gleamed with a sinister splendour.

A piece of jagged tin can slice a throat, sever an artery or cleave a limb. A tin tack falling from a great height can pierce the skull or knock out an eye... The Farrier pulled the guillotine lever down. Even when he'd put the old German prismatics on him, he'd still not seen anything irregular. The crowbar went in, found a purchase, levered out a chunk of metal and sent it hurtling downwards with a crash. Even when, at random intervals throughout the day, he'd watched him through the binoculars, nothing about his apprentice's actions gave him cause for doubt. Nor should it—for Michael had spotted the binoculars along with an old photo of Pop in army dress uniform holding the ceremonial spiked axe with which farriers had despatched injured horses in times gone by

So whenever the old Farrier (pierced by suspicion) took a notion to put the glass on him, Michael would either desist from mining his claim altogether on that day, or else he would work harder on the far side of the mountain where it gleamed in a splendour of enamel, separating the precious metal tossed out on the slopes from its less exotic relations on the far side of the hill; for he had become addicted to the alchemy of plucking petals off the sun. Ignorant to the fact that through sheer delight and in spontaneous freedom, the sun creates its own reflections in the infinite prism of those honest objects that make up this gigantic sculpture that has not yet learnt the dishonesties within art, expressing the perfection in the harmony of opposites in small and great ways, even the simple beauty within the ephemeral elegance of streaks of light and darkness at sunrise and sunset. Everywhere he looked there was always a new marvel to behold; where the metal had reacted curiously to the elements, oxidization had turned vast areas of metal into many luminous colours all glowing with a remarkable radiance. The exquisite details were deeply absorbing as if designed for contemplation but the youth had not come here for that.

Failing to recognise the source, the root of his sense of separation, in the aluminium sunset he swung on the pendulum of attraction and aversion. Once he had been close, so close he might have touched with his breath the innermost and indestructible essence. He used the word god still but did so sparingly now. It showed in his face, which had begun to look shrunken, searching for scraps of pleasure or fulfilment but he could not gather his strength together enough at one point for the validation, security and love it was seeking. Though normal enough desires in themselves they seemed now to the youth superhuman accomplishments. One day when he had come into the lean-to he found a young girl talking to Pop. The girl looked with an eager kind of curiosity at him and he smiled. It was the butcher boys' girl Vicky!

"So it's true" laughed Michael.

"What's true?" said Pop.

"She does live on a mountain or near enough," chuckled Michael, recalling the kid's words to him on East Heath.

"I see you two have met before," said Pop frowning for strange occurrences, as Vicky smiled back at Michael.

"We went for a bicycle ride once", said Michael.

For answer Pop nodded curtly at the girl and said, "Tell ma I'll see to it tonight." The girl turned and with a last glance at Michael she left.

"Vicky's a good girl" said Pop, "I don't know how I'd manage without her, she helps me to look after her Gran." In fact she was his Granddaughter, and had lived with him and her Grandmother since her parents had been killed in the war.

THE WEDDING

They were married in St. Dominic's Roman Catholic Church in Kentish Town. Seán Docherty gave her away and Bridget Ann Kelly became Mrs Marshall. There was lots of confetti and a group photo outside the church and the bride looked lovely in her wedding finery with two of Alan's nieces acting as her bridesmaids. They went back to Raglan Street for the reception.

Alan's family and Bridget's family hadn't met before the wedding, so both parties shared a feeling of unease. "Why don't you open up one of them bottles of Scotch?" Alan suggested to Seán, hoping that the fire water would relax matters. It suddenly got noisier in the front room of number 14 than it had been. The voices of the married couple's families and friends were all raised and when Joe Flynn, a first cousin of Seán's, arrived with his fiddle the place started fairly leppin'.

The West Coast of Ireland is bleak and wild. The soil is poor and when the earth is poor, what wealth can the people generate? And yet this fact has not stopped visits over the centuries by colonial Lords and tasselled Dukes with their gibbets and starvations and deportations and a crimson-coated line stretched out behind them, fifes and horns and trumpets braying, their feet falling to the tap of the drum.

"A greedy, dauntless group," say the historians. But long before they came, those gilded imperialists—long, long before that, came others, unadorned and infinitely more lethal, horrendous blood-letters—the Vikings. Those red and blond haired barbarians, however, neutralised most of their conquests by marrying many of their captives.

When the fiddle thrilled out, the response was startling. It brought these descendants of the Northern barbarian jumping to their feet, captives once again to the pulse of the ancient sound. It was pagan, but it was something more than that. At first the tempo was slow and measured, a sweet quavering, then gradually it quickened, sending the sound soaring to the heights, and suddenly the women's dresses were swirling high. Couples, with yelps of excitement, were nearly falling over themselves with the speed and tempo of the dance. Those sitting at the side clapped out the rhythm with vigour and zest to the yells of voices shrill and high. Some of the younger ones with thrills of laughter were leaping into the air. Now, with the speed of it, they began to pant for breath; but there was no let-up to the frenzy. The fiddler saw to that. Just when you thought the music might slow down, with elegant and brutal bowing it speeded up. It was fantastic—wildly out of keeping with the little Raglan Street front room. Now giving way to ever more uninhibited delight, the leaping became more frenzied, more abandoned, the revellers' faces glistening with sweat. Their breath quickened. Their nostrils dilated. Their eyes rolled, yet still the dance went on and on, ever faster and wilder, under the sensual influence of the dance, with the blood risen flushing the face. All the women, even the less handsome, were pretty as they continued to spin with their partners, locked together by their shrieks and arms, and the swirl of their solid skirts round and round the little front room. While the bridegroom's family stood among the pushed-back furniture and looked and looked, for it was something strange and beautiful and perhaps a little shameful, because they did not understand. Finally the fiddler slowed his hand, the clear high notes fell to a drone, and with pounding hearts and senses the dancers gradually staggered breathless to a stand.

As the dancers rested between waltzes and reels, the bridegroom led his bride out onto the middle of the floor, where, shimmering with that gleam the newly betrothed are blessed with, they completed something of a vision to the smiles and nods of the approving guests, who pushed forward eagerly as their raptures increased, so that there was hardly any space to move but the couple danced in it. The tune was perfect and never better played, but it was not the audience the newly-weds had chosen to impress, as their movements flowed slow and gentle like the swerve of a flame. He, gallant and lavish, she graceful and daring. Sometimes—to provoke, it was suggested— they would almost collide, but like skilled matadors gracefully avert at the very last second, a coupling with serene elegance. Her bodice was perfectly cut to emphasise the slimness of the waist while the full dress of pure white satin almost covered the carpet as she swirled on the spot. The little room was not built to contain so much, it became sultry and began almost to smoulder as the young couple, the light moulding their firm young bodies, gradually began to close with each other in the climax of their dance.

The dance ended to clapping and joyful cries from the assembled guests who also lavished kisses on the flushed bride's cheeks; indeed few there forfeited that ancient rite.

Out on a table in the hallway spread on top of a white cloth were a large leg of ham and roast chickens and loaves and cheese and plates piled high with sandwiches and under the table were stacked crates of bottled beer and spirits. Mary Jane began encouraging the guests to help themselves and very soon nearly everyone there had a plate in their hand and with the other hand were stuffing food from the plate into their mouths in between copious mouthfuls of beer.

Alan went to help Seán unplug a blockage in the toilet out the back, while Bridget went upstairs to change. They were going to Brighton for the honeymoon, and since Alan worked for the railway company they would travel free. Mary Jane was rushing hither and thither ministering to the guests. "Have you had something, Michael?" she asked for the umpteenth time, proffering a plate of sandwiches. At the same instant she heard Bridget's voice calling down to her from upstairs. "Go up and see what she wants," she told Michael, as she turned to help Alan's mother extract a bottle of brown ale from a crate.

Michael bounded up the stairs, tapped on the door and entered to her call, to find the bride still in her wedding dress, standing surrounded by blouses and dresses lying on the bed, stockings and underclothes spilling over a chair. A vast brown leather suitcase lay open in the middle of the floor. He stood there wondering what would be expected of him. While his aunty's face seemed full of a half-innocent, half-roguish vibrancy as she struggled with the zip on her dress. "I'm wrapped up like a Christmas present, Michael," she said, turning her back. "Can you get me out of this?"

The boy was shy of course and too confused with delicious shame to notice, as he slid the zip all the way down to expose her slim back that his heart was racing wildly. "Is it okay?" he asked tingling from the too intimate glimpses.

"Yes, that's good," she laughed, standing up and shrugging her body so that the dress slid down to her feet, and in one graceful movement, she stepped out of it. She stood now in a white slip that was so moulded to her figure that it seemed as if it were the only stitch of clothing she was wearing. "There," she said, shaking her head seriously. The afternoon sun shone through her hair, turning it a tawny chestnut, the image gave Michael a sudden, sensual jolt of delight, coupled with a curious unease, making him uncertain of himself, making it impossible for him to look at her. As he was going for the door, she called gently to him: "Wait yet, I have something for you." He turned. She held out her hand; it emphasised her look of nakedness. He hesitated, moving silently, almost on tiptoe, two light steps brought her to him, she put her hand on his chest and with quick precision slipped a pound note into his breast pocket. "There, you're the best man in the house," she said, hugging him in an excess of affection. A blush of pleasure glowed upon his cheek as he came downstairs to find the party still in full swing. They were singing:

> "Tramp, tramp, tramp, the boys are marching;
> Here comes the Bobby at the door.
> If you don't let him in,
> He'll bash the door right in,
> And you'll never see your mammy any more."

It was a popular Saturday night pub song, a sort of warning lament to draft dodgers and army deserters. From that they flowed straight into a gentle waltz and Alan's brother Harry, with a tipsy bow and flourish was trying his best to encourage his shy and giggling nieces to take the floor with him, while Mr Marshall senior, looking very courtly in his best black double-breasted suit with his grey moustache and iron-grey sleeked back hair, glided sedately round the room holding a smiling Mary Jane in his arms.

Alan sat smoking and talking with one of his relatives at the side. Danny, having made a tactical error in his choice of seating, was gently getting his ear bashed by a woeful Mrs Marshall senior on the trials and tribulations of arthritis. Michael was talking to Freida, Alan's sister and her husband Jack, while their two children played out in the hall with Dermot. The rest of the guests were drinking, larking and tipsily dancing about. When the bride came back down Michael was absorbed in some silent judgement so that he looked away as she entered the room though it did not prevent him from noticing the wink that she gave him to show that they had conspired in some innocent way, though the boy interpreted it differently, since her half-clad figure continued flickering on and off before his eyes. The other guests gasped, at least the males among them did, for the streamlined image she presented in her tight dress. But the woman whose nakedness was only for her husband did not notice. Suddenly there was a bit of a flurry when Seán Docherty, slightly the worse for wear, stood up and began to sing accompanied by the fiddler who with a hand both bold and rapid plucked a few loud marshal chords.

> "O father why are you so
> Sad on this bright Easter
> Morn when Irish men are
> Proud and glad of the land
> Where they were born..."

Mary Jane eagerly seeking a different air rushed over and told him to be quiet or else sing something else. For though the song sounded quite melancholy, half hymn, half ballad, it was not really a song of the hearth, it had more of a danger to it. And in this gathering she felt it might cause trouble since it was a rebel song with an ardent call to arms. After that, with a nod of the head, Mary Jane gave the fiddler the beck to make ready once more, and with a stamp of the foot he set to with a will and another tune sweet and compelling began. Then, four more lively reels by the fiddler brought them to the time for the Bride and Groom to leave. Alan's two young nieces, their voices clear and soaring, sang them out with an enchanting duet—a Protestant hymn. It was beautiful and haunting, and when it stopped the sound seemed to hang in the air.

THE UNFORGIVEN

Mrs Watson often threw stale bread out of her first-floor window to the birds, and often would come down afterwards to supervise its distribution, ensuring that the bullies did not scoff the lot before the gentler species had had their fair share. She was a great believer in fair play.

She also liked to chat and would do so in good weather through the young couple's open window. They had to listen, to repay her for her kindness in providing them with such a lovely garden flat, which she had made ready for them after their return from the honeymoon.

Indeed most of her intentions were benevolent. It was only money that prevented her carrying them out. They liked to sit when work was done; looking at the tiny garden through the kitchen window, talking about and exploring each other's day, warm and comfortable in the little kitchen, was, to the newly weds, the height of contentment.

Though the autumn evening was well advanced, the sun still shone down with sufficient warmth to keep the visiting blackbird's spirits high, so high, in fact that in place of its usual warning metallic croak it was perched sideways, carolling joyfully in sweet melodious tones. Alan was sitting in his armchair by the window, cross-checking the station's timetable and the following week's duty roster, while Bridget stood beside the gas stove brewing some tea. She watched him absently while the kettle boiled. Quite often he experienced a harrowing time sifting through sheaves of invoices and bills of lading. There was usually some freight missing, damaged or delayed. She smiled down at him compassionately; sometimes the problems were stupefying and he would then be up half his shift, trying to solve them. She lifted the boiling kettle from the gas ring and began pouring the water into the little teapot. As she waited for it to brew, she lapsed back to their very first weeks in the flat. She remembered with wry humour how they used to have such noisy discussions regarding their baby's religious upbringing, and how she herself had always thought the child would be a girl and Alan had always imagined a boy. It was invigorating and they would talk most evenings about the child they would have until a routine visit to the doctor had informed them that they might never have a child. And, with perhaps the judgement of Solomon rather than any professional expertise, the medic had gone on to apportion blame (if such be the word) equally, intimating that stress could be a major factor, for he believed that what mattered most in these circumstances was to go at it in a relaxed manner and the rest usually took care of itself. But after the initial shock had been absorbed they did not feel unduly worried by it. They felt sure everything would work out; above all, they felt sure of each other.

Bridget switched off the gas and turned towards the table. As she reached across the table to place the teapot near him, a sudden burst of bright sunlight fell full on Alan's face, so that it appeared to her that his head was encircled in a halo of celestial light. It was an illusion of course, and as the sun's rays continued to play about his head, Bridget turned her gaze towards the garden, her eyes straying to a small hillock in the centre where an air-raid shelter had been sunk for the occupants' protection during the war. She looked back at Alan sitting in the chair. "It must have been a constant worry that the station might get hit during the war," she remarked.

"I was not really concerned," he mumbled.

"You must have had nerves of iron."

"Not especially." His response seemed half-hearted, and she perceived at that moment that his mind was elsewhere.

"Most people would have ended up nervous wrecks sitting in that little wooden office day after day, night after night, not knowing whether the sound they were hearing was really that of an approaching train or an enemy bomber."

He did not answer immediately: he just sat in the chair looking out of the window with a rigid jaw. "It was hit—a direct hit too."

"God," she whispered and came to sit on the arm of his chair stroking his cheek, eyeing him uncertainly. There were areas of his mind she felt that would take a long time to know, she placed a comforting arm around his shoulders to gaze along with him through the window at the tiny garden.

"It looks very nice," murmured Alan.

"It's wonderful," replied Bridget, "To have a bit of green to look out on." In speaking of the garden she felt more at ease. It was a great relief at last to be able to change the subject. Yet even as she thought that, her mind was searching for some delicate way to return to their earlier conversation. "Were you badly hurt?" she began cautiously.

"What?" mumbled Alan absently because it did not concern him yet.

"When the station got hit!"

"No, I was fortunately elsewhere." She could hardly compose herself enough she was so relieved.

"Where were you?"

"The Army," he replied with bewildering brevity, and for a moment Bridget was at a loss for words. She began to move away sensing some thought of which she might not approve.

Then something occurred to her which caused great relieve.

"Of course," she said, "you were called up."

"No as a Railway employee, I was exempt."

"You joined up?" There was a breath of contempt in her tone.

"Yes," he proudly proclaimed, "in 1943 with the Guards' own independent Parachute Brigade—Para one," as if it was the most natural thing in the world.

Outside in the garden a cat sat crouched watching a feathered migrant that had come here for a refuge because it seemed quite possible it might just fall from its safe perch.

And now Bridget Marshall began to remember what she had forgotten. Forced to face an anxiety she had been concealing she registered suddenly a number of unpleasant sensations, anticipating perhaps the razor's edge of life, on which everything is balanced. Memories started flashing through her mind of tales told and retold round the hearth since childhood of the atrocities of the Tans. For to her, as to many Irish people, all English soldiers, were forever tainted by the Black and Tans. Emotion overwhelmed her before she knew it. The fear and loathing was instinctive and she looked at him now in a conflict of worry and amazement. Unconsciously, some ancient Celtic impulse stirred inside her, giving her at that moment a feeling that something had come between them. For in the evilness of the Tans the belief was precious, and his disclosure had impinged on that. But there was no way to say this to him, and slowly she began to dwell on the why of it all, and after some minutes of contemplation, she simply said: "No one in our family ever married a soldier before." Her bluntness turned a confession into an accusation.

He could have been contemptuous as he sat there looking through the sun's waning light at his wife. Then since her words had begun to hint at deeper matters, he rose slowly to his feet. "And no one in ours ever married an Irish person before."

"You never ever mentioned you were a soldier to me."

"You never asked."

"I told my whole family you weren't."

"Then you're a good soldier, you've kept the peace."

'But what if Michael and Seán especially Michael were to find out…' Through the heavy air of the false summer came the cries of a departing blackbird. Bridget looked up, lost in a haze of confusion they both sensed the distance that it had to travel. She was at first frightened to accept, even the man's courage seemed to falter, but eventually, because it was there, at last natural to do so, they put their hands out to each other.

Outside in the garden the little hillock seemed so remote, it was acceptable, for the young wife had sensed its shape looking beyond it into the future, a future into which she was now not afraid to look.

What made life comfortable to deal with in this way was that, preoccupations and scruples, every circumstance of every struggle fell away, stretching into safe years. So that as time passed she no longer felt an impostor, which was logical if one wished to stand amongst one's neighbours without doubts. Light streamed through the open window, a bronze haze, so peaceful in its slow dwindling. She reached out to pick up the teapot and began to pour tea into two little china cups. It was natural, of course, she was obviously a sensible woman, and quite alone now, for her husband had withdrawn, returned to his papers. He already knew the meaning of what they had just discovered together.

AN AUDACIOUS PLAN

"I've been taking a little look around that place," Michael said to Danny one night when they were alone in the scullery. Their mother had gone to Benediction and their father was listening to the wireless with Dermot in the front room. "I got a feeling that wharf is full of rackets."

"Such as what?" Danny asked, still reading his book, not really interested in hearing what he presumed to be the boring minutiae of his brother's place of work.

"All sorts of things are going on. You'd be surprised what happens over there on a rainy day."

Danny shrugged and lowered his book. He was trying to work out in his mind what Michael was leading up to and replied dryly: "I suppose it gets wet."

"They're crafty bastards, them cockneys," Michael continued, ignoring Danny's jibe. "Fat Ernie, the supervisor, is supposed to weigh every vehicle that comes into that wharf and weigh it again when it goes back out."

"So?" said Danny, impatient to return to his book now, since Michael's reference to cockneys in a tone implying distance and difference, worried him, because cockneys were their father's supreme example of treachery and wickedness. This never failed to make Danny feel uncomfortable. He would have been very surprised to learn that his younger brother knew this, and furthermore was using this lever of national identification to inveigle Danny (who was basically honest) into assisting him whenever his schemes and plans called for an extra pair of hands. For the notice still troubled him, the words still had a malevolent power to make him uncomfortable, every now and then, when he least expected it, they would begin to rattle around inside his head.

They seemed to spring out and hit him in the face. They singled him out from the rest of the world:

NO IRISH, NO DOGS

And he had begun to think if there was anything he could do about it. Because the notice, as time passed, made him feel as if it were speaking directly to him.

"So every week, he always waves this black van in as empty. Then it stops over at the engineers workshop and about an hour later it pulls back up on the weigh bridge, and again he waves it out as empty."

"Maybe it is empty."

Michael gave Danny a pitying smile. "When that van leaves the wharf, it's chock-a-block full."

"How can you tell?"

"Because I was up on the mountain with old Pop's binocs, having a look around the other day, when it was spilling down, and when that van came in through the gate its wheels hardly left a dent in the mud but on the way out it was sinking to its back axle."

"Isn't there a police sergeant on duty at the wharf gate?" Even as he spoke, Danny was surprised at himself for asking the question—making himself responsible even in that limited way for getting involved.

"Yes," said Michael.

"What was he doing?" Michael laughed low and scornfully at the question.

"He was doing what any good copper would do when he sees an over-loaded van struggling to get out of his wharf: he was standing in the middle of the road holding up the traffic for it."

"So what do you think is in the van?" asked Danny, suddenly taken with the intrigue of Michael's workplace.

"Could be anything," replied Michael. "They're all at it over there," and then added casually, as if to say only a fool would leave himself out, "I've even managed to find a bit of stuff myself." And he went on to tell Danny about his hidden hoard of precious metal. "Nine ammo boxes full! But I can't think how to get it out," he sighed, giving his brother a sort of defeated look which had the effect of brightening rather than depressing Danny, since the dilemma appealed to his problem-solving mind.

He took up the supposedly theoretical challenge eagerly for the next twenty minutes, and he came up with many ploys, the last being the most ludicrous, that Michael should fake an accident or a contagious sickness, and have the box put into the ambulance as his personal effects alongside him, and then driven, bell ringing like mad, out the gate for all it was worth. "No-one's going to interfere with a basket-case," laughed Danny. When Michael failed to respond, he added dramatically: "For whom the bell tolls!"

"You got a good bell and a big basket on the front of that butcher's bike," said Michael quietly. For a while, all was silent in the small scullery. The white paint on the walls was moist with the rime of the winter evening, rapidly descending, condensation had formed an eerie nimbus round the light. Obliquely, Danny looked past his brother, as if troubled by the fading glare of the electric bulb. "Try it just once," coaxed Michael.

"Once is all it takes," replied Danny mournfully.

Michael yawned and leaned back listening to his bones creak. He'd had a hard day. "You won't get caught first time," he scoffed.

Danny's eyes opened with surprise. "Why not?"

"Because you won't be carrying anything." Danny was about to say something, but Michael continued: "First time, you do a dry run. Pull up at the gate; make a noise, let 'em know you're there, which shouldn't be too difficult. Tell 'em you've got a delivery at the engineers' cottages. They won't bother you on the way in, but on the way out…" He smiled at his brother's serious face. "That fat copper will be out of that office so fast his feet won't touch the ground. He hates being disturbed, and he'll turn you over inside out and upside down and all he's gonna find in your basket is a nice juicy piece of horse flesh, which, by the way, you will allow him to keep, because like most old railway coppers that policeman's a proper piss-pot. According to old Pop, the dog's food allowance goes into the till of the Queen's Arms instead of the Butcher's. That dog's half dead with hunger, that's why it keeps hugging the fence when it's out on patrol—to stop it keeling over."

Danny smiled at the image Michael had conjured. "Next visit, you hand the copper that piece of dead horse on the way in. Then we'll fill the basket with precious metal, and he'll be out there in the middle of the road, hands spread wider than Christ on his cross, holding back the traffic, nodding you on as you leave." He yawned and pulled the sheet over his head. Danny laughed but not freely enough to ease a conscience disturbed by dangers he had committed himself to share in with Michael, who had encouraged him to take the job working for the butcher's in Hampstead. He reached over to switch off the light, leaving a small statue of the Madonna with her hand raised pointing into darkness.

Overhead the sky was clear blue without a cloud in sight to mar it, as Danny braked the bike outside the entrance to the wharf. He heard the bolt automatically shoot back, and the small side-gate was suddenly opened. He pushed the bike inside and stood waiting. The place was empty, he thought. Suddenly, a grey-blackish shape exploded from the gate office and slithered to a halt beside him. Axon von Müller British Railway Authority police dog No.505, known to his handler as Rex, was high in the shoulder, sloping down neatly to trim haunches at the back. His ancestors had been born in some dense, dark forest in northern Germany. He could run faster than a tiger and put any wolf in the world to flight. When the breed had been imported to England, because in a war many things change hands, the British (in their efforts to obscure any connection with anything German) had changed the name from German Shepherd to Alsatian.

The pleasant little tingle of adventure that had previously rung through Danny's blood suddenly started to evaporate. The dog, he was sure, was an animal who would be adversely affected by signs of friendship—familiarity or expressions of tenderness such as attempts at stroking, petting, or any other of the formalities and niceties that one might normally extend to the domesticated breed. He stood, the bike balanced between his legs, hands tucked down into his trouser pockets, trying to contain his nervousness and compose his face into some semblance of unconcerned innocence, while the dog began to circle him, slowly. The only accurate piece of information which that bugger Michael had given him about this whole effing set-up so far, he thought, was that this dog was hungry—ferociously so, it seemed. He said a little prayer, then checked himself when, involuntarily, he went to take his hands from the safety of his pockets to bless himself. Suddenly, a voice shouted: "What you got there, son?"

Danny looked to see an oldish, heavy-set Police Sergeant framed in the doorway. "Meat delivery for the engineers' cottages," he said. The copper, with a bored look, waved him on.

As Danny tensed his right leg on the ground, ready to shove off, the dog sprang round in front of the bike, his mane of wiry grey fur bristling, his yellow eyes staring from the huge head, his long muzzle pulled back in a snarl, exposed his gleaming fangs. Danny froze. "Keep calm," he chided himself," keep calm, start off slowly." But as soon as he made a slight move, the dog dropped back on its haunches ears flattened against its head, preparing to spring at his throat. Danny could feel fear as the voice of the policeman called out: "It's the smell of the meat, son." Then the policeman's hand grabbed the chain collar round the dog's neck.

The word "meat" had the effect of a *kōan* on Danny: it gave him instant realisation of what he should do. Pulling the parcel of horse flesh from the basket, he held it out to the policeman.

"That's very nice of you, lad," said the Sergeant. As the dog sat watching him alertly, he unwrapped the piece of meat and slung it right up in the air. "Nothing he likes better than a bit of dead horse," smiled the cop, as the dog sprang up and snatched the meat in mid-air. "Except perhaps a bit of live one."

"I'll bring him a bit whenever I'm over this way again," said Danny, smiling guilelessly at the policeman, who nodded happily back.

Michael was nonchalantly leaning against an old banger when Danny pulled up. "Blinking dog," moaned Danny in greeting.

"You mustn't tease him," Michael laughed.

"All right," Danny said. His tone was weary and exasperated.

"Load me up."

"This is a dummy run," said Michael, the smile still upon his face.

"I've already straightened the policeman," said Danny, as he took the empty cardboard box from the basket on the front of the bike.

"You gave him the dead horse on the way *in*?" Michael said, looking at his brother warily.

"What difference does it make?" replied Danny. "Just load me up."

Michael took a deep breath and expelled it forcibly. "I don't like it," he said.

"You don't like it?" Danny exploded. "Who the fuck cares whether you like it or not? I'm the one who's taking all the risks!"

Michael gave a sigh. "All right. Give us a hand to pull out this box." As they laboured, their figures etched sharp shadows on the oil-stained earth, shifting and elongating with their own movements and the suns rotation.

"Well, no use hanging about here," said Danny with a show of bravado when the box of metal was in the basket on the bike.

"Be careful," said Michael with fierce sincerity as Danny set off on his solemn journey.

He pedalled slowly at first, then put on a nervous spurt, and in no time at all, he was within sight of the gate. With a stabbing, sharp clarity, he closed his eyes against the horror of the moment. The bulky police sergeant was standing just outside the main office, the door pulled out behind him, signalling for Danny to stop. Danny hesitated a moment, weighing dangers. "What if I just keep going straight out the gate?" he thought. But even as he thought it, he knew it would be no good.

"You got some hasty pudding down you today," growled the policeman when Danny pulled up at the doorway. "Thought you was going to ride on out without saying 'Goodbye'." He looked at Danny with a cynical, all-knowing eye.

Danny heard the sound of a train going past, and wished he was on it. The sergeant had his hand resting on top of the cardboard which concealed the ammunition box of precious metal underneath. Danny was rigid but he managed a grim smile. "I'm a bit late, Sarge," he said.

"Sure, sure," said the police sergeant, fawningly. "Only wanted to thank you for the bit of dead horse."

Danny nodded. "Fetch you a bigger lump next time."

As Danny pedalled off, Michael made his way up the side of the mountain to observe his brother's progress from the top.

The summit gleamed gold in a burst of brutal sunshine as he stood among those iron stones, some of which were slimed with oil enriched with a patina of bronze which dripped to tawny puddles. Below him light and shade distorted by distance and angle poured between the wire fencing, shackling the circumference of the wharf in a dazzle of tantalising patterns. In the alternating light the metal was changing colour.

Great fissures were beginning to appear among the alien crags on either side of the sharp metal but the mind, drawing on its stock of memories, began to imagine among that deformed metal, a castle in corroded elegance with its protrusions and crenellations, turrets and even a couple of gargoyles shaped out of the twisted sockets of an old Austin's battered headlights. Rust encrusted iron railings, tied in the middle with short bits of barbed wire were stacked around like sheaves of russet bracken. The sun, a ball in the last light of temporary departure behind a sudden cloud, hung there in the sky, lovely and luminous, a red glowing sphere. In the afternoon warmth the scene had a fairy tale enchantment. Nothing could intrude on the serenity of the structure even the hardness of its sharp edges were softened by a gentle light.

He was calm and happy and less concerned to be exact for details. Something of sleep and dreams was in that scrying light, and in a swirl of mist a young female's form emerging. Her hair was of a golden copper hue and hung about her dark iron features before cascading in a shower of glistening coils onto her dress of silver steel, which shimmered so enticingly upon her substantial metal breast. His eye dwelt with some avidity upon that beauteous orb, a girdle of mist encircled her waist, there was a gold tiara too which could have been a piece of salvaged bronze. The gilding blazed on the braided wire that secured her crown as she stood, her iron nipples hard, beside a pool of purest purple. Serene her mineral eyes a-glitter amid those oily patches, undulating with mauve ripples as the breeze grew stronger, making the dust skip and metal leaves of sulphurous green swirl around and twitch her dress' hem patterned with delicate slivers of aluminium, pried back in silvery strips which had became part of its embroideries. And he who had the power to control iron with fire and hammer now brought with him also, as he gazed, the thought that he might reach out and touch her little hand. Those wired limbs, such tender weavings which in the waning light had become a fistful of delicate bones, as he listened to the metal murmur he remained entranced.

It was natural that the sun should shine just then on the image, sunlight edged with tin struck making it humanly radiant. Dew had moistened her lips which might have smiled if their shape had allowed while metal leaves continued to swirl with an almost sensual rustle around her dress' hem and slither round the steel buckles on her shoes; coloured metals spun with golden threads disintegrating into fine dust fluttered down. Light had sunk its beams into the iron core. Birds stopped in flight on recognising a ceremony; delusion beckoned achingly. Until the youth slowly roused from his trance by a crow's harsh caw, looked up. All was metal; still he saw, acres of tin yellowing to rust. And even were it warmest flesh and blood, between dreamers what can be the relationship? They may dream about each other but then who is to stop the dreaming? He smiled. One would need a steel penis to enter her bronze womb.

The mountain laughed, it sounded like a laugh, a rackety laugh or perhaps it was the wind's caprice. He continued his climb along the southern rampart which was so precipitous that in all its breadth no easy path existed up its sheer face. The metal is old here among the jagged outcrops, begrimed by time. Perhaps such places should not be entered but he pushed on anyway: he did not wish to invest the mountain with mystery. Halfway up, he stepped across a crevice between two rotting water tanks. Trying to avoid a treacherously placed axle-rod, he missed his footing and grabbed at a cable wilted by petrol fumes. His body strained to regain balance; for just an instant he thought he might avoid a fall. He had a sensation of something sinking inside him, then flinched in anticipation as he fell forward, catching his face on a piece of jagged tin, buried like a dormant root. It split him open from his forehead to his chin.

As he lay, sprawled among the folds of dark metal, the blood running freely from his face, old Pop began calling for him, away down below the far side of the mountain. Stiffly, with exaggerated care, he tried to lift himself off the jumbled metal; but at the last moment he slipped and fell back down. Rigid with shock and pain, he considered lying there and giving into sleep, losing himself in the drowsy spasms that were threatening to engulf him. Yet even as he thought that, other thoughts, more powerful, flashed across his mind. Images of hidden treasure, the lorry and the crane it would buy. It filled him with intimidating excitement, acted as a goad. He grabbed hold of a length of railway line which lay wedged against the disembowelled innards of a lorry's engine. It was crimson with rust. The fierce heat of many summers had blistered the paint and the wind darting in with freezing stabs had scoured deep into the metal, so that the bolt heads, like buds, thrust themselves brazenly up out of the engine block like iron flowers on their thin steel stems.

He leant his weight on it and pulled himself up slowly; stood, crouched, panting with the effort, the blood streaming from his forehead into his eye. Inch by inch, yard by yard, avoiding the garlands and tendrils of barbed wire he eased himself down the reeling mountain, until finally he reached the ground.

"Where you bin?" shouted Pop, as he heard the sound of Michael's footsteps behind him, then gave an exclamation as he turned to see his face.

Old Pop the Farrier disguised his concern as he put his young protégé sitting on a box, holding a grubby hanky to his face; then rushed over to his house to phone for an ambulance. Michael would have preferred less ceremony for the occasion: the disordering of his plans seemed to undo him. But it was out of his hands now. Injury has its own rules. He sat, searching for some sort of sorrow he could not feel, as a hot, glittering, fiercely burning flame of metallic sunlight suddenly pierced the lean-to.

While waiting for the old iron lord to return, the apprentice watched the mountain at a place where harsh chunks of iron stood out framed within the leaden morning among that metal mass. Viewed from the safety of the lean-to all these objects were now more believable as lumber; meaningless fragments in an alien environment unconnected to a source or to each other. Here and there evidence of a more practical function still clung to some of their ruptured forms. A tangle of pig iron rapped mournfully on a battered piece of tin, notes of lamentation perhaps from a pagan goddess or maybe sounds of joy, of celebration for a blood sacrifice to a barbaric idol, plucked on a giant harp. The subtle vibrations reverberated ceaselessly throughout the mountain. While all across that black escarpment barbed wire threaded its reliable web since man and elements are forever trying to tear it bit by bit from its accustomed place. Never before had he realised the mountain was so complicated and immense; whole areas remained unclimbed. He stared out at it in awe while from its lofty heights the mountain glared back at him ferociously with eyeless sockets. Temporarily daunted he withdrew his gaze back into the protection of the lean-to.

Perched at an unorthodox angle held by some iron deity's invisible hand or merely by some quirk of gravity, oil dried rags fluttered from the protuberances and furled trumpets of lead and copper piping with which the mountain's flanks were capriciously furnished. The perverse decorations flapped against the lopsided metal with the sound of tiny drum taps, seemingly beating the lazy sun to quarters—to speed its slow climb up the mountainside. As the metal deflected the golden beams outward down into the salvage pit below (had he still been conscious, the injured youth might have felt he was witnessing some ancient rite), as the sun shone down upon the pit dispelling the dark glint into ceremonial rays of celestial light, creating a vivid scene of hostile splendour. The drum major was a stern south easterly wind and those gaudy pennants rose and fell and kept their time by its comical caprices. An idyll might have prevailed had not the wind suddenly dropped, silencing the drums. Left without the pulse of the drum the sun broke off its upward march or it could have been because a bank of cloud had just then obscured the sky. On every surface, whether of earth or iron, a large shadow had begun to spread a cold shroud, while flies had begun swarming about the lean-to, greedy for the trickling crimson before it clotted on the still warm flesh.

Vicky opened the door to her Grandfather. "Boy who helps me has had an accident," was Pop's reply to Vicky's puzzled frown; and was reminded of his own grim prediction as he lifted up the phone.

Once out on the road, the weight was not a problem, since the route taken was flat all the way. The bicycle rolled along under its own momentum; the basket was built to carry a dead steer. After weighing the box of metal in at the scrap yard, Danny pocketed the money, turned his bike towards Hampstead and pedalled like hell for that Borough, hoping to make his last delivery before it became too late. Finally, with breathless, anxious tension, he reached his destination. He leaned the bike against the wall that surrounded the big house, and rang the bell beside the front gate.

He liked the girl at this house, and sometimes when the gate was open he would go right in without ringing. It was an excuse to walk through the lovely orchard, and in summer to smell the apples on the craggy, leafy trees, and if no one was watching, to pick a few windfalls off the ground on his way out. He would have been surprised to know that this was the same house where Michael had been arrested for doing the very same thing a few years back. Apples and girls are a terrible temptation.

He was over an hour late, or at least that was the amount of time he had been missing from his proper place of work. He waited, with the leg of lamb in his hand, hoping against hope that the girl —who was about his own age, or maybe a bit older—would open the door today. After a few moments, the door was pulled back. The girl stood before him, tall, sweet and wonderfully slender. But he did not notice these things about her today; instead he began mumbling as if nothing had happened, to try to convey the impression that all honest people are decently and a little distractedly employed; as if perhaps nothing in the world existed for him now except getting on with his work, his hurry so great that he couldn't even meet her eyes. She took the joint from him, surprise showing plainly on her face, because he half threw it into her hands in his haste to be gone. But she regained her poise quickly enough when he tried to dart off. "Oh don't go yet," she said, stepping out through the gateway behind him, "my Dad wants to see you." Her eyes were still holding him in a steady gaze.

"Who? Me?" he said, in a tone of utmost surprise, putting as great a distance between himself and the subject as possible.

"Yes," she said gently. She felt slightly disappointed. She had made furtive studies of this nice-looking boy and until today had not found him wanting. But now he seemed to bear out the opinions of her father and the girls at her school who firmly believed that working class butcher's boys just couldn't be trusted.

"What for? I mean to say, I got work to do, I got to be getting back to the shop," he gushed, looking now at her face. But she stood back adroitly, blocking the gateway, preventing any undesirable detours. Uneasily, he took hold of the handlebars of the bike, holding it as a sort of shield, and walked into the garden.

Formerly tall and straight, the man that confronted Danny sat in a wheelchair, a mere shadow of his former self, after a car accident. "Where the hell have you been?" he yelled. "I've been waiting all afternoon for you to get here with our blessed dinner."

Danny did not reply; what with all the business of conning his way past the cop and the dog on his way into the wharf, then going out past him again with the stolen metal, and dealing with the half-gypsy fellas at the scrap yard, and the exhausting run of cycling he'd done since this morning, he felt done in. The man continued venting his spleen on the boy before him, and Danny stood there not really hearing; his eyes, though they seemed fixed on the man, had taken on an expression of lost attentiveness. The man suddenly noticed this, and trembling with temper, asked Danny where he had been.

By withdrawing into his self the boy might have been trying to resist piling up the purgatories but his adolescent body stood as if he almost didn't care.

"I am trying very hard to understand what's going on here, lad," said the man, when he'd got no answer to his question. "But my understanding," he jeeringly added, "is not yet sufficient."

"Perhaps he's been ill," said the girl, trying to deflect her father's hostility from Danny. His failure to offer a suitable apology had begun to worry her.

The sound of her voice rather than recurrent questioning jolted Danny from his lethargy. With a sudden, sharp pang of fear, he realised he must not lose his job. He must speak: try to reason with the man; apologise, even. But his throat kept constricting, he had to clear it several times before he could get the words out.

"What's that?" demanded the man, eyeing Danny intently.

"Sorry. I had a puncture coming up West Hill, sir."

The man listened with a suffering expression—every word seemed to make his eyes bulge that much further.

Danny was surprised at his reaction, since this seemed as good as any excuse to offer. Seized by desperation now, he continued: "Had to stop at the White Stone Pond to fix it, sir…" his voice trailing off when the man's head started to shake. The girl cried out in alarm, as Danny suddenly sprang forward to grasp her father's head with one hand, at the same time grabbing a letter-opener off the writing desk with the other, which he forced into the man's mouth, pressing it down on top of his tongue to stop him swallowing it as he went into a massive seizure. (He was inspired to do this by an article he'd read the previous week in a First Aid magazine.)

The girl stood anxiously beside him after the convulsions had subsided, Danny withdrew the letter-opener from the man's mouth. Then, getting his hands under the man's armpits, Danny pulled him out of the chair and laid him down gently, flat on the floor, while the girl's brown eyes looked on with alarm. "He'll be more comfortable like that," said Danny.

"Yes," said the girl, glad to let the boy handle it. She felt weak and frightened by the suddenness with which her father had been rendered incapable. The noise of a car pulling up outside snapped her out of her daze. "That'll be mother," she cried, rushing over and opening the door, to see her mother laughing at something the taxi-driver was saying as he handed her her change.

As Danny knelt down to push an extra pillow under the patient's head, the man opened his eyes and looked glassily up at him. He lay staring in this way until the two women, fear etched into their faces, came rushing in. The wife immediately knelt down by her husband; then, seeing that focus was coming back into his eyes, began wiping the spittle from his mouth with her handkerchief in an agony of relief.

Sensing that the worst was over, Danny stood up and put his hand into his trouser pocket to make sure the money was still there. Some time later, when the full focus had returned to the man's eyes, Danny, helped by the girl's mother, lifted the man up off the floor and back into his chair; and by the time he had settled himself into it properly again, and his consciousness had returned to normal, the whole question of Danny's misdemeanour seemed to have slipped from his mind.

"Can I offer you something to drink?" asked the women, turning towards a glass-fronted wood cabinet full of bottles.

"No, thanks," said Danny, "I better be off." And, heedless of the woman's entreaties to indulge in a cup of tea at least, he made for the door.

"Please," said the woman. Danny turned to look at her. "Let me phone Mr Liekmann, I want to let him know of your sterling work here." She picked up the phone and began dialling. "We've all had a bit of a shock this afternoon."

"Yes, come on, sit down here," said the girl, suddenly brightening and patting the side of the settee.

Danny smiled at the way she was bossing him.

As Danny was settling himself on the settee, the man began to make little gulping noises, as if he was having trouble swallowing air. The girl turned round hurriedly and went to him. Her mother turned sharply at the sound of her daughter's movement. Her husband had got a touch of the dribbles. "Pour father a drink, Isabella." The girl gave a final mop to his chin and turned to the cabinet to fix him one. Suddenly, the mother's attention was taken up with the phone again.

"Hello, Mr Liekmann, it's Mrs Chalfont… Yes, thank you, we've got our order… No, I'm afraid we've had some trouble here… Yes, my husband has had an epileptic fit… No, everything is fine now, it's just that I want to let you know that your delivery boy… Yes, of course—he's right here with us now." Then she said something in a dazed way into the mouthpiece about forgetting introductions, and turning to Danny, "I'm awfully sorry…" she whispered sheepishly.

"My name's Danny—Danny Docherty," he told her.

She spoke into the mouthpiece again. "Danny has been an absolute life-saver," and with almost celestial praise she went on to extol the virtues of Danny. By the time she put the phone down,

Danny was squirming with embarrassment; yet at the same time, when he saw the looks of admiration that the girl kept giving him, he couldn't help feeling flattered and very pleased with himself. So much so, in fact, that he wouldn't have minded if Granddad over in the chair there (slurping his Scotch and from time to time eyeing him vindictively) was to start frothing at the mouth and throwing another wobbler.

"Now, I'm going to get you a nice cup of tea, and there's some cherry gateau to go with it in the fridge," said Mrs Chalfont when she had finished on the phone.

"No, it's okay," said Danny, making to get up off the settee. I've got to get going now."

"Oh! Danny, you can't do that to us!"

He hesitated, awkward, undecided what to do, since her tone seemed to imply 'you must let us worship you'. Then Isabella smiled encouragingly, and he sat back down, like an obedient servant.

Three cups of tea, two glasses of lemonade, and one rich chunk of cherry gateau later, Danny said goodbye to her parents, and, escorted by their daughter, walked out of the house, across the garden towards the gate. Strolling along the grass, under the arched branches of the apple trees both had become shy to the point of dumbness. The girl was the first to speak.

"Are you okay?" she asked quietly.

"Yes." They had stopped under one of the trees.

"I'm sorry. He gets irritable like that whenever his illness becomes too much for him."

"I'm not bothered about it," said Danny.

"You were marvellous," she said, "I don't know what I would have done if you hadn't been there."

He did not quite know how to handle this easy and friendly attention, along with the closeness of the girl, coupled with his relief at not losing his job. He suddenly felt very light-headed.

She put a hand on his arm involuntarily. "Are you all right?"

She wanted to say something else, but before she could, Danny replied affectionately, "Yes, Isabella Chalfont." She looked at him with mild surprise, and he smiled at her teasingly, continuing in a provocative, half-scolding, half-indulgent way, "What a mouthful —found it hard to get my tongue round that."

She did not answer, so he shrugged to satisfy his youthful limbs as the sensation of uneasy intimacy he had first experienced began to evaporate. Though neither of them looked each other full in the face there was still a spell of closeness in the heavy air. The motionless trees exuded a pungent smell, in the stillness before sunset the air became impregnated with their sap.

Suddenly, as the sun's last rays lasered through the branches of the tree above them, he found her lips pressed down on his own in a long, smouldering kiss. It seemed like an eternity that they were locked together. No fruit in that orchard was as sweetly flavoured.

"Didn't have much trouble getting your tongue round that!" she whispered mischievously as he hugged her to him.

MICHAEL'S ACCIDENT

They stitched Michael's face up in the hospital and took x-rays of his head but when the nurse returned with the results which were not good the patient had gone.

He had made his own way home. As he sat on the settee in the front room, Mary Jane could only stare in fascinated horror at her son's almost Biblical mutilation. "Oh Mother of God," she whispered, "Mother of God."

"If he'd kept to his books like I was always trying to tell him," mumbled his father, "he would have been in a nice quiet office instead of…"

"Shush," said Mary Jane, quelling Seán's righteous cruelty with a reproachful glance. The boy had never been so closely stared at. The angle at which he held his head showed he had not yet become reconciled to such attention, his fingers, rubbing at the stitches which held together the rejected tatters of his cheek, offered some distraction.

"Does it hurt much?" asked Mary Jane and before Michael had time to answer, Danny (who was sharing their solemn study of the injury) gave him a sly, confidential wink. Michael responded with a strained smile.

"I better go and have a lie down," he said, with a sigh that was a good deal sadder than he felt. And his mother, with a look of benediction, nodded, full of doting sorrow for the perceived torments of her son. True, he had a throbbing going on inside his head, probably severe concussion. But his torments did not so much derive from these at the moment, but rather from the prospect of an imminent meeting in the bedroom with his brother.

Every bone in Michael's body ached, and the throbbing in his head was more pronounced as he climbed the stairs to his room.

On reaching the landing he stood before the open door, breathing heavily to catch his breath before entering.

Certain that the scar would be trifling after the hospital had done its work, he stood before the small mirror on the bedroom wall. A kind of pallor came over Michael's face as he gazed at his reflection. He was rigid as stone.

"Don't worry" said Danny roughly to stifle embarrassment. "Pretty women will not bother you any more," for the mark took precedence over all other reflected details.

Michael turned away from the mirror and threw his jacket on the bed, laughing at the same time, as if to say that it would be all the same to him. But from now on his biggest fear would be—to be caught out by his reflection in a mirror.

Under a picture of Christ, who stared down, stabbed and nailed, Danny felt greatly relieved as he handed Michael the wad of money he had received that same afternoon from the gyppos for the metal. Danny was expecting perhaps a half-share of the spoils for his own part in the scheme, but would not have objected to a quarter, and was therefore surprised when Michael handed him the full amount of money back. "I want you to keep it. Put it in the bank," said Michael. "And when we've got the rest of the metal out and sold, we'll buy a lorry."

Danny was so shocked by this second surprise that for a moment he was speechless; and into the ensuing silence, Michael poured his ambitious dream. They would buy a second-hand lorry and Danny would offer himself and the vehicle to the Borough Council, who were looking for contractors to take on the work of digging up old lamp-posts in the streets. Since they were made of cast iron they had a high scrap value. Michael scratched at the stitches in his face. His skin seemed to have turned pale. "After a year, we'll trade in the old lorry for a new tip-up-truck, on the never-never!"

Danny was about to protest that he didn't want anything to do with the plan, but Michael (assuming his objections were only about points of detail) replied: "Remember this. While we are buying the new tipper, we will be living on its profits." Michael rested his head against the bed board. "No reason for anyone to worry about a set-up like that, is there?" he asked quietly.

Danny had a dozen reasons at his fingertips why he was worried about a set-up like that, each one more pressing than the next, but he was not given a chance to produce them because at that moment their mother came into the room to see if Michael was alright and he said he was. Then, after reminding them both with stern affection to be good boys and not to forget their prayers, she left.

Danny couldn't find the right words at first; a whiff of antiseptic made his nose smart. He beamed at his brother with the air of one about to impart a revelation.

"Imagine it, Michael. I've just this afternoon been kissed by a girl called Isabella Chalfont. And I probably saved her father's life, too!" He got a picture of himself on errands of mercy during a national catastrophe. Michael did something with his face that was a cross between a grimace and a smile. "So you can see how I don't want to mess it up with this bird!" He spoke flippantly; he didn't want to appear disloyal.

Danny's trouble was that he had survived what he regarded as an epic ordeal with flying colours. That a sort of sod's law— divine justice or whatever—had prevailed at the last moment to provide him with his dream girl was not something that Michael could have intended, nor indeed take any credit for, and he was not going to take another risk with that fat copper and his dog with those white unyielding fangs. Even soldiers at the front got compassionate leave, he thought.

Michael waited a few moments out of respect. Then, in a sad voice, he informed him: "Dad would be very unhappy if he heard you intended to spend all your hard-earned money on some cockney tart."

Danny blushed. He felt uncomfortable. "It's got nothing to do with money, and Isabella's no cockney—she's well-educated, well-spoken, and she lives in Hampstead."

Michael's head drooped. It was a weary but graceful gesture. "Danny," he sighed, "they're just cockneys with pantomime voices. Officer cockneys." He spoke like a man shouldering a dangerous burden that no-one else was prepared to take on. "And it would finish Dad off completely if he ever got to hear how you was running around saving their lives. What they have achieved in life they achieved from an unfair start. Privelege rather than merit is what put them where they are; that is why you will always be the butcher's boy and she the lady."

"No, it's not like that", yelled Danny staring angrily at his brother, "not like that at all". But Michael could see how he was duped.

"Danny; we don't get a proper education like them and so they will look down on us for the rest of our lives because of it".

Danny prefered not to listen, so Michael, realising the difficulty of the situation relented; adding gently,

"I could be wrong of course."

His face grew abruptly serious.

And Danny, who had never been sure that evil existed, now began to wonder whether he was involved in it.

"So, you're still alive!" said old Pop leaning against the edge of the guillotine, smiling as Michael approached.

"Yeah," replied Michael curtly, coming to a stand. He gazed up at the metal mountain, his eyes settling on the summit where its jagged protrusions, clawing at the sky, filled him with some feeling he couldn't quite articulate. He picked up a long crowbar.

The old man averted his eyes from his apprentice's face. He would carry that scar for the rest of his days. Unconsciously, he glanced at his own hand. He began rolling a smoke. He'd been about the same age as Michael when it happened. He'd been more approachable though. He nodded at the memory. He liked this lad. He liked this lad very much, even though he was very quiet sometimes and his eyes seemed full of anger. A fickle wind was blowing around the mountain which, in the course of its meanderings, was burnishing the metal so that it bloomed with a golden coppery hue. While the tin twisting and glinting under a fiery yellow sun began to rattle and shake, the old Farrier halted in his musings. For a moment he was temporarily possessed by a sensation of impermanence. The wind whined among the metal as he reached for his Thermos flask. He filled the cup. "Mind, it's hot," he warned as he handed it to Michael. He took an empty jam jar and rinsed it out under the stand pipe; satisfied that it was fairly clean, he poured tea into it and sat down opposite Michael on one of the old car-seats under the lean-to, where oily rags littered the floor like rusty moss.

For a while he watched the sunlight flashing off some broken bits of glass and then he said: "Didn't expect you to come in today." Michael looked at him. "So take it easy for a while, eh? Could keep five forges blazing with the lumps you throw down." And Michael, who felt that he might have left himself a bit too open at certain times during their relationship began to realise that he had not yet achieved permanence.

When he did not reply, the old man continued. "I'm thinking of selling this piece of the wharf back to the rail company."

Michael experienced a sudden, frightening stab in his chest.

He felt the two selves he knew fighting for possession of him. It seemed doubtful now whether he would ever succeed in communicating through either. The mountain was erupting in bursts of kaleidoscopic images before his eyes, while he sat scratching at the hardened scales of iron that coated his skin.

"When?" he whispered. It had a metallic ring.

"Oh, I haven't decided yet," said old Pop in a light, off-hand tone as he noticed the anxious look on his apprentice's face. It went very quiet. The old man's words seemed to change the texture of the air. The iron lord did not speak again but turned his face away. Then they both sat gazing into some separate place of their own. Seeing his future dissolving out of reach, with those he had depended on, Michael found himself wanting to question Pop about all this, to wonder why he should do such an awful thing, but the words were impossible to frame. And he sat there his shoulders bent under a great burden of bewilderment.

Just then a clap of thunder smote the sky, startling the two men beneath the lean-to. The wind began to rake the sides of the mountain with increasing fury, the iron strained and groaned under the savage lashes of the flapping tin. A long thin tongue of lightning flashed, it flickered brightly on the metal and seemed to prance along the top. Then the heavens opened and rain poured down upon the mountain, as it sluiced down the funnel of its iron throat it trembled slightly and heaved its Gothic sides. But the old Farrier who was peering out from under the lean-to up at the suddenly clearing sky did not notice the mountain move because he was gazing directly into the sun.

By the time they had both finished their tea, the rain had stopped and the sun's first tepid rays had become strong enough to light up the mountain's metallic colours like a mosaic on a cathedral dome. Michael left down his cup and picking up the crowbar hefted it like a sword onto his shoulder. His head ached. This was a blow to his plans, and he was angry that it had ever happened. The wind began to gust in forceful blasts, the mountain swayed, flaunted its metal throat and growled. Disdainful of the threat, he smiled with vicious scorn, crossed himself, and, like Pizarro, launched himself at the metal Andes tilting his crowbar at the sun... for he had set his foot on the path made smooth by that conquistador.

Suddenly he seemed frightened by the mountaintop's unfamiliar summit, where on a grander terrifying plane it might have been a vast altar, its scope and size in keeping with a ceremony.

He looked about this sea of iron, along the pathway of the sun shading his eyes with one hand against the sun, which would itself have been a ball of iron, if it had not shone with such celestial brilliance. He turned away. It had become oppressive. His eyes, which once had offered frankness, now held secrets in their shifting depths. He sometimes felt the need to bruise things as if to punish someone or himself, he could not accept the smallest thing on trust. Yet he could be warm and humorous with people, and with women he allowed friendly and flirtatious relationships which are simpler to handle than attachments that demand love. He edged his way along from car to burnt-out car, he had learnt something of the transitoriness of things. He looked at that metal which had once been things, tortured into abominable shapes, full of rust and ugliness from which all the beauty and goodness had been squeezed. When there is nothing left to respect he would have liked to discover something here, some fabulous treasure, some secret perhaps.

He felt himself on a pinnacle he had never reached before and he gazed with wonder upon the vast valley of the wharf below, dizzied by the immensity of the view. He gazed about, as though to acquaint himself anew with this metal world: a world where he might some day have great success. He had grown, his limbs were long from striding through and tossing iron. There was no doubt in his mind now that the summit was very near.

He peered down at the houses and gardens below with their clothes lines blowing in the wind. Flying the engineers' newly laundered boiler suits and their women's voluminous blouses and private garments, which sagged rather, from the weightiness of married life. A small black brassière, pegged haphazardly, was flying bravely from Pop's line which looked quite assured though all alone. And he began to wonder about the girl who wore it. Was she as flighty as the thing upon the line? From his vantage point he could afford to be contemptuous. He could put his hand on iron, it was hard and substantive and he went forward quickly now to touch something that he knew. But metal does not feel. It submitted however, as he began to lever an old engine block towards the mountain's edge: long and narrow, taken from an Army lorry, it weighed around two hundred pounds. When finally Michael had manoeuvred it to the edge, he glanced briefly up at the sun, then down at the ground; his eyes focusing with a hawk's knack of instant orientation. Satisfied with the accuracy of the tilt, he gave one last sweeping glance around the wharf. Then for the first time he began to doubt the quality of his strength, his own boldness made him shiver, he stepped forward still trembling.

For a moment he stood, outlined against the very rim of the world. The sky moved down and the earth shrank. As the sun descended, the mountain crouched, arching its back against the horizon as he shoved the metal block over its side.

For a few seconds, there was no sound, as the block plunged through the empty air. Then, the sudden bomb-like blast as the metal block hit the roof of the lean-to, causing every bird on the wharf to take to the air in panicked flight. Then the sound, which had been born out of silence, and during its life span had been surrounded by silence, died back into silence. The consequences of the action were not immediately seen for the dust raised by the block's impact darkened the air. It was a while before it settled, and what now became visible aroused both terror and compassion in the Farrier's apprentice. The sky was stippled in crimson there was blood on the sun.

On the day of the incident, Vicky was upstairs in the bedroom of her grandparent's house, assisting her terminally ill grandmother into her oxygen mask in readiness for her nap, when she heard the noise of the metal's crash and felt its juddering reverberations run through the house. While her hard of hearing patient began to rouse herself from any attempt at sleep into a frenzy of emotion, a surprise in one so frail and old, she attempted to jerk the oxygen mask from her face. Vicky the nurse, who was also a blood relation, tried to subdue her rebellious patient, at first with soothing sounds and then with physical strength, enough, that is, to get her Gran to accept and retain the life enhancing halter. But all to no avail.

'She's either a compulsive thrill addict or else a raving nut case or maybe it's just another way of trying to commit suicide,' the distraught young girl thought, unable to fathom and locate the cause of her grandmother's distress in her present state of anxiety. Until the patient got her head as best she could out of the entangling contraption, pointing not as Vicky had first imagined vaguely in the direction of the window where a red dust of metal was blowing across the sky, but instead at the oxygen mask, croaking for her remiss nurse to swab the mouthpiece. Which, with recovered calm, the probationary began at once to do, scraping clear a yellow slurp of custard pulp and an off-white splatter of mash onto the marble-top washstand. After she had finished sponging away all evidence of hygienic misdemeanour Vicky rinsed the offending mask under the tap and returned to the bed where Gran was waiting, laying in a foetal position with a martyred look on her grey wrinkled face. If it was intended to cause a pang of guilt for some tardiness in the performance of a ritual, loud incessant banging down below spoilt its effect as the overburdened nurse, after harnessing her now mollified charge into her spotless respiratory aid, took a deep breath and rushed downstairs to answer the knock.

A few moments later, she opened the front door to a distressed Michael who might have spoken his whole message in French; all she heard was two words: hurtling around inside her head. 'Pop's Dead'. Vicky began to cry. Tears had already streaked the grime on the youth's face, mostly on the side that was scrunched like a piece of battered tin.

As Vicky continued to sob, quiet and subdued, Michael lifted up the phone and dialled. "Can you send an ambulance to the Coal Wharf? The Farrier has met with an accident – yes, it may be serious," said Michael into the phone. "He's dead."

Vicky pondered over this statement with dull astonishment. Nothing could be more serious than death, she thought. She felt herself confronted with impossible visions of responsibility, and felt suddenly frightened; but when Michael, after replacing the receiver, turned to her to offer his support, a great burden was suddenly lifted from her young shoulders.

The old woman, when informed by Vicky of her husband's death, had replied somewhat stoically, "There have been more violent deaths on this wharf than I care to remember. Not a month has passed without a broken limb, a severed arm, a scalding burn." Wearily, she fumbled with the mask attached to the oxygen cylinder that stood beside her bed, then continued to speak (or rather, to mumble) about the dangers of the metal mountain. Too dazed to assess the situation rationally, she supposed she should sell it. It was not very clear, and Vicky was not that interested. She guessed vaguely that it might be of some concern to Michael, but at that moment she was too preoccupied ministering to her gran to give it much thought. When Vicky leant over to assist in placing the mask on her grandmother's mouth, she lay back down, breathing laboriously, her eyes beseeching tenderness at the end of this day of death. Normally she would have worried herself into sleep with the next day's little frets... but tonight there was only a past you couldn't change and a future you couldn't see into.

Some men came, men in sharp suits. They stood in a little group smoking and talking for a while. Then they poked about a bit at the mountain's base before going away again. Despite the immense event that had taken place at its base, the mountain did not seem disturbed certainly not by death, for that was why it had been created, to wreak havoc and bring death, much death dropping from the skies. That had been its sole calling, sanctioned by the people of course, with the blessing of their god.

The old Farrier had only his grand-daughter and Michael to mourn him at his graveside, since all his other relations were dead. Vicky, now being the only living relative, had promised her sick Grandmother that she would stay on at the house on the wharf to look after her, despite the fact that while she was at the graveyard one of the engineers' wives had kindly volunteered to keep that vigil for her. It was a wet and windy afternoon, and after the short service was over and old Pop's body had been committed to the grave, Michael accompanied Vicky back to her house, where Mrs Turner, the engineer's wife, was busy making tea for the old lady.

After Vicky took over from her, Mrs Turner left to go back to her own house, to prepare tea for her own family.

Michael sat at the kitchen table looking through the window at the mountain, while Vicky gathered up tea things and placed them on a tray. Peered at through the distorting rain, some barbaric necromancy made the metal mass appear to undulate in convulsive, heaving spasms, snorting through its metal nostrils like some prehistoric beast. The sound of the raindrops trembling against it disturbed the evening stillness, as they trickled down its iron jaw.

Vicky put the last of the tea things on the tray and began arranging them neatly with perhaps more care than the task demanded, then finally, with Michael trailing behind, climbed the stairs to her Grandmother's bedroom. The old thing looked thin and shapeless, one of the living dead in her corroded mask, until the nurse touched a lever on the iron bottle, skilfully ratcheting the oxygen up an amp or two, then the bones began to put on flesh and Gran flicked into life.

The old woman and Michael had not met since Pop's death, and a thrill of horror shot through her when she saw him. "Oh dear," she said, her eyes pinned to the scar on Michael's face, as if it had been stitched together with steel thread. "it's a perfect monster of a mountain!" Then she asked him about her husband's death. She was more astute than he had imagined: she questioned him not harshly, but with bewilderment, so it was difficult to see her angle. But since Michael could not console her with any consoling details, she wanted to let the agony of it all release itself in a scream; instead, she sighed and said, "Certain things were best not dwelt upon." Michael was not quite sure how she meant it. He fixed his eyes on the oxygen cylinders that stood by her bed. It was, thankfully, distracting. Were they the same as the ones used for cutting the metal? He mused. The metal gleamed, the shadows hardened, the night had become raw and dark. Vicky put the light on. As she drew the curtains, Michael heard the loud moan of the wind outside as it grated on the evening. He stood staring at the cylinders, the sudden light stressed their shape. While the nurse busied herself fixing the blankets and fussing around the bed, her Grandmother gazed at Michael. None of them seemed to notice the absence of conversation. They seemed firmly tied to their own, disturbing thoughts.

"She's a good girl," said the old woman, suddenly breaking the silence, as Vicky trying to arrange the coverings into more artistic folds patted flat the bumpy areas of blanket on the bed. "I'm going to leave you the house," she continued.

"Oh Gran," said Vicky, laughing uncomfortably for something she sensed without entirely understanding, "you're going to be around for a long time yet, I'll see to that." Gran ignored it.

"For a sick woman who only wanted to end her days in peace it's just too much. The Railway can pay for my funeral. I shall sell that nasty heap of metal back to them, it's so big that place has the dimensions of hell." She was in a sadistic mood, prompted by her husband's sudden death and the realisation of her own short future. Michael felt his chest constrict painfully; the muscles of his jaw were taut, making the scar stand out, giving him a fiercely alert look. It came as a shock to him to realise he was holding one end of the blanket in his hand, yet he had no recollection of picking it up off the bed. Vicky and her Grandmother were staring at him, or rather they were watching his hand, which was squeezing the cloth. He placed it carefully back on the bed, pretending to be preoccupied with smoothing the coverlets, as Vicky had been doing earlier. A little care was needed now. He'd have to be wary with this artful old creature. His eye focused with weary familiarity on the bottle's gauge as Vicky began going through the ritual of harnessing the woman into the oxygen mask. He smiled gently at them both, torn between self-interest and the dreadful alternative. The old woman longed for the sanctity of sleep because the afternoon had made her physically vulnerable. There was no more now to say, the figure with the damaged features at the foot of the bed was irrelevant anyway to the trussed up figure on the bed as it tussled with the restrictive sheets. Downcast eyes however did not conceal a certain gravity of expression; beset as she was, she could not yet accept all this. She had discovered other problems. Though her top half had received from her lower parts a vague promise of motion, she was loath in the presence of the stranger to suffer the indignity of asking for the chamber pot. But the intuitive nurse leaned over to slide the pan under her with practised ease and shook the folds, restoring the coverings to their original shape, releasing her patient with an almost sensual rustle of rippling linen which seemed to lash their destinies together.

When eventually the old woman had dropped off, Vicky took Michael downstairs to the kitchen, where she made up a fry of bacon and eggs with plenty of good thick slices of bread to mop up the fat. After finishing their meal, Vicky washed the dishes, brewed more tea, and they went into the living room to drink it. For a while the tea, the girl and the warm room were thankfully distracting to Michael, but in the end it was not enough. The sensation of feeling threatened would not leave him. The old woman sleeping upstairs held his world in her hands. He would have to get back up there somehow. He looked at Vicky sitting beside him on the sofa wondering what to say. "Would you like to hear some of my records?" she asked with sudden gaiety.

"Not half!" said Michael, with contagious enthusiasm. This was one way of staying in the house that could offer a possibility of achievement.

"We'll have to keep the door closed and the volume down, but I'm sure Granddad wouldn't have wanted us to sit here all morbid."

Michael smiled, nodding his agreement vigorously. Music and precaution brought them together.

After Elvis had warned them not to step on his *Blue Suede Shoes*, and Lonnie Donegan's *Sweet Sixteen* had told them about the dangers of putting on the style, Sonny James brought them closer together on the settee with *Young Love*. Vicky gazed with thrilled revulsion at Michael's face. He looked like one of those Crusaders whose masculinity seemed so brutal, she thought, pictured in the history books she had read at school. And yet he'd been so kindly after Grandpa's death, when she'd been close to despair. Bill Haley and the Comets were playing *Rock Around the Clock*. Unexpectedly, she grabbed him, her eyes sparkling mischievously, "Let's do it!" she whispered to her templar as she held him by his undefended wrists.

"What?" he said, slowly climbing to his feet. He rose so stiffly he might have been enclosed in mail. He was trying hard to appear sophisticated, but his voice revealed the struggle he was having with his inhibitions.

After expending a considerable amount of energy on trying to jive noiselessly for fear of disturbing her Grandmother, Vicky replaced Bill Haley with a slow, gentle ballad. They swayed more or less on the spot to it, Michael holding Vicky round the waist and she cuddled up with her head on his shoulder. The situation was ripe.

Just as his pulse began to quicken, the girl pulled away from him. He looked at her with some surprise. "I'd better check to see if Gran's all right," the nurse informed him, suddenly remembering her vocation.

Though instincts of the flesh had been kindled in his growing bones, the youth curbed his desire, reflecting soberly that he had made his plans too carefully to abandon them now. He listened in spite of himself to the sounds that came from upstairs. After a while, when Vicky did not come back, he opened the door and went down the hallway to the lavatory out in the garden, where rain was falling in torrents from a black sky. While all around the mountain a lamenting wind was roving. When he returned, Vicky was standing in the room with a blanket and sheets. "You can't go home in that," she said, shaking out a sheet and laying it on the settee. "Anyway, no-one can walk through the wharf now, because the dogs are patrolling loose."

He lay fully clothed on the settee listening to the sound of the wind and rain outside the window of the front room. He heard a cat mewling and then it (or another) gave an unmerciful screech.

Distressed with impatience while he waited—giving Vicky time to settle in sleep—he fell off himself, until the deep, guttural barks of the two German Shepherds woke him with a start. Instantly he rose and, opening the door noiselessly, stepped into the hall.

It was all silent and cold. The moon was touching with brief beam the banisters on the stairs. He stood for a moment staring into some dark secret place of his own, then he nodded and mounted the stairs. He climbed with the stealth of a cat; halfway up he stopped to listen: silence. He moved on, eyes slitted, trying to penetrate the darkness. He reached the landing. The door immediately to his left at the top of the stairs where Vicky slept was open, as was the one opposite where the old woman lay. The possibility of being caught and the enormity of what he was about to do sent a shiver through him, even though he knew he was not acting out of malice, but because there was no other way. He turned towards the open door of the old woman's bedroom to take the final fatal step.

"I'm in here!" The voice startled him.

The whispered words sounded thunderous they made the hairs on the nape of his neck stand up; his nerves were stretched almost to breaking. He spun round. Vicky was standing in her bedroom doorway, wearing nothing but her pyjama top, her eyes glittering cunningly, thinking of how he had earlier feigned such indifference to her amorous advances. She smiled knowingly at what she perceived as deceit.

He could feel her passion, her warm breath on his face; she was kissing his lips and his throat. He had to struggle with himself, willing his actions to switch suddenly into this new role. Abruptly she pulled away from him, threw off her pyjama top and ran, breasts bouncing saucily, over to her rumpled bed. He shed his clothes and went to join her.

As raindrops pattered against the window pane, he pulled her down on her back. She wriggled provocatively, he kissed her lips, he ran his hand gently down her young body, she murmured happily as he eased himself into her, trembling.

Michael lay still in the warmth of the bed. It seemed as if the wind had swept away all the air in the room, so that all the sounds, however feeble, were magnified. In the silence, even the girl's faint breaths became a rasping bark. As he edged his body to a sitting position against the headboard, Michael could see the northern tip of the mountain through the bedroom window. Under the shine of the moon chunks of mauve metal, some like huge boulders, stood out against the skyline, giving the illusion of Nature's own pattern. He looked down at Vicky who lay still sleeping beside him, her thick, dark hair spread over the pillow, shone where shreds of light torn in courtship gave it a blue, metallic tint. He rubbed his troubled eyes. He resisted the urge to lay back down again. It would be easy to allow himself to give in to sleep. He checked once more to make sure that Vicky was still sleeping, then crept out of bed, pulled on his trousers, and slipped out onto the landing.

It would be easier now, and practically undetectable, and almost painless for Gran. Like old Pop, she had only herself to blame. She'd bought herself an early funeral by voicing her intention. No one was going to take this mountain away from him. He didn't want to end up like his father, beaten before he started, scared, always moaning about them Cockney bastards having all the best bits, watching over his shoulder for anyone in authority (whom he quaintly called "the forces of the Crown"), sitting, black and brooding, in the armchair, looking for a roll-up, spitting his frustration at the grate. Michael nearly laughed. It was half-humorous, half-tragic. He crossed over to the old woman's bedroom, entered, and—silent as a shadow— he stood waiting until his eyes adjusted to the darkness and he could see the outlines of the furniture. A few moments more and he could see the figure on the bed.

Outside, the wind blew and the metal whined with cold. And still he stood, hesitant in the unending twilight, hearing the howling of the German Shepherds as they hungered under the northern sky, while the night protested frequently at the jubilance of lurching tin. He looked down at the pathetic figure sprawled under the rumpled bedclothes, the lower half of her small, bony face covered by the mask which rose and fell with each laboured breath. He reached over, fingers curling round the lever on the oxygen bottle by the bed. As he started to alter the flow, the old woman gave a little whimper and opened her eyes. He instantly froze. She was looking up at the ceiling. The impulse to flee was almost overpowering. He couldn't be sure she wouldn't see him: she only had to turn one eye. He struggled painfully to breathe noiselessly. Then, as suddenly as she had opened them, the old woman closed her eyes again, and (incredibly) began to snore. Swiftly, with one deft movement, he turned the lever, cutting her artificial lifeline completely.

"What are you doing?" The voice gasped.

Recovering from the first shock, he was not prepared for the second, but he kept his head and his hand steady, switching the oxygen supply back on, his experienced fingers twisting the knob with just the right amount of adjustment required. So that the eyelids began to flicker while the pinched nostrils began once more to relax. As he turned around to face Vicky, he started mentally to rehearse some plausible lines. He had split seconds in which to make a convincing reply. There was a moment of silence. Then Michael blessed himself. "I was just saying a little prayer for your Gran." Vicki's expression was uncertain. "So she won't sell the metal mountain and put me out of a job." There was truth in that.

Vicky gave a burst of almost soundless laughter, then her face grew soft and warm. "Don't be silly," she said contritely, her voice affectionate yet firm. "She only says that when she's upset sometimes, but she doesn't mean it really."

Michael Docherty swayed on the verge of nervous hysteria, recurrent reprieve was becoming too much for him. The disclosure had made him weak at the knees. Outside the faint beams of the rising moon gradually pierced through the mammoth obscurity of the mountain and tinged its fretted flanks with various tints of light, while inside on the darkened landing conspiring shadows began to descend the stairs.

"In fact, who else can work the metal but yourself?" said Vicky consolingly when she and Michael were once more down in the kitchen drinking tea.

Michael remained silent for a moment as if considering his answer. "Yes, I can work it all right." He hesitated, awkwardly, not knowing how to phrase it politely to her. "But who's going to pay me?" To this question, Vicky had no answer, and simply went on sipping her tea with her eyes fixed on the table between them, thinking back over the events of the night. And somehow, somewhere, there was always something that just didn't fit. She began to tap her fingers on the table, the little thud rhythmic and slightly menacing began to play on his nerves. Suddenly she looked up and caught him staring at her. He did not avert his eyes but kept gazing at her apparently thinking of something else before he spoke again.

"Otherwise how am I going to pay my rent?"

"You could stay here with me." When he did not immediately reply, she half flushed, adding: "And Gran, of course." He felt a warm surge of affection rising up within him for this straightforward girl and he smiled, unconsciously following out some inner train of thought.

While upstairs Gran was staring out at the moon as if she might read something from its cold light. It was a brazen young moon, its flickering virility touching things, there seemed room for both good and evil, for destruction or renewal.

During the weeks that followed Vicky fussed with extra kindness over Gran; she was inwardly very shaken and took tea in strong doses. Swathed too tightly between the sheets, she had begun to brood about events, pressing her hands against her eyes to focus the blur of the awful happenings into something more precise. While the only sound in the room were creaky tremblings in the springs of the old iron bedstead, as the night drew in along with the old woman's lips around her gums. When eventually she emerged from behind her hands, she had the answer and realised what she must do, but realised also that she must act quickly without arousing suspicion while she still had some strength left in her bones. Outside the bedroom window dawn was breaking. As the first rays of its grey light began polishing the tin the old woman started to prepare herself for sleep.

Some months later, towards the end of July, Michael, accompanied by Danny, went to collect the second-hand lorry they had previously picked out. Since all had gone well and their luck had held in taking the precious metals off the wharf, Michael had asked their parents to allow Dermot to leave his job as an apprentice toolmaker and come to work with him, promising them that it would work out better. Mary Jane and Seán Docherty had hesitated, for they were more than ever aware of the dangers of the wharf as a workplace since hearing of the violent end of Michael's boss. Mary Jane had offered up many a prayer for him. Yet suffering, rather than safety, was their main concern, for they had recently celebrated Lent. Going to Church at nine in the morning and staying there all day to emulate and imbibe the torments of Christ's road to Mount Calvary by partaking in the Stations of the Cross. Shuffling along in the belief that a doctrine can save one from the purgatories, stopping at each new station to lament with the rest of the faithful, though never arriving at the core of the tragedy.

Mary Jane felt it her duty to test her capacity for suffering at least during the extended period of Lent. As if she hadn't suffered enough with the rest of the poor; all year round—but, they had to feel the splinters in their knees.

She would have liked to touch her saviour's skin, the wound in his side that was more than wound, with the blood running out of it like it was still wet. The effect was strangely fascinating. It certainly looked real enough. Perhaps it was the light gilding the statue, which dissolved the fear which death leaves behind, so that she gazed and gazed until it bled afresh.

To better prepare themselves for this ordeal the penitents had abstained throughout the six weeks of Lent from eating meat on

Fridays and the Holy Days, and on Mondays and Wednesdays Mary Jane herself had fasted altogether, but for a slice of bread and a cup of tea. Going, after completion of this rigorous penance, to benediction where the priest (plump as a summer bumblebee) had administered absolution for their sins.

No, their main concern about the change was whether it would be a wise career move for young Dermot to give up the perceived security of an apprenticeship for the nebulous fortunes of an ironmonger. And Michael, having eliminated the necessity for all acts of repentance managed to convince that it would. Dermot was getting on for sixteen now. A tall, sensible lad with short blond hair, stiff and upright above a chubby adolescent face. He had been quite happy to swap the discipline of the factory for the more carefree work on the wharf, where he took over the job of cutting up the metal on the machine, under a new and infinitely more securely-roofed lean-to. In time, Michael had promised he would show him how to use the acetylene equipment, the rod, the burning element that cut and quartered and would also acquaint him with all other aspects of rendering the metal into manageable size. And so once more, the ching of hammer on bulk of metal could be heard issuing from the lean-to. Meanwhile, Danny with the lorry, had secured a contract with the Council to take down the old cast-iron lampposts that had formerly lit the streets of the Borough. Although the old lampposts had to be returned to the Council depot, many found their way onto the weighing machine of the gypsy scrap yard and in this way helped Michael's metal business to flourish.

The day that Michael and Vicky got married, the old woman called for them; and leaving the other guests downstairs to their partying, they went up to her bedside, where she handed Michael an official-looking piece of paper which he accepted with some gravity after which the shrivelled head fell back to desecrate the perfect structure and the pristine whiteness of the pillows. The old creature sighed while the lips pursed in a gesture that threatened to become vindictive. Her granddaughter was gazing over Michael's shoulder at the folded document when she noticed her patient staring at her husband somewhat sternly. On a day of such importance the attitude made the young bride nervous so that she smiled wanly at her charge. But the old woman seemed to have grown more thoughtful all of a sudden. She was, if anything, even more serious looking than before, so that Vicky was reduced to feeling a little worried by what the document her husband was at that moment reading might contain.

While she was pondering thus an insinuating stench of urine assailed her nostrils so that she was reduced to feeling embarrassed and churlish when she turned with a hint of conspiracy to meet her Grandmother's eyes. The old woman waved her away, however, as she went towards the bed mumbling that everything could wait until the document had been read. The remark, seeming to accuse, hung in the air, mingling with the sharp astringent smell, stung the senses. Vicky began to feel unhappy for herself and her new husband but mostly perhaps for her patient. The document, couched as it was in lawyers' spiel took the Ironmonger some time to decode. Though it was not in the end the unfamiliarity of the legal jargon that surprised the reader, nor, for that matter, was it the pungent aroma. Nor was it the truculent patient who had by now wrenched her mask down and appeared to be smiling at him, though on the other hand she might just be gumming the phlegm. What really surprised Michael Docherty, when he had finished deciphering the formal document, whose unbelievable contents had caused him so much serious thought, was the fact that he had been granted sole ownership of the mountain and his bride had been given sole possession of the house, whenever her grandmother should expire? In her disbelief the nurse, Vicky, leant over the bed to plant a warm kiss on the old woman's cheek.

"There's no need to thank me," said the old girl when Michael tried to express his gratitude. "I'm not giving you a present. That Mountain has put its mark on you. Be careful it doesn't bend you completely out of shape," she continued, a sour smile playing round her thin, bloodless lips.

Vicky would have preferred more company for the occasion. After all, she thought, it's not every day you get left a house and your husband gets left a metal mountain. Then she laughed outright. Perhaps it was the gin. "I'm married to a God now," she giggled. "A Tin God."

Michael laughed at that one, and even the old woman chuckled too.

But the days were melancholy the nights suspect though he walked loosely enough looking down into the maze of reflected metallic light under a sky of iron blue. The mountain contained its own diversions. Sometimes the breeze played simple melodies upon the metal and created leaden waves in the trapped rainwater, while into the iron pattern of the landscape his hammer struck its sharp note. On those days all its shapes were kind, all acts purged. At other times the metal leaves breaking open under the hammer's lost notes swelled and shone with drops of blood which did not seem possible in a world of iron. Sometimes after rain the mountain wore a fresh glaze yet it could not lift the torment. But the work went on, the man, accepting what he had deserved, pulled the brass and copper screws and fittings from the base of the mountain and posts of humbler iron, casting the inferior metal aside like chaff. He worked his way over the rusty brown terrain relentlessly, bending and reaping his iron harvest. His boots and trousers covered with iron mould, while the mountain glimmered and glowed, now silver blue, now dull bronze as the cold light dimmed and brightened over it. One hot day in a hollow he came across some chains, long lengths of thick dark blue coupling chains, medium sized black towing chains and smaller silvery chrome coated lavatory chains all tangled together. He spat into the hollow and heard the hissing sound of chains agitated by hot spittle or snakes writhing in a pit? On slack days he would collect these coiled chains and at once their scaly links slippery with oil would uncoil as he dragged them across the surface of the mountain to the edge where dangling them over the sides he would watch as they slithered like reptiles to the bottom.

BRIDGET'S STRUGGLE

"How was the soup today?" asked Bridget, in her calm acquired accent.

"Heavily reinforced with water," replied the man with malign truculence in the clipped tones of a Belfast accent.

"I'm sorry it wasn't to your satisfaction," replied Bridget with genuine concern.

The man nodded. He wasn't exactly displeased with her answer, but he didn't seem too happy about it either.

"We shall have to see if cook can make it more nourishing for winter," continued Bridget, as the man still stood, seemingly undecided, pondering her perfectly elocuted utterances in the hallway of the priest's house.

"I…"—said the man, falling silent immediately. He wasn't the usual soup-kitchen type slumped drained of dignity; observed Bridget. He was dressed in a sombre dark suit, with a clean white shirt and a dark tie. He had a steady gaze and an open, honest-looking face.

"Was there something you wanted to speak to me about?" enquired Bridget, at the same time opening her office door encouragingly, noticing as she did so the slight limp as the man entered. Bridget sat opposite him, in her clothes of elegant cut. After a moment or two, the man dropped his wary reserve and began to pour out his tale. He had been employed, he explained— since being de-mobbed from the Army—by one of the utility companies as a fitter, but had been laid off when the firm for which he had recently worked claimed that they had received letters of complaint from their customers, stating that they did not want any Irish or Black workmen coming into their homes. He finished by adding that though he was not of her denomination, he would be very grateful if she could provide him with a letter—something to show his former employers that he was trustworthy.

Outside in the Sacristy garden, the bushes and foliage had taken on an eerie presence, while the trees, glittering under the evening stars, held silent and still beneath their weight of snow. But was it the people, thought Bridget, or was it the council, preparing their racism for everyday use now—masking their sinister design under this new, artful guise? If so, since life is based on trust in people, the last trace of affability, even civility, was dead, she mused, and she was startled by the realisation which suddenly dawned on her about the middle-aged man now sitting so forlornly opposite her. His religious and political affiliations, though a positive and dominating factor in Belfast, afforded him no such protection here, where, in the racist jargon of Great Britain, he was just another Paddy. The dark caul of segregation, of official contempt, had begun to sink in. That her own experiences were similar, that she had knocked, and on being answered, was turned away made the incident too familiar and more intolerable.

She looked towards the window. More snow was beginning to fall. In the absence of any wind, the large flakes floated down in slow motion, fluttering against the pane like exhausted moths attracted by the light. "See here." The Ulster-man was leaning across the desk towards her, indicating the official-looking papers he had suddenly produced. "See? Wounded in action," he said, as Bridget took the proffered papers from his outstretched hand. "That's it. You can find your way around a document better than I can," he enthused.

For some reason, Bridget did not want to read his army papers and instead found herself thinking of her own people who'd had to emigrate to foreign lands rather than go to the North where there was nothing for them except oppression. In the complications of feeling that the man was a northern Unionist—that the same thing had also happened to her brother-in-law Seán Docherty—Bridget sat staring at the man with troubled eyes.

Outside, the deep December snow lay smooth upon the rooftops and covered every part in a mantle of pure white, infused with a touch of lightest blue. The air was clear and fresh; you could breathe freely providing you were willing to judge freedom by the capacity of your lungs. In the silence that followed they were united for a moment in the tragedies of the past, the intense nostalgia often helped her to recognise how much ground she'd gained through ambiguous allegiances. She wished she could have supported the despised utility worker but her will had been made feeble by his lack of faith, so she didn't declare herself, though most callers were suspect because they made demands. But he was determined to add a last humiliating touch, to probe a little deeper at the collective wound.

"Though the beast does not attempt to conceal itself, no one will take responsibility for its presence," he said rising from his seat. Bridget recoiled from this sudden assault on her loyalty. As he left she barely acknowledged his departure since her mouth felt dry in the resentful air. It was unpleasant enough to make her wish he hadn't come.

Though before the sound of his departure had faded out completely, she was already drafting out the formal letter that he'd sought. Yet she could not thank him for reopening a wound she had thought healed.

It was agreeable to prolong her exit but eventually she had to get up and begin the long walk to the door. She might not be strong enough. She was tired out from long manoeuvrings round unorthodox angles because it's so important to be safe. Once she'd learned the new language, though, they had been more than willing to hold open the doors which the importance of mundane living had required. Tone and pitch had buttressed any possibility of censure by those who saw at first something to resent even in red hair.

She slipped her fashionable coat over her arm, its flimsy fabric no proof against the weather, turned off the table lamp and became exposed to the black shadows as she trailed the edges of her anxiety across the polished floor, because something akin to immigration was forcing her out. Though this might prove to be the vastest sea she had to cross she would not always be acceptable to those she was trying to assist. There were those who would rather await the natural unfolding of events (however painful) than tamper with the future. There were jobs, many had some kind of roof over their heads now, and if underneath all this there were people who had not enough to eat, who were afraid of something or somebody, who were tubercular or homeless or without fundamental rights, that was no concern of foreigners. She felt a return of the tide of the previous moment's irritation.

Why, when she had everything described as advantages, did she expose herself so rashly? She had no reason she could have represented as adequate except a conviction deep in her heart to fight against an ugliness that was both fundamental and systematic. Her jaw tightened. She could not help being moved as she remembered a tumbledown cottage amid fields full of dock leaves and nettle and the cry of the curlew at dusk. Adjusting her scarf in the hall mirror, her expression appeared so doom-ridden it was almost tragic. Embarrassed, she laughed. It was really a comfort to be able to laugh at her reflection. If from now on she might not be so acceptable to others, at least she would be acceptable to herself.

Eventually she set her mind on forming an organisation that could speak for all Irish people living in Britain.

To think out each move well in advance. To sound out the colleges and Universities to form alliances. It should be equality for all but she knew that would be impossible. She would try for her own countrymen first and if she achieved some success others could follow.

She needed to confide in someone who had experience in these matters, who could explain what to do and what not to do. Some young people with tempers and hot blood suggested rebellion, she listened and returned to words.

She spent a great deal of time wrestling with words to get the council officials' idea of Irish people to match her own but without much hope. Most councillors were deliberately uncommunicative yet even those involved in good works looked away doubting, appalled at the audacity of such an undertaking because, well, because English and foreigners were quite different; it had to stay like that.

There was also the question of overcrowding. Had she thought of that? "Ah, well you see" said those councillors who had studied the situation and discussed immigration with care. "Some immigrants, foreign ones with darker skins and hooded eyes had strange beliefs and even stranger habits which might upset the balance, cause confusion in their overbright and gaudy clothing, more suited to a Christmas pantomime than on the streets of England among civilized people, not to mention the headaches people would get from all the different languages being spoken around them." He gazed at her pale dedicated face. "No doubt you are kind and full of good intentions but it's safer to leave things as they are. Of course England is well known for its marrow and stoicism but we don't want everybody upset and having headaches do we?"

Now Bridget realized what a mountain there was to climb when even the decent people were in opposition to her idea.

She tried to get people to hold meetings about their plight, they had talked about it often enough—but now they began to have doubts.

For those who are uneducated know it is not good to come to the attention of those who are. So there was only one voice for everyone. But people put on a face of surprise or anxiety when approached about anything political, especially concerning immigrants. After those that should have been concerned had decided not to be.

This was the sort of task which could reduce the strongest person to a nervous wreck. Many times she was on the point of giving up, for along with the praise and promises in a pretence of sociability their humour was destructive. The people seemed to have become frightened of gentleness, goodness was mistrusted, dismissed as sentiment emblematic of everything that was weak. But eventually as the years went by, cautious friendships were formed.

Then things began to change, when Bridget wrote an article for London University. It did not deal with anything too controversial, or political, or social. It could be laid aside safely as allegorical. She was invited to give a talk. The intellectual weeklies asked her for articles and interviews. Precise and lucid in her writings and speeches, passionate in her emotions, but controlled in their expression; tireless in her devotion to her work, she struck blow after well-timed blow in her struggle against racism. But for every step forward it was a case of two steps back, yet she wanted to think the best of people because Britain had suffered from the war.

Every year she wrote a letter to the Home Office requesting an interview. The letters were initially politely formal, but increasingly they became more blunt. Underneath that competent exterior was a tired young woman. She began to point out in her letters that the smallest movement one way or the other and an Irish person can be locked up, lose their job, be put in prison, interned, or even killed. But still we will not allow ourselves to be brainwashed into the belief that we live by courtesy of the English.

Mary Jane cast her eyes about the room. The room, like the house itself, had a certain shabbiness about it now. Most of the other residents of Raglan Street had gone—been re-housed in new council flats; she lived in hope of being re-housed in one herself. She'd been waiting over twenty years; surely it would happen soon. The vision glowed seductively; she daydreamed on it. It had ceased to be a vague ambition and had become a necessity, filled with fearful apprehensions, lest something should arise to thwart its fruition. She could not forget the poverty of her childhood, or the grumbling of her hungry stomach during the war when Seán and herself often went hungry to bed.

Mary Jane would have been surprised to know that the Council knew these things, and much else about her too, for her sister Bridget had been classed as an agitator, due to the fact that in a radio interview she had referred to Britain's policy of the unfair voting system in northern Ireland which affected the poorer citizens, a policy which denied many British citizens their democratic rights. Such was democracy in action, it had never been benevolent rule. Re-housing for Mary Jane might now be out of the question, since certain government departments scanned the files of those who had been separated from their roots without seeing them. So that, as the years passed, they forgot those who did not fit comfortably enough into their social scheme—they were of no importance.

Mary Jane began fumbling around until she found a match box. She lit the votive candle that stood on the mantle piece under a statue of the crucifix. Its little flame trembled on the wick as it slowly lit the briar crown which was pricking the flesh and tearing the brow. It was clear that all possibilities were contained for her in the form of Christ's death on the cross. Perhaps more symbolic than necessary, it is in any case perfectly natural that the body will die. Though the blood flowing out between the barbaric nails in his hands was divine. That much was proved, if one dared accept its blessing. So she continued to gaze with some rapture at the figure on the cross who had such easy intimacy with death.

She was stricken by the suffering of saints which her emotions had made her own. She might have taken on a different body and at that moment would have recognised the absolute if she had seen it. Because even in the most exalted existence suffering can be found, it was enough to move about the old house in her flowered apron and perform the simple task of living while she waited for the council to pass judgement. Soon she heard the front door being opened. Then Seán came into the room. He looked at her as he took off his jacket, and rolled up his sleeves. All his movements were slow now, since the accident. He was tired and his back ached. He sank into his comfortable armchair. Mary Jane liked to see him relaxing after a hard day's work, for the simple reason that he seldom got much work now. A bit of painting from time to time, but his injured back prevented anything permanent. She brought in his dinner, a good hot stew. She had not known what time he would be home and so had already eaten.

As she bent over him he smiled and kissed the mild hollow of her throat. Such actions came spontaneously to him now since soldiers no longer marched through the shadow of his dreams and their drums seemed silenced forever. "Ah," murmured the surprised woman, laying the tray down sharply on her husband's lap, so that her home-made gravy shimmered on the plate's edge and her dumplings wobbled. Being kissed always made her feel awkward but it was highly satisfying to have the washing all done and the house cleaned and to be able to sit down and put your feet up if you liked without having to worry about where the next meal was coming from. This was what made Mary Jane extremely contented. She revelled in the knowledge that Seán had some form of employ now, though she was not quite sure how secure the boys' employment was, but she consoled herself that she had brought them up to know right from wrong. So she never did ask herself why some of their work-mates never came to the door in broad daylight. If she did show too much interest in something that was causing them to talk to each other out of the sides of their mouths, they only hugged her and gave her a funny smile which made her wonder what secrets they were withholding.

Alan watched the two birds swooping lower—dark and elemental, this pair of carrion crows had taken up residence near the station some weeks back. He continued walking along the line as the train disappeared in the distance. The two great hulking corpse-eaters had landed and were swaggering along between the tracks. They had learnt, like the shark who follows a stricken ship, that trains often leave dead or dying things in their wake. Merciless killers of any small or helpless thing, they called querulously to each other now as they spotted something small and furry struggling on the ground. The young vole cried out pitifully as the crows probed it with their terrible beaks. In a sudden burst of savage anger, Alan picked up a stone, then just as suddenly dropped it as the anger inside evaporated at the futility of interfering with nature's plan.

It had been a tiring day. Ever since the Area Super had informed him vaguely that someone would be calling to ask him some questions he had been disturbed. He remembered that he'd just cleared the 12:30 freight for Richmond to go through when the Super had walked in with two men. They were both very tall, beefy and red-faced, and in spite of the ordinary charcoal grey suits they wore, only the very innocent would mistake them for anything other than police officers—which indeed they were, although their jurisdiction did not extend further than the end of the line, since they were only British Transport Police. They had been unusually polite and repeatedly commented on the responsible and important job Alan was doing for the Government. At first he'd thought that they might be Royal Equerries and that the Queen was going to be visiting the line until it slowly began to dawn upon Alan that, having not made the responses that courtesy demanded, these men— neither of whom seemed anxious to explain their presence—would not be behaving as they were unless they had some distasteful duty to perform.

"We've moved on a lot from the old days of instant dismissal for fiscal dishonesty," said Detective Sergeant Hoskins, settling himself on the edge of a chair. "There's even a classification table now that ranges from stealing a locomotive to being late for your shift." He smiled but his attempts at humour failed to deceive. "Everything seems to have its league table of tolerance nowadays, right on down to a warning—and quite right too, I say."

Alan's eyes moved without haste from one policeman to the other. "This is all very interesting, but what is happening? Am I suspected of some crime?"

"Absolutely not! Your character, as far as we are concerned Mr Marshall, is beyond reproach. Indeed your whole family's character is without blemish: your father was born and bred here and has also rendered sterling service to the company, we've been told. A man's family should rightly be an aid rather than a hindrance—especially a man's wife: the power behind the throne as they say."

The Detective pulled out a packet of cigarettes and offered them around. Alan declined, as did the officer's partner; only the Super accepted one. They all looked at his hands. "May I?" he asked; though it didn't look like he would wait to be permitted. "I know one cannot always escape the fate thrust upon them by circumstance," continued the plain clothes man after he'd lit up.

Something about his voice alerted Alan that the conversation was taking a dangerous turn. The policeman withdrew the cigarette from his mouth, flicked ash onto the floor, and plucked a loose strand of tobacco from his lower lip, all mechanical acts designed to gain time. "I believe your wife's Irish." The sergeant's tone was innocent. But the stationmaster struggled to hide his annoyance at the impudence. "She certainly is," he replied in a level voice. "Why?"

"Well, it can be a factor—a two-sided one—in any Government job."

"How's that?"

"It can lead to promotion, or, it might lead to something else." The Supervisor, who up to this point had been idly fiddling with his long-service watch that was hanging from a chain stretched across his paunch, was suddenly all ears. The conversation had caught him now, since he believed he had reached the zenith, the furthest rung on the ladder of promotion. He was eager to hear what could lead one to even further advancement in one's post.

"Something else?" said Alan coldly.

The Sergeant ignored his comment. "I have been afforded the opportunity of visiting many different countries in my humble capacity as a servant of the Crown," he intoned and braced his shoulders subtly as his narrative took him into foreign parts, "and, although I've been as far afield as India in my travels, I have never seen the Taj Mahal nor Trinity College Dublin, nor for that matter the Blarney Stone when I was stationed in Ireland." Alan tried to imagine how much more circuitous this man's conversation could have been if he *were* to have kissed the Blarney Stone. "Does that surprise you, Mr Marshall?"

Alan merely shrugged.

"Well, the simple truth is," continued the policeman, "I'm not interested in marble, rocks and stones. I'm far too interested in people to waste my time on viewing inert matter. And do you know what observations I have gleaned from watching these different people all over the globe? No? Well then, allow me to explain," said the man who had been abroad. "Most foreigners are scavengers and so actually benefit from hard times. To bring them on too fast would be to upset the natural order of things. Sure, there are a few social and economic problems here in our own country which must be dealt with, in fact are being dealt with—perhaps at a rate too slow for some, but to imply as Mrs Marshall has recently been doing on the wireless that this country is lacking in democracy is to ignore its recent stand and ultimate defeat of Fascism." He nodded to emphasise the correctness of his statement.

There was a certain calmness within Alan that was apparent. He did not need to prove the masculinity that obsessed most men. He was certain of himself and his judgements in so many ways and yet he felt challenged by the policeman's words, by his unquestioning acceptance that, because a war had been waged and millions of lives had been lost, the world had somehow been miraculously put to rights. He began to dislike the smug assurance of the man. A smell of earth and flowers came lightly through the half open window and suddenly he felt he wanted to be away from it all, outside in the presence of trees and sky flowers and birds, walking by the track. But the day had aged the station master.

As he pushed open his door, Mrs Watson's cat glided into the basement flat before him. He shut the door and turned to find Bridget standing in the hallway smiling at him. For a moment he was lost for words. She hesitated, concerned by the stricken look he gave her, then her arms went around him and she kissed him: not passionately, just fondly. Suddenly he stiffened as something touched his ankle.

"What's wrong with you tonight?" asked Bridget kindly as the cat wound itself round his leg.

He averted his eyes, unable suddenly to look at her. "I had a visit from the police today," he said off-handedly, trying to make this piece of information sound unimportant. He took her arm, still without looking at her, and steered her into the kitchen.

"What did they want with you?"

"They wanted to know about you." A jolt of adrenalin shot through Bridget. She waited for him to go on. "They asked me if you spoke Gaelic. I told them I didn't know."

"Why did you tell them that?"

"Because I wasn't sure." Bridget thought Alan's expression looked foolish. Each of them was threatened since details were not apparent.

"Christ, have you ever heard me speaking anything other than English?"

"Yes," he said with gruff suddenness.

"What?"

"I've heard you say things in Irish: remember when you told me about 'open the door and close the door'." He tried to soften his words but she had captured the tone.

"For God's sake, Alan!, cried Bridget, 'oscail an doras' and 'dun an doras', imitating her original language, which she could not speak. Two phrases, my whole vocabulary in Irish! Anyone who could call that fluency in Gaelic needs their head examined."

"The police could."

"Yes, anyone who can speak two words in Gaelic would be capable of anything as far as they're concerned." Bridget shook her head in despair. "What sort of daftness are you playing at?" she snapped. Very seldom her devotion and determination failed her.

She looked at him with the sudden despondent feeling that comes from not knowing someone you ought to know well.

"I was trying to keep your options open." Bridget looked at him closely, as he went on: "Suppose you did speak Gaelic fluently, and I told them you didn't and you told them that you did—well, you can see…"

At first, Bridget couldn't think of a creditable explanation of why he should want to do that. Then she realised that this meant Alan thought they would soon be questioning her, and a tremor of fear ran through her stomach, as she became aware that Alan was trying to provide her with an alibi. But an alibi for what? She felt something tugging away at her inside. It was guilt. Guilt for somehow involving Alan in her crusade. Bridget took a deep breath and expelled it with a sigh.

"They told me Seán Docherty's father was shot by the Black and Tans," continued Alan, "and said that that's one of the reasons why you are stirring up anti-British feelings under the guise of petty residential permissiveness." She gave him a quizzical grimace. "Council housing, digs, rooms to let, call it what you will."

"So that's why I'm being followed."

"You're being followed? Why didn't you tell me?"

"I didn't want to worry you."

"Who's following you?"

"Obviously they're policemen, but I don't really know." Her expression betrayed the idea that she was immune to shock.

"But Bridget, anything could happen to you! I don't like this at all."

"Well there's not much I can do about their following me."

"You could give up lobbying the Home Office; that would go a long way in helping to put a stop to it, I'm sure."

Bridget gave a hollow laugh. "Christ, anyone would think I was involved in sabotage and high treason!" Alan's embarrassed smile showed that he found her attempt at humour misplaced. In an agony of conflict, she took his hand.

"It's not as simple as that, my love. Leaving aside the wider issues such as jobs and housing, there's a million other smaller reasons: it's in things like Mary Jane destroying the bunches of shamrock my father used to send her for St Patrick's Day—she didn't want the children to be subjected to violence or nastiness for wearing their national emblem. It's so as young Irish men and women can come out of an Irish dance-hall in this country without being arrested by the police on the pretext of their being drunk and beaten senseless into a Black Maria. Their faces distorted with hate, their eyes gleaming insolently with lack of shame, it's—Ah dear," she sighed. "There are certain sadnesses in people that are sometimes difficult to share." Alan glanced at the window.

"Perhaps you've become a victim of your own eloquence," he said.

Bridget paled with fury. "I seek only equality, equality for all."

"There is no cause more dangerous," snapped Alan.

When Bridget failed to reply he continued.

"There'll be more of them following you from now on if you don't give up!" Alan was beside himself with worry for her and couldn't help showing his irritation.

"What do you mean?" asked Bridget, trying to sound casual.

"They have a notion you might be in the IRA."

"No." Her mouth hung open in disbelief. In the breathless silence that followed it seemed ages before either of them moved, she wanted to go to him, to say something to break the nightmare quality that seemed to hang over the room. Alan began to roll a cigarette. She looked at him, too shocked at what she had just heard to speak for the moment. Alan lit up and took a long thoughtful pull on his fag, as he looked for evidence of insurrection, but found only a young woman, his wife with sheer green eyes that had not yet recognised evil.

He was never confused about his own place and role but realized complexities must set in if you were an immigrant. Just as Bridget had a vision of what might be so did he and what he saw made him cold and afraid since he realized now anything might happen. That same week a German goshawk escaped from its enclosure at Regents Park Zoo and was now flying free while the firm favourite in the Cumberland stakes *Trojan Prince* a powerful stallion lost to an outsider, *Cloverfield* an Irish mare bankrupting half the bookmakers in Britain. Meanwhile Victor McLaglen's old role about an informer was suddenly showing again at all the main cinemas in Britain.

When the two detectives called at Bridget's flat the following week she was out, as they already knew she would be: for the political branch of Scotland Yard's Serious Crime Squad had learnt from experience that it was an excellent ploy in some cases to create dissension between the suspect and their landlord. The double pressure from outside and inside the home, especially in low priority cases such as the present one, very often helped to snap the suspect's nerve.

The job of this particular unit was to combat the work of refugee organisations throughout Britain at this stage; their task was mainly to hassle any politically motivated immigrants. Of course, if, during their investigations, they uncovered any real threats to the State, then the case was automatically passed on to MI5.

When the bell rang, Mrs Watson thought it might be one of her tenants that had forgotten their key, and was surprised, on drawing back the front door, to find two casually dressed men standing on her doorstep. One of them, although not that old, was completely bald, while the other seemed to be covered with hair—at least, his head had a thick black growth and his face was sprouting short black stubble. She wondered if they might be builders, and was surprised indeed when they showed her their identity cards.

"We'd like to speak to one of your tenants—Mrs Marshall," said the bald one. And when Mrs Watson told them that they'd just missed her, they didn't seem too put out.

"Perhaps we could ask you a few questions while we're here," continued the bald one, and when Mrs Watson nodded her assent, he asked, "Does Mrs Marshall strike you as the sort that might have one or two boyfriends?"

Mrs Watson was astonished. "But she's got a husband, Alan, a gentleman. He's been with me for years."

"What my colleague is really trying to say," said the dark-haired one, with a primness that bordered on the obscene, "is does she have men calling here at the house?"

"Oh no, oh dear no, this is not that sort of house, sir," cried Mrs Watson, adding with a confident toss of her head, "and Mrs Marshall is a hard-working girl."

"A hard, working girl in more ways than one, if you get my meaning," grinned the bald one.

Mrs Watson gave a little gasp.

"I know. Comes as quite a surprise," he said. "Of course, it's all circumstantial at the moment."

"It is unbelievable."

"I know," said the policeman "But over a period of time one hears a word here and a word there, and very soon you've got a sentence."

It was obviously his intention to withhold details.

Mrs Watson stood there, looking from one man to the other in a state of shocked bewilderment.

"We have not yet actually caught Mrs Marshall in... aah... *flagrante delicto*," continued the officer.

"I beg your pardon?" said Mrs Watson.

"In the act, or, in this case, if you will pardon the expression 'on the job'—I don't feel justified in being more precise than that," he answered somewhat nobly. She was incredulous and held her front as if her dress might not contain the force of her anxiety.

"However, we must ask you to keep this quiet for now," said the hairy one. "We've got good laws in this country, and a person is innocent until proven otherwise. So if you would be kind enough to let her know we called today and ask her to pop into the Police Station as soon as she gets home, we'd be much obliged."

About five o'clock that evening, Mrs Watson rose from her armchair where she had been dozing and began to make her way downstairs to the basement flat, considerably agitated by the fact that she, an honest, decent Englishwoman, might be dangerously close to tripping over a bucketful of filth. It seemed an age since she'd set out, her hand held fast to the polished rail was numbing at the wrist. She lurched, biting her lip as something gave beneath her foot—the carpet perhaps? But she was not deceived, the rods were old and suspect too. She continued hesitantly on her doubtful descent into the silence of the basement where it was proposed she should intrude on one who had not appreciated the flat for its proximity to a garden but for other purposes.

"If I were to fall and sprain a bone," Mrs Watson could have said, the suffering will not be mine alone. Though she trod more carefully now, stopping every now and then to shake her head for some unpleasantness. Fright and pain apart, it would be an inelegant position to be found in, with a carpet rod tilting at your thighs. After some initial fumbling in the dim light for the banisters' reassuring touch she continued to descend the hazardous stairway. Negotiation had become a slow and solemn duty now. But Mrs Watson, who was the landlady, did arrive finally at her tenant's door.

She stood in the strict space by the doorway, feebly resisting the moment, because there are certain conventions to be observed when dealing with a sitting tenant or a bawd. But there was no visible disorder or disturbance so she tapped with her arthritic knuckles, because it was inevitable, on her lodger's door. When the door drew back the brightness encouraged exposure. The old woman looked at her tenant and in the distraction of the moment found herself confronted by a blaze. The shimmering glowing mass of the younger woman's hair, a smouldering flame of golden copper which the fragile doorway might not be able to contain. Indeed the landlady had become quite hot and bothered, but before taking refuge in her anguished breathing Mrs Watson, gathering her awkwardness about her, passed on the policeman's message without mentioning their distasteful suspicions, as she had been instructed. But the young woman did not seem to hear, or the matter that had been referred to was too improbable to grasp. And when she smiled and thanked her, then something of pity touched the landlady for one who did not perhaps understand all that a summons to a police station might imply. As she stood there, looking at Bridget, Mrs Watson was suddenly aware that she was trying to visualise her as a lady of the night, ready for anything and capable of most, but somehow, she couldn't manage it, and she blushed both from embarrassment and fear of this role that had been thrust upon her.

Her first impulse was to warn Bridget of the policemen's suspicions, but she checked it, then stood for some moments contemplating in silence until Bridget asked her if she would like to join her for a cup of tea.

"How nice of her," thought Mrs Watson, and found herself suffering from the temporary illusion that the policemen had not really said those terrible things to her about Bridget at all. "It was probably that I imagined it." And yet she heard a voice—it was her own—refusing rather fussily Bridget's offer of tea. So Mrs Watson, who usually enjoyed a bit of a yarn, had become quite old, and stiff, and depleted from having taken part, as she turned to make her way back up the stairs. She wished that it had never happened. But it had happened; already the little hallway could not contain it. And since the policemen's visit Ethel Watson seemed to have shrunk, though her tenant seemed to have maintained a tolerable shape.

Bridget looked at the jumper she had been knitting for Alan, which, while she had been engaged at the door, had somehow ended up on the floor. She knelt, occupied now in the task of sorting the components of her art, retrieving the ball of wool and placing the front and the back of the article into some semblance of order. For a brief moment she seemed to be looking at the tangled items for some sign of division in herself, while Mrs Watson's cat sat with a contrived smile on its face, watching from the top of a cupboard, and now that she was warned, she felt suddenly tired she threw the half finished jumble on a chair. It was too involved for her to continue its unravelling.

She began tidying her hair, gripping it by the handful and pulling it back so severely that it strained against her forehead and temples as she pinned it beneath a green scarf. Her face seemed drawn and aged yet without loss of dignity. Unconsciously she picked up her knitting and placed it in the cupboard, while the cat began to mewl for some injustice sensed. The sun was spinning spidery shadows in the dust as she put on her coat to leave the room. The fact that the sun would rise, would blaze again with light, aroused the reverence in her, yet she was sufficiently enough in doubt to bless herself in hope all the same.

At the police station, beneath a naked yellow light bulb, Bridget sat while two plain clothes men watched her under this other sun, in a room that was bare except for three chairs, a table and the corpses of flies. The man to her left had a pale, alert face with blond, thinning hair and wire-framed spectacles of the sort that a child might get on the National Health. Their eyes met. He had a knowing expression. The other one was taller, straighter, like a soldier who was decaying gracefully in middle age. He kept glancing at her legs. She could see his interest was not political, despite the fact both men worked for MI5. After the insincerities of greeting, the struggle to preserve her own honesty increased confusion, so that if their motives for summoning her here were sensed rather than reasoned, it was natural that she should wonder if she had committed, perhaps, and then forgotten some former misdemeanours. Was she fearful? Discontent, she would have said, if she did not suspect that such an admission would have made her vulnerable. All were looking at one another, wondering rather than judging, for what could be concealed in that bright room, from every corner of which an actual or suspected crime might arise. The men had become absorbed with their clothing, fixing a coat cuff, straightening a tie. They were innocent enough acts in themselves but she doubted their motives. In fact, sitting as she was at the centre of the room, the woman gave no indication that she noticed them. Her glances and expressions were reserved for the furniture which stood with crude directness. A table, some chairs, their solidness was comforting and in many aching moments her mind would return to dwell on those innocent things. Yet as the silence increased the woman began to have doubts.

But these men did not pay any particular attention to what others brought to this room felt. As they waited with heads held, to listen for words that people had never before dared to utter. And sometimes they heard incredible things. But now the woman had returned to where she had begun, where thoughts left with little to hide behind must forsake their secrecy and come out into the open, into the hostile atmosphere where the air remained undeceived, in this room, which appeared quite functionless. But that of course was its strength, it had numerous purposes, this apparently functionless room, where they sat listening for whispers and questioned each other in silence. For they knew, these two men who took her presence for granted, from experience in this and many other bare rooms that the new or the timid or those not in favour of making full declarations must first be encouraged with silence because once uttered in a moist warm room statements bred others.

There were several versions of the same moment which made the silence echo far more audibly, until eventually the blond man pulled a small notepad from his pocket, opened it, cleared his throat and looked up at her. Each of these solemn acts were performed without undue haste. She waited for him to ask her a question, but he chose to begin another way. "You're a regular at the Magdala Public House." The voice was working class, well modulated without discarding firmness.

"Hardly," she replied tersely. "I've been in the place once."

"Nostalgia?" He quipped in his insinuating tone.

She ignored the jibe. There was fine sarcasm in the last remark.

"In a way, I suppose, I was curious to see the scene of the crime for which the last woman in England was hanged. Wrongfully now, as I remember."

'Is that all you remember.' they asked.

Bridget Marshall refused to indulge them in the subtleties on which they thrived, though as time passed she grew more afraid, while her inquisitors grew more impatient and expectant because they had not yet discovered her weaknesses.

"Michael Collins, one of your compatriots, used to use the pub as a drop-in too, metaphorically speaking," continued the detective, looking at the woman, whom he found disconcerting, through the wire-framed glasses that he was compelled to wear.

A redhead without freckles was hard to accept.

"I'm sorry, I'm not with you."

"That's right, you're not." The taller one made a little snickering sound and recited in a sing-song tone, "He that is not with me is against me and so on and so forth." These two goons had a priceless routine.

Her pretty features wrinkled in puzzlement as she leaned forward. "I don't understand what you're talking about," she replied with a firmness unexpected in one so gentle. Then she sat back quietly in the straight-backed chair. The two men, who were nourished by mystery, watched her small slender hands—those unconscious tale-tellers that so often said much more than words, but they were folded calmly and neatly in her lap.

Blondie tried to make his face look kind but it was too far gone to achieve that. It could never quite achieve the expression towards which he was feeling his way. The woman's senses stirred unhappily inside her. As she concentrated on the situation that must be faced, his eyes went beneath her clothes. She blushed as he looked for something he could recognise in the immoderate glare. She was not wearing stockings, that, and the absence of lipstick, might have suggested anarchist tendency, but the paint, peeling in the vagueness of bare corners did not collaborate. Perhaps there was nothing of sufficient importance to be withheld, yet his suspicions remained as he continued to gaze at her bare shins.

"Maybe you don't, some immigrants take more time than others to see where their bread is buttered and who is responsible for buttering it for them."

A spasm of anger shot through Bridget, temper nearly made her reckless, fortunately she mumbled instead. "Shouldn't everybody be entitled to a morsel of food and a bed?"

"That's the way it usually starts," said Blondie to his colleague, talking to him as if Bridget were not in the room, "the boys always begin by demanding specific social goals—better housing, higher pay, equal rights with those who've fought for their country, if you don't mind. Soon as they're given them, what do they do? Why, they just become more radical, that's when they come out with what they *really* want, that Great Britain, if you please should give up yet another part of her Empire.

Bridget was just about to tell him angrily that she was not in the IRA, then stopped short, halted, as a chill ran through her from the realisation that he had not mentioned the IRA but instead had used the euphemism "boys." The light blinked as if the bulb were wearing out. Bridget felt claustrophobic in this place where both truth and fiction mingled freely. She could sense the resentment in objects; although nothing had been confessed or denied. She said very quietly, "We need an equal race law here."

"You could get yourself in a lot of trouble. Baiting governments to mandate a reckless charter isn't safe." It was the tall one now that spoke. Something in his tone made her look at him closely. He wouldn't meet her eyes.

"Don't push, don't shove, don't raise your voice. You seem to want the Irish people to emasculate themselves," she said.

Blondie sighed. "Look: what is wrong with giving up something when it becomes unsafe?" The light was striking the steel rims of his spectacles.

"Because some things cannot be given up. And if you do, you

lose a bit of yourself," replied Bridget with terrifying calmness. She would not allow herself to appear frightened by their threats. She had discovered other fears. The unsavoury walls looked less than innocent, the cracks in them were hiding something ominous— pink flakes of plaster dangled like disintegrating flesh. Because she was afraid of falling into a number of traps she refrained from trying to decipher the hastily scribbled messages blurred in the chalky texture.

The blond agent, whose mind usually worked very fast, was at a loss for some subtle reply that would ease him over this… this jarring note that the woman had struck. He ran a hand through his hair with a tired sigh. Hearing other people's troubles might have made him sensitive, as he bent down in the unsanctified confessional encouraging, with suitable gestures and expressions, confidences with which to conjure. They were desperate for such words that helped their calling and would have heard them eagerly, though were experienced enough to know it was improbable that, at this stage, such an opportunity would occur. The agent informed her, "Any country that dares institute reckless charters would face a serious backlash."

Bridget began to be aware of her isolation, which caused great unease in the room from which it was not possible to escape. The plain clothes men had seen the strong position they were in, amid the warm glandular smell that pervaded the brazen light of that inadequately furnished room. They searched around for some way to take advantage of it, looking at the young woman almost as if they had been lovers.

The blonde agent peered through his glasses trying to read the answer to his own suspicions but his gaze was blurred by an intimidating silence while doubt continued to express itself. It might have continued like this if it hadn't been for a conspiracy taking place between silence and the unknown. Since they were not yet ready to translate her silences into pronouncements their gestures appeared innocent of motive, but they gradually began to limber up as she began to explain the insignificance of her work.

Then Bridget heard questions, she heard shouts. The lamp was so placed, she could not see their faces as their voices grew angrier, menacing, friendly and finally monotonous. But she did not speak because she did not care enough in this bare room where emotions as deep as fear and even terror, and blood and urine had stained the floor, while the walls of flaking paint gave evidence of unconcern. Because before even the most willing can collaborate they must first be enticed. The light was of such intensity now that the woman flinched as if scorched. That was the attitude her body had taken. Her face was giving it painful shape, for in that naked glare not even the eyelids provided a refuge.

"Your husband told us," said the blond detective, "That he is worried you will get him the sack."

"My husband would not have said that."

"Why?"

"Because it's a lie."

"Why would he tell such a dangerous lie?"

"It is not him that is lying," replied Bridget. Somewhere in the interior of the building a dog barked. It was a neutral statement so that, for the moment, they could remain detached in this room, which had at first appeared to Bridget inadequate.

To perceive simplicity where everything was so uncommonly complicated had been unwise. Yet it was a common error committed by nearly everyone who came to this place. Now she would have looked out of the window if there had been one. Instead she began to trace with her eye small patterns on the rugged table and studied the grain and counted the whorls in the gouged wood, while her whole body rejected its promise of permanence which was anyhow flawed by its misshapen legs and vandalised surface, graphically dramatizing diabolical perversions, which seemed reflected in the men's wooden faces as if they had ceased to exist in themselves except through the wood, so that the table was a link, linking them physically, bringing her into their circle. As they moved through their séance, doors closed or clanged shut, voices called and were answered or not; it was not so clear, muffled by the distances from which they had travelled. While a couple of cockroaches shook the dust from their prehistoric skulls as they emerged from their den and scuttled along the rim of the skirting board. Doors opened and closed, closed and opened, the day shift was changing. A spider web stretched taut across the bottom corner of a wall began vibrating frantically; on the body of a fly the roaches had discovered a wound. Outside the world was getting on with the business of making its dinner, unconcerned about insects, whether beetle or fly.

And yet, faintly, ever so faintly, somewhere someone might have screamed. It was not improbable. The older policeman cocked his head on one side and smiled while the blond haired man's eyes became fixed on a thin rubber band which he would pick up sometimes and examine through his steel rimmed spectacles. Bridget saw all this and more, she saw, in particular, the ages that had elapsed since first she'd entered this room when behaviour had been more or less predictable.

Soon Bridget saw that the two men would stand up, the blonde man and his military accomplice. In fact, they were already preparing, removing their elbows from the table. She could hear their chairs scraping the floor and the breath heaving in their silent mouths. Then she could see their legs straightening and their bodies unbending until they were standing over her. Aware of the motion of her breasts visible outside her dress as she was gathering breath, she wanted to look away because of their common eye which was measuring the hopelessness of honest existence. She would have liked to look less conspicuous; but that was not possible; she knew that she was still numbed from sitting too long alone with them in this isolated room, where honesty bred dishonesty. Her hair, unkempt now under the green scarf, was striving to break loose, her clothes were not fresh, her buttocks were pinned too tightly to the chair, and she waited with the agony of what she knew must eventually happen.

They continued staring at the subdued woman seated on the chair, nothing of what had taken place could prevent that. In defending her convictions she looked peculiarly dejected but thankfully could avoid seeing by not looking. It was necessary to disguise feelings. There was no room for anything other than raw presence, so that at times her breath went in and out too fast and other times when it seemed to refuse to flow at all, but none of this halted the inevitable.

Suddenly one of her interrogators reached out with his hand towards her, flicked a switch on the lamp beside her plunging the room into darkness. Though it seemed a thoughtless act, to quench that which might help illuminate a moment of truth, it had been fully premeditated. And yet the room was not quite in darkness for the peculiarities of the men's profession did not allow for uncertainties, though during the varying shades of shadow its atmosphere of indifference remained waiting for identification.

In the afterglow, which should have had no possible connection with any part of her, other shapes threatened. Bridget could see the man's face close to her own. Under the wire-rimmed glasses the wrinkles had tightened round the edges of his eyes, which had begun to focus on her purposefully. His lips parted, their breath intermingled distressingly. She saw his mouth opening while her own mouth moved in a series of soundless flutterings of protestation. His eyes incorrigible, forceful and assertive had turned to slits. She became reduced; resistance was slowly seeping out of her as his voice kept asking, insisting encouraging her as if she were a child.

"Are you going straight on home from here?"

"Home?" The question startled the woman who, suddenly roused from her compelled inactivity had no ready reply. The two men waited, they did not appear ruffled to discover that the one who should have known the answer didn't. In spite of warnings she hadn't been prepared for such a ruthless exit but did recover her identity enough to nod as she stood up.

The three figures stood there. The woman faced the two agents as if there had been no darkness. They could have been remembering the silences which they had failed to penetrate. They badly needed to justify themselves but the woman had upset their timing she was without mystery now there was nobody left to accuse. The tall agent said. "I'll get the car." He could have called the duty driver to help them out of a difficult situation but he liked cars. He liked driving. He could turn a car on a sixpence.

Later that week an M15 agent sitting in his office scanning a young Irishwoman's file that had just been placed on his desk jotted down the word SUBVERSIVE.

A GARDEN PARTY
AT THE CHALFONTS

It was little more than fifty yards from the bus stop at Hampstead to the big house at the top of West Hill. But within a minute of leaving the bus, Michael Docherty was in a quandary, for the surroundings seemed somehow very familiar. For a few moments perhaps, there had been an illusion that this could not be so, but now, as he walked into the orchard through the open gate, he realised that this was indeed the place where, as a child, he had been arrested. Under the deep shade of the apple trees it felt almost cold after the sun's fierce glare, as Michael, conscious of his rising excitement and a sense of uncertainty, stood for a while leaning against one of the trees.

He had not wanted to come here today, but since his parents could not come and Vicky had to look after her Gran, Danny had implored him not to let him down by staying away from his girlfriend's birthday party.

He continued looking at what, to a former trespasser, might amount to an immoral luxury. The trees all around were laden with apples, most not yet quite ripe. Michael stretched up a hand to take one. As he did so he heard a voice rise in laughter from the direction of the house, and other voices followed, joining in the merriment. He began walking towards them along a path margined with white parsley and stitchwort. Violets, speedwell and ground ivy spilled their blue on the hedge-side bank. The chapel clock struck the hour on Christchurch Hill. A breeze blew from that quarter and it brought the three notes' clear peal.

There were about twenty people spread about the garden, chatting and laughing in little groups. Most of them seemed a little drunk. He spotted Bridget talking to his brother's posh girlfriend, Isabella Chalfont, while Danny looked on. Suddenly

Danny spotted him and waved him over to where they stood. In the middle of the lawn a large table had been spread with plentiful supplies of cold meat, shellfish, sausages on sticks, pâté, sauces of every variety, and in the middle of these dainty dishes, a monster cake with twenty-one candles took pride of place. Bridget looked at the layout with befitting admiration.

"What kept you?" said Danny, adding, "I thought you might not come."

"He's here now," said Bridget smiling holding Michael at arm's length for a moment while studying his face. She had felt a certain fondness toward Michael ever since the days he'd trudged round with her trying to find a room.

Isabella held out her hand. Michael shook it. There was something of a sex-shyness between them, which made them awkward in each other's company whenever Danny had brought her to their parents' house. "Happy Birthday," said Michael, "when are you getting married?"

"What do you want to know for?" laughed Isabella as she looked at Michael, but her tone held an invitation to ask more.

At that moment, Mrs Chalfont came forward with a bottle in her hand. She greeted Michael cordially, without any inkling of the past, adding (with an eye to her future son-in-law's prospect, perhaps): "And your business is prospering?"

Michael was not slow in surmising the cause of her concern and some remembered kindness made him soften, either a word in a drawing room or the mute direction of an apologising arm cutting a swathe through the shadows in a long ago summer hallway.

"Doing great, thanks to Danny's help," he said.

She didn't reply. She was wondering about the scar which had disfigured his cheek and brow; a slim-hipped man with fine eyes and wavy chestnut hair. 'A handsome fellow if you liked them lithe,' she thought, 'perhaps dangerous.' She didn't like the bold way he looked at her. And yet, since the War, one had had to make some unavoidable compromises. She inclined her head, he planted an austere kiss on her proffered cheek and she began to circle the garden once more replenishing her guests' glasses. After which, Mrs Chalfont encouraged everybody to take plates and help themselves.

It suddenly seemed like a pack of wolves had gathered round the table. The breed was mainly a friendly, talkative one. Between its chatter, it sipped at glasses, ate shellfish, nibbled sausages, blew smoke, and shrieked with laughter. Soon the table was empty, but for the odd crumb. Hunger appeased, the guests reformed once more into their respective little groups, and, drinks in hand, wandered back to hold their own patch of garden.

But Isabella's group, made up of Danny, Bridget and Michael, kept on wandering, stopping every now and then to admire the numerous shrubs and flowers of the massive garden. From the walls hung dark green tresses of velvet lichen. The air was fragrant with the scent of summer. "What are those called?" asked Michael, pointing to a cluster of pretty pink flowers growing in amongst the crumbling wastes of a part of the wall.

"They're known as yarrow," answered Isabella.

"They're lovely," said Bridget.

"According to legend," said Isabella, trying to be a dutiful host, "Achilles used Yarrow to staunch his wounds. And thereafter the God Zeus decreed that those whose garments were woven from Yarrow would never meet death by human hand."

"Did it work?" said Michael, bending to examine the cluster with interest.

"I don't know—anything's possible in legend."

High above, a wood pigeon began to coo gently and a mistle thrush answered with piping song.

"God," said Bridget, "it's lovely here. It's like being back home." She was full of a subtle joy; indeed all of them seemed to have gone into a trance of fulfilment. But the bliss had its shadow. Dark clouds were gathering which looked like they might block out forever the blazon of the sun.

They continued to amble. Their progress was slow amid gusts of wind that lifted the leaves and ruffled the grass. There were many species of flower and shrub to be examined and other guests to be greeted and wine to be drunk… And in this leisurely fashion the afternoon moved on. There was a bit of cloud, but otherwise the threatened storm seemed to have passed over. The garden had survived the first terrible tremor, things except for the tattered spiders webs had begun to resume their natural shape while the darkness drew back at the coming of the sun.

"Thanks be to God we're saved" cried Bridget. Michael smiled wryly, not understanding altogether what she implied since he could no longer believe in the promise of salvation for himself, because he no longer felt acceptable to God; he was too clearly marked with the sign of His disapproval, so that if at times his face appeared well-scrubbed and at others not so clean at all, it was simply that he had ceased to look in mirrors since the accident when he'd reacted toward his reflection as though he had suffered the amputation of a limb. Yet he was faced all the time by his ever-watchful image, though metal gives a more distorted view. Sometimes he would think of the words that his mother had taught him. Then his eyes would become hooded and unseeing because he could no longer see how they might lead him back to God. But there were other Gods besides his mother's pale god a prisoner of other people's sins, whom his father often spoke of, the pagan Gods of Ireland's Viking ancestry. But some maintained there was no God—no God at all.

The bones in his face became dark and shadowed.

"Wait" said his young aunt gently. He was awkward, all words had become suspect because he knew that certain things were not intended, as she touched his face—brushing his hot cheek lightly with cool fingers. She smiled and said, "that's got rid of that old bit of fluff."

The sun had begun to shine bright across the blue expanse of sky a rainbow traced its graceful arc. The grass was thick with clover, which deadened footfall and made for reverence as Michael made his way over to the house to use the toilet. He walked slowly over the grass where white wood anemones made a spangle amongst the green, keeping a wary eye open for the gardener, if indeed such a fellow still existed. Some of the guests had left now. He noticed that the groups had become fragmented. Yet Mrs Chalfont continued on her rounds, dutifully replenishing the glasses of the diehards.

There was a smell of dust and age and stone and wood, and also a human body. He was sitting in a wheelchair, head back, eyes closed, resting. On a small table by his side lay a pipe, along with a tobacco pouch, matches, and newspaper. Even though the skin was shrivelled now and speckled in places, the head bald, yellowing beneath wisps of grey hair, Michael could not mistake the face of the former army officer who had taken him to court over an apple.

Suddenly, Major Chalfont sensed Michael's presence. His eyes sprang open in uncertain wakefulness. "What do you want?" he demanded with an irritated croak because he had been taken unaware.

"May I have a peek at your paper?" enquired the intruder amiably.

"Yes, you can take it," replied the Major brusquely.

Michael reached over slowly, picked up the paper, and stepped back, resting his buttocks against the table. Major Chalfont watched impatiently as Michael rifled casually through the pages. "I see somebody's had a little go at the crossword. Clever." said Michael sweetly, as he continued searching through the paper. "Sorry, I'm looking for the latest metal prices," he continued, conversationally, as the light from the latticed window waned and the shadows in the room piled up.

Major Chalfont did not like the ironic tone in this young man's voice but for the moment he didn't know how to combat it.

"Always check your metal prices," said Michael in a tone of mock-admonishment, "then you'll never go far wrong." When the Major did not reply, Michael continued: "Of course, I understand you're probably not interested in metal prices. Okay, let's see what the fruit prices are doing. That's more up your street—or should I say, *orchard.*" He smiled.

Major Chalfont lowered his eyes. He sensed something sinister in this jocularity, and had the good sense to keep silent, biding his time, waiting for his wife or someone to come in from the garden.

"No, can't find anything," said Michael, bunching the paper and throwing it on the floor.

Suddenly, the major couldn't stand the youth's words any longer, (holding as they did something of a promise of pain under the guise of fun). "Get out of my house" he snapped. He tried to make it a roar, but the illness had robbed him a long time ago of anything remotely resembling parade ground volume.

"Take it easy, Granddad," said Michael affably. Then, calmly putting his hand into his pocket, he pulled out an apple. The Major glared at it. He didn't speak. He seemed to be trying to, but couldn't. He just continued staring, as Michael, with provocative deliberation, began tossing the apple in the air.

Up to this moment, the Major had been unattached in a sense to his anger. A Teddy boy who couldn't hold his drink? One could forget it. But now he felt a personal affront. This man with the terrible scar on his face had violated his sacred orchard. Gurgling with uncontrolled vexation, he tried to push himself up out of his invalid's chair. But the effort was too much. He flopped back into the fettering shadows, puffing furiously.

"That's it Granddad, you sit down and have a nice little rest for yourself. No sense in getting worked up over an orchard full of maggoty apples." At the mention of the word 'maggot', the Major's eyes started to bulge. "I never knew," continued Michael, pushing himself upright, "that such small apples could have so many maggots in them."

Major Chalfont was by this time practically frothing at the mouth in his efforts to articulate his anger, but the only sound he managed to emit was a sort of gurgling croak.

"I know," said Michael in commiseration, while at the same time examining the apple, "it defies speech."

The Major felt a piercing thrust in the lower part of his back. The tremor travelled all the way up his spine to set his head in motion, so that it began to wobble around on his thin neck like a nodding doll in a toyshop window. Almost sick with rage now, he kept trying to get up from his chair to reach the cord that hung from the wall which would ring the bell in the garden, while Michael, tossing the apple in the air, walked calmly out of the house back into the fresh air.

After the shadowy cool of the room, Michael found the sun's warmth more soothing than before, as he strode through the garden. Isabella's group had grown since he had been gone and had now developed into a regular nature ramble. She seemed very happy strolling up and down, sharing her botanical knowledge with the more sober guests. Conversation with the inebriated was not compulsory—it was justifiable to wave and pass on.

Michael caught up with them at the edge of the orchard where Mrs Chalfont was sprawled in a deckchair, an empty wine bottle beside her, sitting with her face to the sun, eyes closed trustingly. She had discarded her shoes along with her duties and her hostess' tray. And, were she a soldier, her clothes might be judged to be in some disarray. Vaguely she became aware of their presence, and gradually woke to their chattering voices. For a moment she stared with sleepy absent-mindedness at them, she might have been gazing into an evening of her own youth, and as her eyes began to focus she became tormented by a sense of somehow being unfairly trapped. But when she focused fully, she saw that her daughter was smiling sweetly at her, as were the rest of the half-dozen or so people that stood, some bending in an attitude of utmost friendliness and gentle concern. Her daughter Isabella squatted down by the side of the chair, holding her mother's hand delicately as if searching for some diagnosis, forming her words with slow care as if talking to an invalid or a child.

Mrs Chalfont sat poised somewhere between annoyance and embarrassment as she placed an arm across her chest to hide her breasts. To be woken so suddenly had for the moment left her mentally confused. She was tired and sleepy from rushing around in the sun all afternoon. And something was digging into her thigh. She reached down and pulled up an empty wine bottle. For a moment she stared at it, then vacantly threw it, with slight vexation, upon the lawn.

"Another dead soldier," laughed one of the guests and Michael smiled inwardly at the remark.

Although she never drank, Elizabeth Chalfont was familiar with the jargon of the Officers' Mess from the many reunions she'd attended over the years with her husband, and for some reason found herself sharply annoyed by this remark. Then, for the first time, as she felt her drowsiness evaporate, she looked directly at them, understanding for their awkward concern suddenly dawning. She began to laugh, with bell-like glee.

Gradually the guests began to depart, their "goodbyes" and "wonderful party" ringing in the otherwise still evening air. And very soon all that were left were Isabella, Danny, Bridget and Michael, standing around Elizabeth who was still sitting in her deckchair on the edge of the orchard. When, Bridget and Michael's token offer of help was courteously refused, they too made their farewells, and, leaving Danny and Isabella and her mother to clear up the garden, walked towards the gate through the orchard, stopping every now and then whenever Bridget's interest was taken by a flower or a tree.

It was a soothing feeling to walk along the narrow path amongst the mist blue carpet of hyacinths. Under the trees the evening air was still warm with the pleasant scent of flower and fruit. The sun had bred fantasies, and fantasies had lingered on into the evening glow. While Bridget strolled along this path another landscape was unfolding to reveal a whitewashed cottage with her father sitting at the open fire and she sitting by the well with Alan in the soft summer light. There was a baby in this fantasy too. Remembering her husband, she glanced back to smile. Had the path been wider the man and the woman might have walked side by side on this path. As it was not Michael walked behind his aunt who was torn in her thoughts between reality and fantasy. Suddenly as she bent over to peer down at a spot around which foxgloves hung their dappled heads, Michael was captured by the beauty of her bare legs. He had never seen them so exposed. The skin so delicate stressed their shape, while the soft pink crinkled lips of the foxgloves, unconscious of their own vulnerability offered themselves trustingly as, swaying delicately, they brushed the skin on her long white legs.

The light was fading fast now here in the orchard amid the trees, where flickering insects had become obsessed by brooding leaves, when suddenly the sound of bell chimes snapped them both from their respective reveries. One by one the urgent sounds fell leaving hardly sufficient space for each to die away in distant echo before the air was filled again by repetition of the iron knell. Bridget straightened and turned towards Michael.

"Is that the church clock ringing?" she asked.

"Sounds like it," he said.

"That's a queer timepiece—it's not quite six yet and perhaps it gave a dozen peals."

For a moment or two, he stood in silent contemplation.

She was pleasantly disturbed by the abstract, unhurried watchfulness of his blue eyes.

"Maybe it's a Protestant church."

"Oh, is that the reason?" Bridget laughed.

"Could be," shrugged the young man who was her nephew.

"And what would you know about it, eh? Sure, you never go near any church." The lilting jibe lent her speech a rich and vigorous charm.

His expression was guilty but it could also have been pleased.

"Hey! I used to be an altar boy," he cried, "I'm the world's greatest Catholic, in fact I'm rated number one! The Pope himself begged me to come to Rome."

"Really, it took you all your time to come here." Bridget laughed as Michael stood gazing at her silently for a moment, she continued, "wasn't it a lovely party though?"

Michael's jaw tightened. "If you like old soldiers."

"Ah Michael," she sighed as she patted his arm, "I know where the hate comes from."

"You do," he cried, grabbing her quickly round the waist, and in one deft movement, with his free hand supporting her legs, lifted her clear off the ground. She gave a spirited giggle. They looked like a couple of lovers in a Boucher or a Fragonard as he whirled her around and around the rococo ferns and foliage. She felt a quick thrill of fairground fear as he began spinning faster. Bridget was laughing with nervous confusion.

"Aah, now Michael, be careful you don't drop your poor Auntie," she cautioned. But he was spinning on the spot too fast and overwrought to reply. In an awful way, it was funny: with Michael holding her in his arms, tottering on wobbly legs, laughing hysterically. She managed a wan grin, but her face was drawn and strained and she was becoming very dizzy. Michael started gasping for breath. His eyes had turned to blue slits and the scar across his forehead and cheek stood out grey and puckered against his smooth pale skin. They were spinning, spinning then the world tipped as he knocked a clumsy foot against a stump. His legs gave way, and clutching Bridget to him, he toppled backwards to the ground.

She lay for a while in shocked bewilderment, the intense silence almost stopping her breath. Then, lifting herself to a sitting position beside him, she stared down at his motionless body until her senses settled and her heart returned to bearable beating. The dark shape of clouds was changing all the time. She called his name, and when he did not respond, a chill touched her. She leant over, putting a hand on his cheek to try and rouse him, but his body continued to lie sprawled in a shocking stillness.

The emptiness of utter sorrow was slowly beginning to settle in her eyes when suddenly he sprang up. She gave a gasp as he grasped her shoulders and pushed her back onto the ground, smiling at her with playful cruelty. Annoyed that he'd fooled her she started scolding.

"You're pure daft!" she cried as he sat looking down at her, "do you know that, Michael?" She was foolish enough to ask.

"Were you worried about me?" he replied softly. She blushed with honesty but did not answer.

He gazed down at her, captivated by her face, haloed by masses of tawny waves. Her green dress wrapped her limbs tightly, her hips and thighs were rigidly outlined, emphasising the slimness of her waist, while the bodice of the dress seemed strained against her breasts.

It was an intensely physical moment, their two shadows joined upon the ground trembled in one shape. As her nephew looked directly into her eyes, the thin crescent moon seemed so close just above the branches of the trees. Every tree had the light of the moon upon it. Their leaves had become helplessly exposed.

In that moment she might have received a full kiss on the lips. She turned away her mouth. She did almost scream but went instead into a more private mumble to prevent any such indelicacy. A smell of wild bluebells permeated the air which, in a more civilised garden, might have served to redeem.

"Let me up now Michael," she announced, as though it might still be possible to exercise her will. The feminine tones of her despair did not serve to restrain him, but made him if anything more eager to carry out some act of which the gathering gloom still disguised intention and made the mood more difficult to assess. The impression was increased by the privacy of their surroundings. They might have remained there forever, frozen in tableaux if the man had not suddenly been unable to bear his own reflection any longer. The trees which had begun to sense the approach of the intolerable twitched and trembled. Though the mood was still playful the wind was gathering strength. While leaves fluttered others fell, for the wind would not be deprived of its intention. The moon shone brighter. In the moist air the darkness lifted to reveal the pale bare limbs of a tortured tree.

As bones became stretched taut under galvanised flesh, lying on the ground amongst a scattering of dead leaves, brindled by light and shade, everything came back in the orchard where he had first picked the forbidden fruit. Seized again by powerful longings to possess, he gazed at the pale tender skin of her uncovered throat then stiffened suddenly as the cry of someone that has reached the climax of emotion rent the evening air. He felt Bridget tremble, as another agonising scream followed. In its ugly rage of echoes, the church clock began to chime the hour but it was the wrong hour since the clock was broken.

There was a thud of breath and limbs, muffled by leaves and blossom, as the two figures scrambled to their feet in the darkening orchard under the apple trees, in the shadows of the tangled copse, by the little hillock where bluebells lay ravaged by dusk. It was a common problem in this dark place full of breathings, as they tried to disentangle and clamber to their feet at the same time. The man was so full of concern he wouldn't let her reject him so she accepted his help, though not as fully as he wished. The darkness and unevenness of the earth was spilling them against each other, whether they liked it or not. As they silently headed towards possible horrors in other directions, with assumed meekness, the man dropped back and hid his ravisher's hands inside his coat. She began to blush for the shockingness of it all and stumbled as she attempted to run faster in her hobbled dress.

Now the youth was really alone. It was the most frightening accusation of his betrayal. Tormented, he ached to see his vision drawing away from him. Yet even though their breath in unison was being sucked in and out too fast, it would never be allowed to merge in subtler intimacies, as they continued to run or stumble in the direction from which the screams had come.

In their common breathlessness the two figures finally reached the house to find Major Chalfont sitting blocking the doorway in his wheelchair. Regardless of discomfort, his head was thrown right back and his eyes were wide open, to catch a possible intruder or like someone who has just had a surprise: which indeed he had— he'd just died!

"God," exclaimed Bridget, "what happened?" And her nephew, who had come up behind her, shook his head sadly from side to side, thus giving his arrival a moral tone.

Mrs Chalfont stood by the doorway grave and utterly motionless, while her dress of fine fabric, which had become severely gathered in cold pleats around her waist, made the breath tight in her throat.

"The Major," a lump caught in her throat, "my husband is dead." Whereupon Isabella began to cry. Up until that moment she had consoled herself with the thought that her father might just be having one of his fits.

Danny put his arm round her comfortingly as her mother continued: "The wheels of his chair seem to have become wedged in the doorway as he was trying to come outside." Isabella lifted her tear-stained face to look at her mother questioningly. Here Mrs Chalfont's voice seemed to fade and a tear wet her eye. "He must have leant too far back when he rang for assistance." She paused to dab at her eyes as she gazed at the little group who looked back at her with terrible held-in tenderness, though one of them did not appear too concerned at all. Was he grinning at her or was it perhaps illusion produced and heightened by the terrible scar? She trembled slightly with anguished breathlessness. To stoop and hold her husband's lifeless hand was some distraction. Even the wind seemed to have died with appropriate sympathy, but Bridget had become greatly disturbed as she remembered the papers had mentioned that Mr Levy, Old Pop, Michael's boss had been an ex-soldier and he too had died suddenly and now this man, both ex-soldiers in strange circumstances, with Michael in the same place at the same time in both cases! She began pondering on that but all her sinister imaginings dropped away when she suddenly remembered that Michael had been with her and the others in the garden all afternoon?

A great wave of relief washed over her as she looked at Mrs Chalfont and her daughter holding the dead man's hands. Because everything seemed normal and as natural as it could be, but of course it was not and could never be. In the end all that good feeling of forgiveness of his actions towards herself became overlaid with anger, that became also fear as, she remembered with a chill that Michael had at some point left the garden and gone over to the house alone. It turned her blood cold, she began to think in a panic. She could not mention her suspicions to anyone, least of all Alan or, God forbid, Michael might... But that she dared not think about, the horror of it was too much.

Two days later she received an official letter embossed with the Crown's seal and after reading it, found she had been granted her long-awaited meeting with a minister from the Home Office. Though still disturbed by her ordeal at the hands of her nephew, since nothing further had occurred, she began to think that Michael's involvement in the two deaths was somewhat far-fetched. But the memory continued to occur, it rose up into her mind, attached to the dead man's face.

She threw herself into her work, writing to the papers and magazines telling them of the meeting and reminding them of its aims. Some wrote back with promises of support. A group of London University students telephoned; they said they would like to be involved and they would help in seeking new legislation. She met with them at the University.

There were six of them: four men and two young women. She looked at their pallid faces. They seemed to be dressed in clothes that even a rag merchant would have refused. But their eyes had a look of great self-assurance in them; and so they might. Between them they could count in parentage an Admiral, a General, a Scientist, a Bishop and a Lord. For a second or two she thought they might be Irish. But they greeted her, these youngsters, in over elocuted BBC voices. Bridget smiled: this, then, would be her support group—fire fight fire!

They adjourned to a pub near the University. Bridget could not quite remember all their names, so she asked the young man sitting nearest her, wearing a threadbare black polo-neck pullover and blue jeans.

"I'm Hadrian," he smiled. He seemed to be the spokesman for the group, and so she asked him what he thought about their chances of success. "Actori incumbit onus probatio" he cautioned pompously. "Yes of course" replied Bridget "on the plaintive rests the proving but are our proofs strong enough?"

"In instances of this sort," he said, "it seems clear that Time will put a stop to these abuses." His colleagues nodded sagely.

Bridget was beginning to think she had made a mistake in coming to meet these youngsters. There are times when it pays to speak your mind; others when it does not. She asked instead: "But what do you intend to do?"

"We," said Hadrian with his casual air, "will assist Time."

The matter was impersonal to them; third year law students. They were, in military parlance, unblooded; trying to get a new law instituted or an old law repealed would provide something in the nature of battle practice for the furtherance of their careers. It was as simple as that.

That year, Britain experienced one of the coldest winters on record. The building trade came to a standstill as cement froze on the labourers' shovels and plasterers with trowels poised betwixt board and wall saw their mortar fall: rigour had already set in before it hit the floor. The sky was shrouded in grey, the earth was wrapped in white—the trees and shrubs, their edges fringed with snow rime, whipped by icy winds, black whorls of driving sleet swirled and stalked the land. The roar of the wind grew to a scream. The whole country lay at its mercy as it stamped its shivery limbs.

The days were all the same. Light came at eight o'clock. At noon the sky was brightened by a tepid sun, followed by a short, grey, dismal afternoon, which merged some four hours later with sombre twilight before fading into darkest night. Remote and alien, motionless as a lunar landscape, the whole wharf had an eerie silence about it. It seemed a dead place under shackles of ice. A world which had frozen in rejection of all things human.

Yet there was life. Outlined against the white expanse could be seen the dark uniform of the transport police officer and the gaunt, sliding shape of the Alsatian that ambled along the strategically cleared perimeter path by his side. Every so often the young Alsatian stood and gazed about it, seemingly to marvel at the snow in its capacity to change the very face of the world. Then it would lift its muzzle, scenting the wind, before continuing after its handler, its lean sinewy body giving no indication of its lethal strength as it flitted like a shadow over the snow. On the hour, every hour, with precise and regular monotony, unawed and indomitable, the two servants of the crown exhaling white breaths continued their slow prowl around the perimeter fence.

Along with the wharf, snow also coated the mountain in powdery sheets of grey that hardened throughout the night, the metal groaning with cold… In the relative warmth of the day, the snow crept back up the mountain. As the soft scud retreated, its thin seep blotched with brown and streaked with grey trickled over the metal and down the mountain sides to form little rivulets at its base and force its way on life.

In the blink of a sudden sunburst, the glowing sheen seemed almost benign; but the conditions were too treacherous. Even the most daring would baulk at the idea of a midday climb. Yet snow was not the only peril. At any time the mountain could spring a sudden surprise. From its frozen summit, vicious wind blasts hurled down chunks of solid ice—some landing in the salvage pit where Michael worked, absorbed in cutting up old vehicles while waiting for the Spring thaw.

As though the end were nigh, the wind rose during those months to tempestuous proportions. The mountain responded to the boisterous wind in wild tossing, jumping and rattling, an island of iron buffeted under a great isolation of sky. Then gradually there was an almost tangible something in the air, invisible yet felt, a warmth was creeping into the atmosphere. With it came the sound of ice cracking and splintering into crystals, dripping and glittering like a fall of white diamonds. But Michael Docherty was unimpressed by jewellery. In the increasing light as the snow and ice melted away a sense of relaxing came over the whole wharf, of the former frost locked mountain stretching, of life returning, coming back from what had been a stricture. He still laboured like the damned—so much so that when he got home in the evening he could hardly sit up. He would drop into bed and fall fast asleep, while Vicky would lie there beside him, listening to his fitful breathing. Sometimes snuggling up, she would kiss his damaged cheek, for his sleeping form gave a confusing impression, as if it were uttering a prolonged and inaudible sound. As if it were silently screaming. At 7:00 am he would wake. Then his face, grown strange in the night, would become almost familiar again.

THE WOLF PIT

It was coming up for 8:30 on a fine May morning as Michael left the house for work. He was a bit behind today, and he strode out fast. As he came in sight of the lean-to, he noticed someone sitting underneath it in one of the old car seats, and his manner became slightly hostile as he drew near.

"What are you doing here, mate?"

"Just having a little breather, son. The old lungs ain't what they used to be. Caught a gob-full of gas in the first war. Priority job kept me out of the second war, and—God forbid!—I never want to see a third." He took a deep breath and expanded his gas infested lungs.

But his confidence remained immense in resettling his big buttocks on the seat for nothing short of a long stay. The ironmonger grimaced, he was not in a mood for interpreting the subtleties of priority jobs and military exemption.

"Look, Pop," said Michael, searching his pocket for some loose change with which to send him on his way, "I'm sure you've been a very brave man. But I got a lot of work to do. Can't stand around here listening to war stories all day." The stranger's gaze was so fixed upon the mountain he might not have heard, he was trying to fit the pieces together it seemed, wrestling with some problem of perspective. Only when he had completed his calculations was he prepared to acknowledge the existence of another.

"I know how you feel, son." He said at last. 'Some of them old timers' war tales would bore you to death. But I got other stories. One in particular, which I think you'll find very interesting. Course, I'm not sure of all the details yet, but no doubt you'll be able to fill me in."

His tone was slow and measured, as if it were the symbol of some conspiracy between them. Though his voice was gentle and his eyes downcast, Michael Doherty was not altogether convinced, and for the moment was conscious of the narrow space in which they were confined. The narrator's memory was so vivid, it seemed unlikely he would need assistance with its powers of recall. And even if he did the young ironmonger's expression showed he would be unlikely to assist.

Suddenly there was something unpleasant in the air.

"Who are you?" said Michael, coldly. The wharf had not completely thawed.

For a moment or two, the fat man did not reply. There were always considerable advantages in keeping people guessing. So he straightened his tie and cleared his throat, before checking the seams of his leather elbows and the cuffs of his sports coat, but did come to it finally by degrees.

"Just a passer-by, so to speak," he said at length, his voice thick with catarrh or gas. "But one time I used to be in charge of Security round here, back in the days when old Pop was alive." He took a slow drag on his fag. "You must have seen me toddling about." Michael took in the big frame, the large face and head and the process of memory began its work, for somewhere in amongst the ageing flesh—though the eyes were like pinpoints and the smile was fixed—the face of the former Gate Sergeant without the uniform which previously proclaimed his authority began to emerge.

"Course, I've retired now, but as my old lady (God bless her, she died some years back)" He took a fit of coughing that brought tears to his eyes. "As she always used to say: A good copper is never off duty. Funny—I still miss her; but it was best. She was in a lot of pain. Yet the end was remarkably peaceful: fell asleep and never woke up again. Not like old Pop! Terrible business, that. Head crushed like a melon, I heard. Which set me doing a bit of thinking I can tell you."

He reached into his pocket, pulled out a hip-flask, took a good slug, smacked his lips appreciatively, then continued. "And now the business is yours. And somehow two and two don't make four, if you get my drift." In spite of riveted interest, the ironmonger hesitated to encourage more from one who might arrive at it by intuition. Instead his eyes turned to focus on the mountain mesmerically, watching its metallic colours mingling lustrously, glowing brighter with the climb of the sun. Suddenly the whole of its eastern flank kindled into leaping tongues of flame. He averted his gaze. What had at first offered pleasant distraction ended in virulent glare. As the stranger continued to look at him, Michael Docherty took care not to utter a word, fully aware that in such a situation the smallest slip could have disastrous consequences.

"You must excuse me if I sound dramatic," said the fat man, concealing a sly glint of anticipation by lowering his eyes.

"It was all very unlucky," mumbled Michael cautiously.

"Unlucky?" queried the other. "Surely not—no, I'd say you got to be very lucky. Or else you had some plan."

"Plan?" said Michael quietly.

"In a manner of speaking… Of course, there's a word they got for this sort of thing it's called 'premeditated'."

Michael Docherty was silent. His vocabulary did not include the word 'premeditated'. For a moment he turned away in a state of bewildered disbelief. He would have loved to flee but it is difficult to escape from words. Words, especially official ones, pursue.

"Thought out beforehand. They got a Latin name for it, them lawyers, but for the life of me I can't think what it is offhand. But *plan* is simple enough to understand for simple folk like me." He took a drag on his cigarette. "But that's what the courts call it: premeditated. Course, it's better if it don't go to court, because that's a topping offence. Then again, a smart lawyer might get it down to manslaughter, diminished responsibility and all that, but I wouldn't bank on it; and you'd still be looking at a lot of time." He paused, nodding his head sagely up and down as if he might approve. Though exact details had been omitted, he now began to embark more thoughtfully on something of which he certainly could not approve.

"Let's see if I've got this right," he went on, "I made my own little picture of it putting this and that together; an engine block— an inert lump of metal—glides all the way over the top of the mountain, then lines itself up right above the exact spot where old Pop is working, then suddenly just drops." Michael Docherty gazed at him in shock. "I'm trying to envisage it as an accident from a detective's point of view," continued the old cop, "but I'm afraid my imagination doesn't seem to run to it." His hand, which he'd held aloft throughout his narrative to emphasise his tale, now dropped with a resounding smack upon his huge substantial thigh. The fat man had woven his spell.

Michael Docherty, the iron lord, became very still now, as if dimly aware that something almost indecent was required of him.

While his mind scrambled after phrases in exasperation, his face was shadowy and smudged by the sweat and grime that clings to iron. It flickered desperately out of a shimmer of metal. He wrenched his eyes away from the mountain suddenly for fear his thoughts might be reflected in the tin. After the first few moments of hesitation he began to move his tongue over his dry lips. Snatches of sound came from out of his inadequate vocabulary, mercilessly remote.

"So what's your plan then?" He managed to ask with vulgar dignity, after the first shock of discovery had begun to subside.

"Well," said the policeman, with devastating politeness, "I tend not to make too many plans, son. They always seem to have a nasty habit of going astray. Of course, the war changed a lot of things. People's values; points of view; morals... even my own ethics have been stretched from time to time. But always with the best intentions, I might add." His language seemed pompous in the rough and rugged clearing under the shadow of the metal mountain. His politeness had become daunting.

"What you after?" growled Michael tersely.

The newcomer heaved round, beaming with mock enthusiasm.

"Straightforward, no beating about the bush, I like that, I can see we're going to get on well. He settled back in his seat with sinister composure. To answer your question: I need a considerable amount of money in the shortest possible time. Not for myself, I must emphasise." Michael looked at him with make-believe surprise. "I want to erect a monument to the fallen."

"The what?"

"The fallen." His voice became reverent. "Those brave souls that went out to face the panzer, and are now no longer with us. Them that fell in the line." The ironmonger hesitated a moment, disorientated by this fat man with the small eyes and the bulbous maroon veined nose, who in no way resembled an erector of monuments or even memorial plaques, but whose proposal despite the unusual way it was phrased, was very clear.

The man climbed slowly to his feet. "Mind if I use your lavvy for a minute?" he said, walking over, opening the door and stepping inside without bothering to close the door behind him. After relieving himself, he pulled the flush turned and came out. "Got all the mod cons over here now," he said as he walked back to his chair. "You see," he continued, settling back, pulling the hip-flask from his inside pocket again and taking a good long swig, "I cherish the eternal values such as honour, bravery, and of course, loyalty to the Crown."

Michael Docherty's hammer lay where he had left it, on top of an empty oil drum a foot or two away from the cutting machine. He could see it from the corner of his eye as he stood, gazing at the ex-copper with hidden fury. The hammer was an extension of his hands, he was accurate to the point of splitting a hair with a blow from it with either hand. He turned. There it was in front of him. He was aware of the size of the gamble, the stakes he was risking, and he knew he was not strong enough to pick up the hammer and murder the policeman. And he despised himself for his weakness.

"Sorry about this," quipped the intruder as he returned once again to the lavatory.

The salvage pit had become very quiet as the ironmonger gazed at the black escarpment where the raw wounds of wreckage, harsh chunks of iron, bashed crooked, jutted at improbable angles from its flanks. A slight breeze began to play over its sterile surface as the man came back out of the lavatory. Michael Docherty looked away as the anger and frustration hibernating within him began to thicken his blood, while the fat man, advancing with his stiff-hipped waddle, returned to the conversation and spoke as if something had been agreed between them.

"So I'll need half the takings to fulfil my obligations to the fallen. I'll collect every Friday and don't worry too much about keeping records of earnings for me, I'll check at the weigh-bridge to see how much metal goes in and out." He smiled, but Michael felt no inclination to return it, although there was a perverse comfort in his demands—it bore out what he thought of the police.

"Whatever the actual turnover turns out to be," continued the copper settling down in his seat and gazing slowly around, as a sudden sunburst lit up the salvage pit, gilding the scrap around the lean-to with a bright metallic sheen, and bronze dust hung trapped in a column of light (it had reached that time of day when the sun deceives with gold).

"I'm sure we can force out of this place a higher yield." The policeman predicted as he began to rise ponderously once more. "But we mustn't try and take on too much at once though. Well, that's what my doctor keeps telling me. So I'll just use your privy again—slaughtered with the old prostate, pissing all the time." He remained grumbling a while about the situation but finally, by a massive, creaking manoeuvre got himself to his feet. The younger man watched silently—not that he didn't have anything to say, he'd just lost the will to say it.

But he was still the Farrier, drugged with the music of metal. When he held the fiery rod against cold iron, flame leaped sparks flew, the air around the metal trembled. Yet, he walked, later that day over areas of concealed wealth, head down as if in fear of secret thorns, while in the early evening light the sun declined and dusk weaved its pale patterns on the night's edge. In the high bright moon, tilted, slanting naked girders, down, sunk, submerged deep in the mountain's unfathomed depths grasping at the wind, succeeded only in tightening the hug that bound them.

The light steadied itself, held onto surfaces, then wavered delicately, altering its patterns, slashing reflections out of the mirroring metal. The man squinting in the general bedazzlement of the iron landscape continued to climb precariously towards a line of burnt out shards strung out along the mountain's ridge. Invariably he would turn dizzy if he stared too long upwards at its scintillating crown. An old bedstead, its ruptured springs hanging in rusty coils, their jagged edges setting traps for clothes and flesh, lay strewn before him. He picked his way carefully around it, pausing to survey the surrealistic scene. All that region of iron and steel belonged to him. He went on over his peculiar territory, clambering over the savage iron rocks every so often hitting with the bowl of his hammer some object, just to experience its reassuring ching. Long strands of barbed wire draped this part of the mountain, their tendrils criss-crossing whole sections like iron veins that transfigured the metal so that the rust glinting scabbily in the glaring moonlight looked like blood-brown leprous flakes. It was an alien world of grey destruction and yet there were many treasures concealed below its austere surface.

He picked his way between the heaps of blue metal, acid green where dripping car batteries had over decades eaten into its iron core, forming dark brooding pools of sump oil below.

Always looking for pleasing shapes, he would often try where the mountain had cut across the evening, to escape, by hiding behind objects of beauty. Perhaps drowning in a burst of lingering yellow sunset, listening to the sound of metal swaying gently, jingling and tinkling in a soft and friendly breeze.

As the evening grew darker, day died away on the mountain's towering summit leaving only thin pale fingers of light lingering on its slopes to reflect its diminishing freedom.

He stopped finally beside an old lorry cab where a spider web hung rigged by silver threads to its shattered wing mirror. Easing himself onto the front seat, he sat concealed, watching, while he waited, the wind worrying a loose sheet of bright tin so that it twisted and turned, illuminating a small patch of shadow among the anonymous tonnage of metal. In the warm darkness the mountainside seemed flecked with crisp white snowflakes that sparkled and glittered. Those motes of light suddenly seethed alive with flickering wings as thousands of moths rose above the warm metal in the purple splendour of the spring evening.

But there were moments of laceration when the metal dug into the flesh and the sun was in his eyes as he felt his way around the mountain's simple shapes, while the hammer rang with the peal of an untuned bell. He was trying to remember his first glimpse of the mountain when even the greenish glimmer from the luminous dial of the speedometer on a half submerged wreck, or a last white flash of reflected sunlight from an old wing mirror at sunset filled him with joy but now confusion blurred his vision.

He would have done something destructive but because he was unsure what he owned he did not dare. The waning light had magnified the objects on which it lingered without belittling or destroying into separate forms. But now the objects had become lumber it was doubtful whether identity would ever be restored and in the end even iron will crumble. As the darkness lapped around his ankles he listened warily to the tinkling of the insubstantial metal, haunted by a face that would return—not to accuse but to command.

The following Friday, Michael sent Dermot out scouring the mountainside for old car bodies and engine blocks, in fact any large heavy pieces he could find to throw down, while he himself took over the job of shredding them up in the lean-to far below, working as he waited for the ex-cop to call.

All the previous week his mind had been in turmoil— tormented by visions of the ex-cop's face. It appeared before his inner eye, sly and gloating: the small, dark immobile eyes peering out from between yellowed folds of crinkled flesh.

He looked up at the sky. He could hear the screeching of metal as Dermot, somewhere up above, levered an engine block or some such towards the edge. The light was tentative as he stood there contemplating the mountain. With only the merest light, the molten core had begun to glow. All around him was the sound of creaking and straining. The mountain was preparing, reshaping itself. Once it rose so high the sun turned it into a burning blob. In this state, although shrunk to the size of a pinhead, the whole universe seemed contained within it, until cooled by its descent, it began to expand, to reform once more into its original form. Balanced between elation and dread, the hammer became an extension of himself. It wouldn't be discarded. He stood among the opposing influences trying to recapture the sense of ownership, until the intense heat suddenly struck him full in the face, singeing his hair which was billowing in waves of corrugated bronze. The stench shot up his nostrils, feeding the anxiety already latent in him. The day was full of doubt.

He went back into the lean-to. A car bonnet lay across the table of the guillotine. He could just make out his distorted reflection in the enamelled paint. He struck it with tremendous force, he heard the scream of metal as the sparks flew from its pulverised sides he struck and struck until he was arrested by a voice.

"Nice day for it, son."

Michael Docherty's thoughts were jerked back to the present. He looked up to see the old cop standing outside the lean-to, smiling his old cop smile. And he was not alone. A large black German Shepherd stood alert and watchful by his side.

Michael turned. He did not want the cop to come in under the lean-to, and so stood blocking the entrance, the hammer still clutched tightly in his hand. The dog looked up. There was the slightest possible stiffening of its body as it fixed its baleful gaze on Michael Docherty: and Michael stared back. The cop gave a humourless chuckle.

"Bit big for a bitch, ain't she?" he said, ruffling the dog's mane with his fist. "Still, she's got the gate dog on the pant—been following us around the wharf. So I want to get off quick as poss."

Michael put the hammer down, took up an old rag and began leisurely to wipe the grease from his hands. The cop pulled out his hip flask and took a quick hit.

"Things ain't been too hot this week," said Michael, finishing off his manicure and throwing the rag onto the ground.

The cop replaced his hip flask in his pocket. He took a few seconds to reply.

"Yeah, I know," he drawled, "but like I said, this place has got potential for a higher yield. So let's hope it picks up soon, eh?"

The veiled threat was not lost on Michael. He gave a bleak grin. "Take a cheque?"

"Afraid not", smiled the old cop, with wary tolerance. "We'll transact all our financial affairs in cash."

With the cop standing outside, Michael took his time counting the notes into an old envelope while the cop continued to stare at the golden walls of metal. After Michael had finished counting he leaned out and offered the envelope to the policeman, to satisfy an agreement he was unable to avoid.

"Count it if you like." His eyelids might have been covered by metal scales.

"God love and bless us all, I trust you," replied the other warily, and, putting the envelope in his pocket, continued: "Keep an eye on Bess here for me while I have a quick pee."

Once inside the place where his sad bladder had dragged him, the cop pulled out the envelope and checked his loot. Satisfied, he replaced it in his pocket, took another hit from his flask, and begun unbuttoning his fly. He congratulated himself. His eyes were sharper than a fox. He had the knack of seeing crime before it was committed. He'd not liked the cut of that young fellow either, and, alerted by old instinct, he had brought along the dog. If that same finely tuned instinct had failed to spot that his new business partner was also beyond alliances...Well, his prostate was playing him up.

For fully half a minute he couldn't piss and he horrified himself by suspecting impotence also. The lines in his forehead gave evidence of the intensity of his efforts. Uncomfortable and awkward, it produced some of his worst moments, while impatience almost frustrated his attempts. But now, at last he felt sure that something was moving despite all previous deceitful overtures. He lifted his head, parting his lips to smile, it was a vague, private sort of smile, his heavy breathing indicative of approaching orgasm rather than a penis searching for a focus point above a chipped toilet bowl. There was a distilled smell like the smell of old engine blocks that have lain to long in the sun followed by the anxious trickle. Then, such relief as he experienced the flow! Such a thick flow he noticed grossly standing, the arcing urine accentuating his vulgar abandon, flinging the water high in a great spout then the lightning leaped as his veins filled with fire, two hundred volts of raw electricity shot from the toilet bowl, using his urine as a conductor to race all the way up through his penis to his spine. Mercifully he was scarcely conscious of what in ordinary circumstances would have struck him as extreme pain. This fact which might ease the conscience of a murderer did not concern him though. He was dead before he hit the floor.

Although there had been hardly any sound, Michael Docherty knew he would have to be quick as he picked up a pair of insulated pliers from the bench, and, clutching the hammer in his other hand stepped out of the lean-to and walked towards the lavatory. But before he had covered a couple of feet, the dog began to growl menacingly. She knew that something awful had happened to her master, and every so often she lowered her muzzle to snuffle the man's face.

Michael edged forward cautiously. The dog smelt fear, but it was not so much fear of the dog that gripped Michael. He was gripped by something else, something more dreadful: he must get into the lavatory to disconnect the live wire from the toilet bowl at all cost. But the dog did not know this: all she knew was that she must protect her master who was lying helpless on the ground.

After a few false starts, Michael switched tactics and began to circle the dog, trying to get behind her. The dog's eyes followed him, but the beast did not move. If only he had a piece of meat—anything with which to distract the dog's attention. The need for haste weighed heavily upon him, and as he looked into the dog's eyes, he knew one simple fact: he would have to kill this animal quick. He turned and went back to the lean-to, and taking the lid off the dustbin, walked back over, hammer in hand, to face the dog.

He walked straight at the dog, who had never ceased to fix him with her eyes, veering neither to his left nor to his right, holding his makeshift shield in such a way as to ward off any frontal attack. The dog, realising that she could not get at the man through the dense object that had suddenly sprouted on his body, backed off, lips curled, snarling with hate. Michael stepped over the dead body into the toilet, and, placing the dustbin lid against the wall began to disconnect the live wire from its lethal and incriminating position behind the cistern. After he had done this, he replaced the bulb in its socket, gave one last look round, picked up his shield and went to step out.

But the dog had repositioned itself right outside the door of the lavatory; and because of the narrowness of the doorway, Michael realised he would have to come out sideways, since the dustbin-lid was too wide. He hesitated. His side would be exposed, and somehow he felt the dog knew this. It stood, slightly crouched, growling, every fibre in its body bristling with hate, preparing to launch itself at the man as soon as he stepped out from the protective cover of the doorway. There was also the additional complication of the dead body, lying immediately outside on the ground. At all costs, he must not trip…

But in the interval between seeing and doing he suddenly realised he was safe. He was safe from detection now—with the electric wiring replaced correctly, he could afford to sit it out until someone came along; then they could call for assistance. It would be easy to explain a murder without blood. He heard the man fall, he'd gone to see what was wrong, and the faithful animal had taken offence. He began to smile at his own acquittal. There was nothing to do but sit and wait.

And as the mountain grew scales over its solid flanks sunlight soaked the metal without warming it, he suddenly remembered something. In all the confusion of the morning's events, he'd completely forgotten the money he had just given the copper it would be in his pocket along with the envelope on which he had made rough calculations that could be incriminating.

As he was pondering on this, the big Alsatian bitch suddenly sat back on her haunches, her ruff expanding until it became a huge amber aura, framing her face. Her body stiffened until she seemed to be made out of black shining steel, then she threw back her head and howled the burden of her plaint at the sky. The wolf had wakened and was calling its mate to its aid. There was something disturbing about that sound. He took a deep breath. Then gripping the hammer tightly, he struck. With frightful daring, he threw the dustbin lid at the dog's head and sprang over the dead body into the open—while the dog, snarling furiously, leaped to one side to avoid being hit.

Michael was standing where he'd landed, calculating the odds of the bitch springing at him if he chanced bending down to pick up his shield, (now decorated with ochre of mud and grime) when he heard a sound coming from the direction of the mountain behind him. He turned his head glancing at the high dark skyline towards the threatening ridge which reared its head in sudden menace to see he was now confronted with an additional and possibly greater threat. It had come silently on soft pads as was its nature, like a shadow, a dark shadow from which all the ferocity in the world seemed to be glinting from its eyes; he was almost transfixed by the fearful gaze of the gate dog; and in that distracted moment the bitch, whom he had forgotten for an instant, sprang at his throat, missed, grabbed an arm with her teeth and started to drag him down.

But an arm is not a throat. With incredible agility, Michael spun round, catching the dog under its muzzle with a flying kick. The pain and shock caused the animal to release her hold for a moment, and in that moment, with a speed that gave no warning, Michael brought the hammer down on her head, shattering the skull with the force of the blow. The bitch's legs buckled beneath her as she fell to the floor.

The gate dog, furious with rage at the man for attacking its mate, had already begun its leap, and only the fact that at the same time Michael stooped for his shield, prevented the dog from sinking its teeth into his neck. Failing to connect, the dog's own momentum hurled it over Michael's head, and it came to land on its feet a couple of yards in front of him. Almost immediately it turned and sprung into a crouching stance, the hair along the ridge of its back rising in fearful spikes.

Michael stood panting for breath, soaked with sweat, the blood running from his damaged arm; but he felt quite calm. It was good at last to confront the source of his unease. Now there were no nameless fears lurking behind him: there was only a clear-cut enemy in front. He found himself surprised at the terrible beauty of the dog's face and head, its thick, wolf-like coat, its black and tan belly. He made a feint with his shield at the dominant muzzle, but unlike the bitch, this dog did not blanch. He was faced with a more determined animal now.

He could not hear any noise; there were no familiar sounds of metal scraping against metal coming from the mountaintop. The arm of the crane swung out over the lean-to like a gallows, the monotonous rattle of its machinations silent now as its rippling chain dangled idly form its jib. He realised that Dermot must have gone to dinner. Everybody was elsewhere. He felt very weak. He seemed to have been abandoned even by his shadow. He tried returning to the protection of the lavatory, but the dog would not allow it. He saw how it circled the pit as the dust danced in the sun between them, blocking his way whenever he tried. Even if the dog was unaware, the wolf in it was performing some instinctive ritual. It was stalking him relentlessly. It was a different animal now from the one that had slunk furtively into the clearing ten minutes ago looking for the bitch. It was slyer, keener, more deadly. It had been given the opportunity to rehearse. The dog knew now that it was fighting for its life. In the late afternoon, the metals at the top of the mountain revealed a curious brightness like clusters of glittering coral, but below them some trick of the light, of perhaps reflection caused the metal to appear from a distance even brighter, almost to the point of illumination with garish splendour like torches round an arena.

Kept constantly on the alert by the circumstances of his situation, the reluctant gladiator watched the dog's eyes, looking for some clue as to when or how it would attack, and he realised he could not continue indefinitely to keep his concentration at this level of tension. He was panting heavily now he could feel the sweat running down his face the taste of it on his tongue made him purse his lips and spit. He was losing blood rapidly. He looked hopefully toward the lavatory. Should he chance one last mad dash? Suddenly it seemed so far away, and with sickening clarity he realised it was too late now: he would never reach its protective walls again. This thought induced a touch of despair. The dog sensed this: and, interpreting it as fear sprang at him so fast that the man did not even have time to lift an arm. He tried to pull away from the whirling bundle of fury, but the dog was all over him, snapping and snarling. He brought up a hand to protect his face, and felt the animal's teeth sinking into his shoulder. It felt as if a million white-hot needles were piercing the bone. Their awful struggle had produced a vast scattering of dust. He had the dog by the scruff of the neck now, trying to strangle it, but he was far too weak to achieve anything, other than to grip its neck in an effort to keep its teeth away from his throat. The dog was all rib and muscle. They were locked in a terrible bond. He could smell the foetid breath on his face as the dog brought its back legs up, nearly disembowelling him with its claws as it fought for a hold. Suddenly the weight of the beast, coupled with the delayed momentum of the impact of its lunge, whipped him back on his heels, causing him to fall against a heap of metal that fringed the salvage pit. In the shadow of his non-alertness the mountain had taken on an ugly shape. Time had mapped the mountain with several fatal flaws so that his encounter was as shocking as it was unexpected. He let out a gasp, which did not betray sufficiently the violence of his affliction as an iron railing pierced his back, the spike forced its way through his body.

He collapsed to a sitting position, stiff with shock at the terrible sight of it, staring in horrible fascination at the point sticking out from his chest. The dog sprung free the moment he fell but now scented something peculiar. Eyes focusing purposefully on what it appeared to have discovered. It leaped back at him with opportunist savagery as he lay impaled, unshielded by ruse, doorway, dustbin-lid or hammer. For an agonising instant the man's mind refused to function, then with his heart pounding in his chest he gave the dog his damaged arm, prompting more eagerly the juices of its festering appetite, ignoring the pain as it sunk its teeth into his flesh, while with his other hand he pulled from his pocket the electrical pliers and during the gruesome communion, as the pain began to rise in terrifying spasms pushed them through a metal ring on the dog's collar, noticing as he did so the Government Crest embossed on the name tag. He smiled with sour contempt and began twisting the chain collar tight with a cold, still wrath. For a little, only the sound of panted breathing could be heard within that fatal circle, as the dog slavered and gulped its mouth foaming with blood apparently unaware of the annoying nagging pressure round its neck. And not until it had become terrible as a vice did the beast reluctantly let go its grip on the hot veined piece of flesh and bone it was savagely enjoying, so as to shake itself free. But this was not such an easy thing to do now, since along with the discomfort, the pressure on its throat was choking it. Suddenly, the dog's eyes began to roll. It tried to make sounds, but could not, with the torture of death in its throat. The man did not raise his eyes during the awful tearing and rending but kept up the steady pressure, twisting the pliers with terrible finality. After a long, last, final embrace from its iron collar the dog's body went limp, gulping uglily its purple tongue lolled out from the side of its mouth, its eyes suddenly closed, and then it collapsed over him. Before the dust of secrecy had time to settle, a breeze, strengthening into a marauding wind: began to prowl among the metal, causing the mountain to tremble at the light of its own reflections.

Michael looked for a long moment at the dog who had scented death. One of its hind legs was quivering, the pliers still dangling from its metal collar above the desecrated crown. He moved beyond its dying body to that of the dead police officer, where flies were beginning to circle—a dark halo above his head.

The sun descending above the metal mountain was streaking the sky crimson in long, jagged lines. The ground around him was smudged scarlet and veined purple here and there by rivulets of oil and stagnant water. He looked at his mutilated arm which the dog had just failed to swallow down. Then his gaze focused on the terrible spike in his chest. It doesn't take much time to become a cripple and even less to die; even when life is worth nothing, we still cling to it. Knowing his own life was being measured in seconds, he saw what a depth he had plunged to in seeking permanence where it cannot be found, so he began to climb once again up the mountain to the sun, while the hammer chimed and sang and chased itself in echoes round the acreage of metal. Everything was respected but ultimately nothing mattered, forms are born to die. Long beams of sunlight slanted across the degraded metal in a bright and honest light while the world swam before his eyes in a clammy mist. As the circles of pain began to widen, the mountain shrugged and stiffened its iron shoulders. He would have liked to get up now and walk away from all this and seemed to be going to try.

He lifted his head up as the pain tore through him, while insects rose in a lazy hum, breathing hard as the blood bubbling up in his throat suddenly spumed out from between his clenched lips. At a spot beneath a piece of tin where shadows roosted he looked up at the mountain it had been his intention to conquer. He pulled what looked like a piece of bracken from his pocket; his head drooped forward onto his chest; his fingers relaxed and a sprig of milfoil or what Isabella Chalfont called yarrow fell from his fist.

After a while the shadows started to emerge from beneath their cold canopy and began hopping and fluttering from ridge to ridge, evidently intent on investigating what could turn out to be a ready feast. The four corpses would certainly make a substantial meal but the crows hesitated; they would have preferred their carrion leaner—faster rotting. Too long a wait would thin them out. They rattled their strong wings irritably for the discovery before becoming expectant, their blue forms rapt once more as if cast in lead.

A QUESTION FOR THE HOUSE

Bridget's feeling of disappointment was so painful that it made her feel weak. She could not imagine why others had failed to show up. She looked at her watch. The meeting was scheduled for three o'clock. It was now five-to. This came as some kind of relief to her, she could only be strengthened by encouragement as she stood upright and alone amidst the visitors and tourists. But no one would share in her moment of faith, 'what is this equality that she's after'? They said, 'It is not possible.' So she continued to wait. Big Ben began to strike the hour. The crowds looked up; all the faces were expectant, hearing in its chimes a sequence of positive future changes.

Then the woman began to walk forward rather stern but graceful in her sensible shoes to meet those who had the power to bring such changes about, while the chimes continued to echo, vibrating with her own convictions to mark the stages in her progress, clearing away all superficial doubt, so that her being became peaceful.

Within the huge porch of the House of Commons she was confronted by a very tall Police Sergeant who gave her a cursory glance that covered her from top to toe, and after checking that her credentials were in order, signalled for an usher to escort her to a waiting room. "If you would wait in here, Madam," said the lackey, "someone will call you soon."

Bridget entered an antechamber and heard the door close behind her. For the first time since she got the letter granting her an interview with the minister, she felt nervous. Little by little she had carried the battle into the enemy camp. Now she was here. She made herself sit down slowly. She began to look at the tapestries on the walls of that room at which on entering she had only glanced, where light was falling on those scenes, its dust-filled rays were roving across villages and battlefields of medieval times. Yet that same light that splintered on contact with serf and vassal seemed to blaze against the painted nobles so that they shone with colour, became almost animated by it to convince, it seemed, with glittering pageantry all they had done in the worlds that they had conquered. Indeed the whole room exuded an importance which refused to be renounced. Most people resisted the tapestries' shadowy extravagances but were absorbed into its mysteries by a sense of respect. But Bridget Marshall did not accept their ostentatiousness, for she saw that the monks in those scenes might have achieved a permanence which the warriors' showy postures could not dissolve, since their hard yet humble faces told of conquests other than those brought about by the sword, and then she was strangely comforted and in her solitude she offered up a prayer.

Before she'd finished she heard footsteps; the footsteps halted outside. She rose slowly to her feet as the usher opened the door. He stared at her impersonally. "When you're ready, Mrs Marshall, the Home Secretary's aide Mr Asp will see you now." He escorted her down a stone-flagged hallway.

They walked in a straight line of silence all the way along that massive corridor, where the historical relics of a thousand years of empire were authentically preserved. Rigid, leathery and masculine. It was impossible to ignore the austere splendour.

At the far end of the hallway, they stopped. The usher showed Bridget into a room. It was high-ceilinged with dark, mahogany panelling and floor-to-ceiling paintings mounted in ornate gilded frames, which depicted English monarchs surrounded by determined looking nobles on beautiful horses of bold and spirited mien. But centre place on this billboard of glory, right behind the Home Secretary's aide's head, was reserved for Oliver Cromwell, who seemed to stare down at Bridget in frozen, puritanical dread. She might have regretted her impulsiveness now but had to continue since the judge had already taken his place.

Mr Asp was seated behind a large desk. The immediate impression he gave was of a fair and freckled University student who occasionally indulged in mild campus parties though nothing could be further from the truth. In later years he would be ennobled to Lord of the Realm by her Majesty the Queen for his severity and single mindedness in carrying out her laws—often at the cost of justice.

Though convention might not have approved, the woman smiled as she offered her hand.

Mr Asp rose briefly from his chair but only to frown formally before sinking back into it without a word, whether innocently or to indicate his disapproval would never be that clear.

She stood before the table awkwardly until the usher after first handing a folder to his boss, indicated for her to sit on a chair to the side.

"Mrs Marshall's file, sir," he said. Then he stood back respectfully as Mr Asp opened the folder. The ministerial aide coughed slightly or laughed; whatever the sound, it seemed to have been dragged up from the depths of his lungs, it might have destroyed whatever intimacy there was in that room. The woman, though, seemed unaware of anything but her own calculations. As she began her count, eight hundred years meant nothing, worse hatreds had been solved, it is the next moment which might bring the thing right. So she was hopeful, though her eagerness could have destroyed her respect for convention, leaning, as she was, right over the table so as not to miss any details.

Her gesture had been spontaneous but misgivings set in as she strained to watch the Home Office man scanning her folder. Though his expression neither denied nor reassured, there was a cold and formidable formality about him as he flicked through the pages. She heard the leaves protest. The sound hung above the table. Their fanned echo, once set in motion, had its own inevitable momentum and she knew that she would fear this freckled man and be included in his contempt for documents.

Suddenly the Home Secretary's aide spoke, or rather it was more of a mumble. Mr Asp hardly ever raised his voice; you leaned forward in your seat, you strained to listen. No one dared ask him to repeat a word, and when the Home Secretary's aide talked so low, who could raise their voice? Yet surprisingly enough, Bridget had got back some of her courage and she said now: "Sorry, sir, I did not quite catch that."

There was a wariness in Mr Asp's eyes as he looked up at her. Bridget noticed it instantly and the Home Secretary's aide seemed to stiffen when he realised he was being observed. By this woman whose impropriety bordered on the ludicrous, crying for a handful of Micks, barbarous descendents of the Northern heathen.

The idea, the very notion that he, as the representative of her majesty's imperial government was going to be held responsible for the past (a past which this woman's countrymen had made into a cult) began to fester in him, doubt took possession of the room as he glanced at her green eyes. Everything in Ireland was too green.

"It's the curse of immigration," he said, tapping the folder with a finger. "One really never knows for sure whether the evidence put forward is factual, hearsay or just plain imagination." Again there was only the sound of the ticking clock in the room as they continued to sit close yet so far apart on the terrible formal furniture. She lowered her head to hide a frown that might give her away too soon. She had been wrong to come here, she could see that now but continued anyway

"Only the wilfully blind could say a thing like that" replied the embarrassed woman. The smell of blood in the room had made her bold. For a brief moment the politician's features were obscured by a segment of shadow.

It certainly was not easy to focus clearly in that room, darkened by so much mahogany panelling to daunt the sparse light.

Mr Asp, who had never been known to lose his temper, replied calmly: "Sorry, I did not quite catch that."

But Bridget did not repeat herself for him. Instead she continued: "Most of the youth of Europe were sent to fight against Germany for classifying other races as inferior. Many of those young people lost their lives in that cause. And yet here in England you allow the Irish and Blacks to be classed with animals—dogs and pigs, to be exact sir. How do you justify the equation?" the thoughtful emissary dared to ask.

"The question is certainly unfortunate," replied Mr Asp. His honest English face gave no clue to his frame of mind.

"And so?" said Bridget. There was a kind of accusation in that. The furniture solid with righteousness stiffened, the drapes hung rigid at their rings.

Mr Asp eyed her bleakly, "...and so, in the absence of concrete evidence, I am hopeful that without any action on our part the points of view of all concerned will be mutually understood and respected, indeed we would do wrong to interfere in what amounts to a process of natural selection." The woman was incredulous. Even the man did not appear to believe completely in what he'd said, so he pushed the file to the side of the desk, signalling that the interview was over.

A paralysing silence had descended on the room. Bridget looked hard at Mr Asp, sitting there amid those pictures and symbols of conquest, searching for the correct words. But, when her mouth would not take the shape that was intended, she quickly realised that no words could express what she felt. In the muted atmosphere she stood up and slowly, shook back her hair, its heavy sweep shot through with bronze and copper weaving, glittered lustrously in the darkening gloom. Then, back straight, slim attractive shoulders stoically squared, Bridget Marshall turned, since there was no cause for her remaining and went from the room and from that house of stern conflicting statements.

THE WAKE

Michael's funeral was a quiet affair. Everybody spoke in undertones and had an ashen face. On a day of sudden showers that had in them a vicious bite of sleet, the cortège left the wharf, passing under the shadow of the iron escarpment. As the procession approached the main gate, a cold sun sailed across a clear gap in the sky, illuminating the mountain and lighting up the quagmire of churned, oily earth around the salvage pit, which an exceptionally frosty night had dried into a hard, muddy scab. Constable Roberts stood with his dog just inside the locked main gates, a tall erect figure with clear open features, who, although with just six months service, was tireless and conscientious in the performance of his duties. The weather, for example, was a matter of complete indifference to him and even if the freezing wind which was blowing across the wharf were to have started hurling chunks of metal down, he would not have batted an eyelid. As for turning away: it was unthinkable. He was a London lad born and bred whose parents had brought him up decently and honestly. But there had been some strange tales circulating around the canteen about the deceased ever since the tragedy had happened. And though he would not be led astray by canteen gossip if he could help it, he had some doubts about what his correct responses should be.

(Some of these strange tales had of course already been discussed amongst the mourners. Michael's parents were silent and would not discuss the matter at all, remembering the weakness of flesh, the hardness of iron and the stealth of wolves.)

He could see the faces of the mourners now looking towards him from the car windows, all dressed in ritual black, faces smeared by rain and tears. As the cortège drew nearer, his natural instinct was to remove his helmet or at least give a salute. He didn't want to appear disrespectful yet he did not want to be disloyal to his own comrades either. As he was pondering thus, thunder, almost deafening in its drum-roll, reverberated throughout the sky. Released from his quandary the upright young copper stepped smartly back into the protection of his office. The wind dropped and for one strange moment everything seemed stilled. Suddenly with a piercing crack a flash of white sheet lightning rent the air. The wind rose now to terrifying heights and with nothing to protect it from the wind's long, savage lick, the mountain swayed, pitching slantwise under a blue black sky. Pulling and tugging at its iron roots, the wind buffeted the metal so hard that sounds sang out around the wharf with strange whining, twanging echoes. Sounds like that of many children crying or perhaps the sharpening of the swords of war.

When Bridget heard about the third man's death in mystifying circumstances she'd felt compelled to confess her suspicions but the priest had absolved her from a mystery that did not convince. She looked at the other mourners in the car, each wrapped in their own mystery, mumbling prayers through respectable lips and a tear wet her eye. She remembered her nephew as he lay in the coffin, a young man with his eyes closed who had once walked with her through hostile streets looking for a room. Since there was no need to express shame in the face of death she looked down in the agreeable silence and saw that his still body was regretting anything that might have occurred.

Indeed what had? Just an untidy scrambling, a confusion of limbs in a clearing amongst twigs.

She would never voice her suspicions now, indeed what use would it be? Seán Docherty might revel in the fact and think Michael worthy of a ballad. But the knowledge would probably destroy his poor mother Mary Jane.

The sky continued to erupt with lightning and in the high bright flashes was revealed a dazzling kaleidoscope of shimmering colour. As the rain splashed on its sterile surface the hearse slid onto the weigh bridge. There was some mild consternation in the hollow minutes of the pouring morning over this unexpected detour but the widow's grief-torn face became livid at what she considered a most disrespectful disruption. And now the old woman—his mother—began to cry, but all emotion was unconvincing, for as Michael could have told them were he still alive, no laden vehicle may leave a government wharf by order of the Crown without first being checked and weighed.

Danny sold the lorry and gave the proceeds to Vicky to help towards the cost of Michael's funeral. Later he heard that Isabella Chalfont, who began to evade Danny, had got engaged to someone of her own class. And Dermot took up once more where he'd left off his former apprenticeship.

Mary Jane often sits quietly trying to recall the Priest's comments at the graveside. In his sermon he had mentioned a place of great Evil; or had he said "We are surrounded by great Evil?" …Or there again, "We are in the midst of great Evil?" She could not quite remember, but if there was so much evil about, she felt certain that many people had helped to spawn it.

But Seán is convinced the Priest was speaking in tongues. He has this recurring nightmare that the Evil he mentioned is soon to come. Its perpetrator: the British Government. He has nightmares where whole families of innocent Irish people—men, women and children—are imprisoned for life, and often for many lives. But hardly anyone took any notice of his ramblings. He had always been a weak man terrified that blame would be laid at his door. So he continued to express his timid life in shouts.

Yet these sinister prophesies do disturb Alan, since he can no longer classify such utterances as complete heresies; but Bridget tries to ignore them. Those possibilities don't bear thinking about; her worries are for the moment more immediate. Vicky, since Michael's death, has started acting strangely. It is not quite six o'clock, yet already Vicky has commenced her nightly vigil by the bedroom window. Through the glass, the metal mountain is revealed curiously flickering pale purple in the moonlight. Some nights when there is no moon, it appears pure black: every fissure and protuberance distinctly carved as if in solid permanence. She has settled her Grandmother down for the night, and though the old woman seems like she might go on forever, she is fading fast.

The engineers have been relocated to another wharf, and now, when Gran has gone, there will be no one left but herself. Alone, she will watch the winter light fade quickly out, and—listening for the hammer's ching as darkness falls—she will try to see his face amongst the flitting shadows. For in the mind, her tin God still roves on darkest nights on this impossible pagan altar. But the old woman could have seen more. Vicky would be surprised to know that Gran keeps night vigils also; only when her ears hear the sound of the hammer's ching, her eyes gaze far above the metal mountain where shadows neither help nor hinder.

In another bedroom in another house moonlight shone gently over the pale forms of a couple lying on the bed. They had held each other tight in love's embrace and despite the earlier sensual joy, Alan had casually wandered into a small gloom. He imagined it had come from being at the funeral, which it had, though some emotions have no respect for time or place. His mouth trembled; it was too intimate, physical and perhaps far-fetched to express for one who made inventories on the backs of bills of lading and did slow calculations in his head. For he had also pondered deeply, questions about his nephew (whose eyes, were shy of mirrors, though he was reflected in other people's eyes all the time) and was both surprised and afraid at the answers that he got. As he drifted in that world between sleep and waking he wondered how much if indeed any did his wife know. For a long time he had forbidden his mind to run those thoughts but tonight he could not prevent them. A great deal remained remote. Yet who can say what is good or what is bad until revelation is complete? For there is only the source, dark in itself, making everything shine. So that everything is known by its reflection.

He put an arm around Bridget; her presence was so familiar to him and now so necessary but she was already deep in that space where mind and senses transcend time and touch, and so she never heard him when he said, "I'm afraid for you."

THE HAWK

High over Hampstead Heath, a huge bird, three feet across the open wing-span, was cruising in circles three hundred feet up or more, watching all below. The hawk dipped and glided lower but still could spot no movement on the heath land far below. Two and a half pounds of instant death, it continued to hover in effortless attentiveness, rising and falling on the winds coursing over the bleak and silent heath. The sun breaking through the clouds enhanced the rugged rural beauty, casting sparkling rays of light on Kenwood.

But now, the huge wings began to beat, its shadow fell across the heath as, altering the line of its flight, the hawk sailed elegantly on a wind current blowing gently in the direction of the wood. Growing impatient now to spot and raise a quarry, not for love of the chase but simply because it was hungry. Wings taut, on it sailed, motionless above the open heath.

The sky darkened, the wind strengthened, bringing a sudden summer storm. Untamed, untrained, neither belled nor jessed, the hawk, with powerful wing strokes, cleaved the blustery rain-swept wind. A flash of lightning lit the sky. The hawk banked, gathering its wings close to its streamed lined body.

As the first clap of thunder raked the darkening sky the hawk began to plummet to the ground. Its eyes two murderous orbs of concentrated fury, it sped towards a rabbit thoughtlessly breaking cover to cross a stretch of open land.

Suddenly the rabbit sensed danger, like a blind human who, though he cannot see, is nevertheless aware he is seen. He froze with fear two inches from a bramble bush. The hawk, a breath away from the rabbit's unprotected back, was forced to veer—too late it saw that overhanging thorny mass: it crashed against it heavily and was thrown onto its back.

The ruffled hawk sluggishly regained his feet. Although dishevelled, he was not disabled and, after a few frustrated pecks at the thorn bush with his gun-metal beak, once more took to the air.

It flew now along the edge of the heath, following the line of the railway track the hawk sailed over the metal mountain, before turning eastward towards Kentish Town West, searching for a certain vantage point to view that area of wooded track.

The storm had ended as abruptly as it had begun. The hawk soared the tracks, startling a couple of crows, who flew panic-stricken across his path making fast for some trees. But the predator, not to be beaten this time, singled out the young female with damaged rear wing-feathers, beak raised in anguish her querulous squawks now silenced by fear. Single-minded, heedless of her mate, the hawk with his massive power advantage soon overtook his quarry, getting between her and the trees.

Her mate cawed harshly as he flew into the safe copse. The young female answered with forlorn cries, fluttering turbulently in the fraught sky. The hawk rose higher to gain attacking height, wings spread wide, a hovering crucifix of death, the summer breeze blowing cold as winter as, closing in, he lashed out with naked talons, catching the vulnerable crow a glancing blow that sent her spinning in a stunned mass of swirling feathers towards the gleaming tracks below.

The hawk let out a piercing scream as it clawed the empty air, and, though it was not yet quite dark, the starlings circling nearby began with mournful cries to roost. No birds wheeled idly now in that expanse of sky as the death-dark shadow continued gliding over all on spread unmoving wings.

From a high tree the feathered flesh-and-bone cruncher took up a sentinel position. Ever observant of all winged movement it turned its terrible curved beak round and round and round, levelling in the summer's evening his remorseless concentration at the ground.

An eerie stillness had gathered where the winged assassin continued, with a fierce unblinking stare to search the ground unhurried, waiting for the slightest move to come spiralling down on his untaken feathered food. The ferns flapped in the late evening gloom before the rise of the moon as the hawk continued to bar access to the sparse copse. The last light of day was fading fast now, yet the bronze hawk still waited—head plumage vaulted, a brooding death-watch.

A creaking sound caused the hawk to turn its yellow eye to focus its gaze on the man closing out the station's office door. Alan's shoulders were stooped now, and his face was seamed with age, as his fingers fumbled with the utility keys, (he looked far older than he was). Although the hawk foraging through its third summer was not concerned with this, it continued to glare, its head tilted curiously at the man's hands—perhaps thinking that they held or would even make a tasty meal. The injured hawk had learned to exist on carrion discarded by humans ever since a flying speck of gummed bark had hardened on its eye, causing it to fly sightless on one side, so that when it swooped at prey now, it faltered—it could no longer judge the fine angle required for the kill. For all that, it had survived. Like the man below, it had come to terms with its limitations and its losses. The day now had only a few more moments to live.

As Alan stood waiting for the train, he thought of Mrs Watson's warning of the year before. How she had ranted and raved that Bridget would bring trouble to her door. But there had been no trouble for the landlady and no more visits from the police. Bridget had died suddenly last winter from injuries received in a hit and run accident. She had been crossing the road on her way home one night, taking a short cut through a quiet street, just as she did on several other occasions, when a sleek black car skidded round the corner and shot through the lights of the quiet London street, leaving a black trail of exhaust smoke and a body laying dead in the road behind it.

The hands braced themselves against the train door. His thoughts paused half-way between criticism and approval. There was always something of this in his attitude to Bridget's cause. He regretted this enormously because it verged on the irrational. His crime had been complacency, because he had his own preoccupations, only now did he begin to penetrate deeper racking his memory. His head bent self-critically. Indifference at first had blinded him to contact with the living moment. The warnings and other subtle forms of tyranny had been contemptuously ignored.

Misgivings now vied with respect, because after all, the warrior must be made of flesh and blood or else take up futile existence in stone or marble, though the man preferred to keep his memory of a beautiful figure descending from a carriage onto a platform at the little station in Kentish Town.

For some time after Bridget's death her friends walked softly even when nobody was there and whispered in dark corners and stopped going out late at night because of footsteps following them which were the echoes of their own shoes while listening behind closed doors to those listening the other side of the door and jumped, caught suddenly by their reflection in mirrors and were careful not to complain, aware of the fact that when the blacks in West London had retaliated after their homes were attacked the police in an effort to conceal the racism had arrested blacks along with whites proclaiming to the Home Secretary that it was merely hooliganism. But eventually some brave souls or those that found that they couldn't stand the shame any longer (solemn promises they had made to Bridget came back to haunt them) began to regroup, they took up and carried on Bridget's struggle.

It could not have been otherwise. And the triumph was complete when Black people who had fought for years against discrimination took to the streets. Then the doors of the nation's universities were flung open and the students burst onto the streets. Former timorous calls for change had now turned into demand. Suddenly every party was united in one ideal, only differently expressed, but their common goal did prevail, when the country was forced to a standstill. The Home Office began to suspect some terrible danger;

there was, moreover an ominous sound that it could not quite fathom, could not trace. It was the voice of dissention.

Though for a while the Home Office was consoled to some extent by the benefit of illusion. It was just a matter of crossing the arms and sitting tight until the sound died away or its source was located and silenced. But the trouble with unfamiliar sound was that it might leap up suddenly in a blaze of revelation. When the singing began the grave men squirmed in their upholstered seats while their unmoving eyes stared straight into space. If they did not communicate their discomfiture to one another, these men who had experience with words, it was because it was either too great to convey or else they assumed that it would very soon go away.

But something almost dishonest was required of them to sit for so long, legs locked and arms crossed, hearing totally different sounds in each ear, while someone was prowling around in the corridor. Yet they were pleased with their inspired deception for only the very wise or the very innocent could suspect that no strength was concealed in those firm looking postures. And so they sat as the sound continued to soar, with their chins gravely lowered, these stern men not best known for clemency, yet now with expressions of some tolerance. To rise and sing—one voice alone is never enough to make the Home Office unfold its tongue, and yet it did attempt to smile. Though somewhat faintly at first because the smile did not properly fit its mouth. But to try is the thing and when the massed voices rose up in sudden spasms of passion (even the hecklers had joined the chorus line), only the very foolish or those without rhythm or soul could fail to be moved. When eventually the sound began to echo across the nation as one, the grave men began to unfold their stubborn arms, and although none of them broke into song, it was noticeable that one or two feet begun to beat time with the song of the people. Then a curious transformation of their features began to take place as the grave men were jerked out of their setting and put on a reasonable face preparatory to participating in great events. All dissension dissipated, as tenderly, lovingly, gloriously trilling sang the clear voice of courage of a young Colleen. Everyone listened to that sound silently. Silence at that hour was freedom, it was a world without image, symbol, memory or vision, sanctified by time-honoured wrongs, for that was the product of yesterday, a world trapped in the toils of centuries, harsh and confused and unclear.

Most of Raglan Street and its people are gone now.

Mary Jane is dead too and was buried alongside her husband, Seán, in a country to which they had never belonged.